SOMEBODY ELSE'S MAN

Books by Daaimah S. Poole:

Another Man Will

What's His Is Mine

Somebody Else's Man

A Rich Man's Baby

Diamond Playgirls

All I Want Is Everything

Ex-Girl to the Next Girl

What's Real

Got a Man

Yo-Yo Love

SOMEBODY ELSE'S MAN

DAAIMAH S. POOLE

Kensington Publishing Corp.
http://www.kensingtonbooks.com

DAFINA BOOKS are published by

Kensington Publishing Corp.
119 West 40th Street
New York, NY 10018

ISBN-13: 978-0-7582-2248-0
ISBN-10: 0-7582-2248-3

First trade paperback printing: October 2009
First mass market printing: September 2011

10 9 8 7 6 5 4 3

Printed in the United States of America

Dedicated
to all the fathers that do!
Daddy, thank you for always being there.

ACKNOWLEDGMENTS

Allah, thank you for making this and all things possible and for giving me the ability to turn words into stories.

I have to thank my two boys, Hamid and Ahsan, who share the computer with me and who have assisted in endless book promoting. One day it will all make sense.

Special thanks to my mother, Robin Dandridge, and my father, Auzzie Poole, for always being there for me, especially when I'm on a crazy deadline. You both are the best! Many thanks to my stepmom, Pulcheria Ricks-Poole, and to all of my extended family and friends.

My agent/mentor, Karen E. Quinones Miller . . . always and forever . . . I thank you for everything.

Allison Hobbs, you know what I went through and you were right there talking me through it. Thank you so very much.

Tamika Wilson, thanks for never being too cute to pass out a flyer for your friend. One reader at a time. LOL!

Ieshea Dandridge, I love you, Cousin. Thanks for coming in and helping . . . no questions asked.

Devon "SuperDev" Walls of Starshooterz, thank you for my great trailer and for all of your help.

To my readers, I thank you so very much for spreading the word and for your constant support of my work. Please keep in touch with reviews, comments, and e-mails: DSPbooks.com, myspace.com/DSPbooks, Twitter.com/DSPbooks, or e-mail Daaimah14@aol.com.

Thanks to all of the Kensington Publishing staff, Audrey LaFehr, and Walter Zacharius.

Last, but not least, I would like to thank all the booksellers. Thanks for always being supportive. I really appreciate all that you do! Nati and Andy of African World Book Distributor, Hakeem and Tyson of Black and Nobel Books, and Khalil at City Hall in Philly.

Much Love,

Daaimah S. Poole

Prologue

"Your father is dead," my mother's voice said dryly over the phone.

"Huh? What father?" I sat up straight, my heart picking up speed.

"Your biological. He passed away a few days ago." Her tone was calm and casual. I didn't say anything. I think I was in shock.

"Nicole, you there?" she asked.

"Yeah, I'm here," I said as I clutched the phone tight and processed that the man I never got to call father was no longer walking this earth. "How do you know?"

"I read it today in the obituary section of the paper. His funeral is Saturday."

"Really?" I asked, knowing it was true, because after retiring from the post office my mother read that column every day, right after checking her horoscope. Every once in a while she ran across a death notice for someone she knew.

"Well, I have to go. I just thought you should know. I'm going out and Ernest got overtime."

"Okay, I'll call you when I'm on my way home from work," I said as I slumped in my chair, dazed. I loved my mother to death, but why would she think it was a good idea to call me in the middle of my workday and give me that kind of news? She was acting like it was no big deal to tell me that my father is dead. Especially under the circumstances. The circumstance being, I had seen my father only once in my life, back when I was thirteen, and that was fifteen years ago.

I never missed having a father until I was in the second grade. I remember my best friend Tia's father coming up to our school and bringing cake, ice cream, and balloons to our classroom for his only daughter's birthday. Tia came back to school on Monday bragging about how she had the best dad in the world. Then this other girl named Felicia joined in and started talking about her father and all the fun they had together. That's when it clicked. Where was my dad? But worse than that—who was my dad? I didn't even know his name. I suddenly realized I had never heard his name and didn't have a clue what he looked like. He was completely absent from my life. I had no pictures, and no memories. I couldn't even recognize him if he walked past me on the street. For years I asked my mom who was my dad, and why wasn't he a part of my life, and she would never answer me. One time she told me he was in the army and the next time in the navy. Then she told me he got killed in Vietnam. I believed her until I found out that the war ended before I was born.

When I was thirteen, I begged her to tell me who my father was, like so many times before. She usually would tell me to leave her alone and get the fuck out her face. But this time I didn't leave her alone, because I had to get an answer. I was working her nerves. And just so I would get out her face she finally told me his name. The words came out of her mouth real slow . . . "Ray-mond Haw-k." She would have been better off not telling me his name because once she did, I had more questions. "Where is he? Where does he live? Why doesn't he come around?" I asked breathlessly.

She explained to me that she met him through a friend when she used to hang in south Philly. She told me that he really was in the army and that she had gotten pregnant with me right before he went to basic training. She said by the time he got back from training, she tried to tell him she was pregnant, but she found out he was already married to a woman he met near his base. She said she confided in his cousin and told his cousin to tell him she was pregnant, but she never heard anything from my father, so she left it alone.

I still wasn't satisfied and wanted more information. So, the next day she went to work and I searched through her dresser drawers for my birth certificate. I found it and his name was on it. I went to the white pages and called a few Raymond Hawks. By the time I got to the sixth name I was tired and hoped I didn't get another answering machine. The sixth name on the list was the only address in south Philly. He lived on Wharton Street in a neighborhood where my mom used to hang out. I figured he had to be the right Raymond Hawk.

I rode the number 7 bus to south Philly. I felt nervous and excited at the same time. Throughout the bus ride, I couldn't stop thinking about what was going to happen next. I didn't know how my father was going to react to meeting me. I wondered if he would reject me, or would he love me like a father should?

I got off the bus, one block away from his house. I walked up to Twenty-fourth Street and made a left. I saw a store on the corner with a big sign that read, "Delicatessen," and brick row houses in every direction. I looked at the address and went straight to 2416. Taking a deep breath, I walked up to the top step and knocked on the door. As I waited for someone to answer I became a little nauseous and my palms were dripping sweat. A woman with reddish-brown kinky-curled hair answered. Her skin was light brown with specks of freckles scattered on her nose and her cheeks. A pair of black, round glasses sat on the tip of her freckled nose. She was wearing a pink terry cloth robe and blue-and-white flowered nightgown.

"Can I help you?" she asked.

"Uhm, is Raymond Hawk here?"

"What's this about?" Her eyes narrowed suspiciously as they began to rove up and down, peering at me through her black glasses.

"I'm his daughter, Nicole," I said.

"Daughter? Raymond only got one daughter and she's in this house playing with her toys."

"My mother said he is my father." I unfolded the birth certificate that was clutched in my hand.

She bent down and examined my birth certificate. "How old are you?" she asked, breathing hard, her eyes narrowed at me.

"Thirteen," I said, straightening my shoulders.

She flung the birth certificate at me. "That's impossible!" Then she screamed at the top of her lungs, "Raymond, get out here . . . now!"

I got the first glimpse of my father as he came to the door, out of breath. He was a tall, beautiful man with smooth, Indian, deep red-brown skin, like mine.

"Yeah, baby," he said, looking out the white screen door to see why she was yelling.

They both stared down at me and she said, "This young lady says she's your daughter. Is that true?"

He looked at me, startled, and then he started backing up a little as he shook his head, saying, "No. No. I don't know her. She's not my child."

"You sure there's not something you forgot to tell me?" she yelled as she swung out and punched him in his side. He bowed over and she walked away from the door. As he was bent over I recognized even more features that looked just like mine. We had the same straight black hair, mink-like eyebrows, and long eyelashes.

"Who told you I was your father?" he asked, frowning.

"You dated my mom, Lois Edwards—they call her Lolo. She was friends with one of your cousins." I let out a breath as I waited for his face to change.

"Lois?" He wrinkled his brow and scratched his head. "I don't know anybody named Lois. Look, I'm sorry, I never met your mother in my life. I'm not your father, but I hope you find him." And then he closed the door in my face. I could hear the woman cussing him about me.

Hurt and confused, I stood there for a moment. I thought about knocking on the door again and demanding that he admit that he was my father. But all the lies my mother had told me over the years started swirling around in my head and I decided to just leave.

As I walked back to the bus stop my sadness and disappointment turned to anger. I was in tears for the entire hour-long ride home. I wanted to kill my mother. Why did she insist on lying to me? In my mind my mother was a stupid, lying whore. How could she not know who my father was? How could she keep this information from me in the first place? I asked myself those questions until I got off the bus and ran home.

I usually tried to stay out my mother's way because she was just so evil. But being scared of her didn't stop me from barging into her room and disturbing her nap.

"Mom, how could you? I went to that man's house in south Philly and he said he wasn't my father," I screamed.

"What man!" she said as she jolted upright.

I explained the entire story to her in detail, even throwing in how embarrassing it was to be told he wasn't my father. She didn't even respond to me as I cried and kept asking over and over, "How could you?" When she didn't respond, I ran out of her room in tears.

Ten minutes later, she came out of her bedroom with a baseball bat in her hand and ordered me to get in the car with her. I wasn't sure if I liked the way she planned on handling the situation, but I got in the car and put my seat belt on. What else could I do? We were at Raymond Hawk's door in less than fifteen minutes. I was surprised that my mom knew exactly where he lived. She blew her horn repeatedly in loud, drawn-out stretches. Then she got out of the car, stomped up the steps to his house, and hit the door several times with her balled-up fist. Two children, a girl and a boy, who looked to be about seven or eight years old, peeked out the window.

"Raymond, open this door," my mom yelled. He came to the door with his eyes bugged out, gawking at my mom like he was seeing a ghost.

"Raymond, why did you lie to this child?" my mother demanded.

Instead of answering the question, he walked away and the freckled-faced woman took his place in the doorway.

"He ain't lie to her, he ain't her daddy. He told her the truth," she yelled, with her hand planted on her small hip.

With her nose turned up, my mom looked her up and down and said, "Listen, you need to mind your fucking business. This ain't got shit to do with you."

"It's got a lot to do with me because it is my husband you are talking about," the lady yelled back.

"I don't want your broke-ass husband. I have a man."

The woman didn't have a quick enough response and just stood with her mouth open. The neighbors and other people passing by on the street were beginning to tune in to the screaming match.

"Could you lower your voice?" she asked my mom in a whisper. I could tell she was becoming a little embarrassed that all her business was being put out on the street. "Do you think we could finish this conversation inside the house?" Freckleface asked, her expression nice and friendly now.

"No, I don't want to come in your house. Tell your husband to come back to this door before he gets a big problem."

Raymond came back to the door and leaned against the doorframe. My mom walked up on him and pointed her finger at the side of his head. Poking him in the temple, she said, "Raymond, one thing you ain't going to do is tell my daughter that I'm a liar." She gripped me by the arm. "This is your daughter and you know it. Now, you asked me to stay away and I did. I don't give a goddamn about you. But you don't ever in your life tell my child that I'm a liar." My mom took a few moments to catch her breath.

"Are you her father?" she asked, staring him down.

Freckle-face shot him a dirty look. "*Are* you her father?"

Raymond looked at his wife and then at me. He dropped his head in defeat and then looked up at my mother. "Yes, I am her father," he said with a sigh. "Now leave, Lois, and stop causing a scene in front of my family."

His wife looked like she wanted to faint. The two little children were peeking out the window, their eyes wide with shock. Freckle-face wasn't trying to hear what Raymond had just admitted. She sucked her teeth and shook her head. "Raymond, you know damn well you ain't got no other daughter. Your family is right here in this house." She turned evil eyes on my mom. "I hope you don't think you're going to be getting any of our money.

My husband ain't never going to take care of that child of yours."

My mom looked like she was about to go off on Raymond's wife. I could tell she wished she had brought that baseball bat out of the car so she could smash some windows and bash Freckle-face upside her head.

"You ain't got no damn money," my mom exploded. "My daughter is very well taken care of. She don't need y'all for shit. And it will be a cold day in hell before she ever contacts you for anything."

And that was the last I saw of Raymond Hawk. No birthdays, no Christmases, no graduations. I never spoke about that day. I knew it was a touchy subject, something I wasn't supposed to discuss ever again.

Over the years, I have had countless vivid dreams about my father. Sometimes I would be so mad when I awoke because it seemed so real. Now he was dead. I took a long sigh. I just couldn't believe it. I really wasn't ever going to get to know him.

I knew he wasn't a part of my life growing up, but for some reason I always thought that our paths would cross again. I had hoped we would get a chance to talk. I imagined, actually I prayed, that one day he would come to his senses and claim me as his daughter. If he'd only taken the time to get to known me, he would have liked me and seen how good I am. But that day will never happen. I will never know him and he will never know me.

CHAPTER 1

I sat at my desk, motionless for a few minutes, still in shock. Then I grabbed a tissue and wiped the falling tears. I cried so hard, the collar of my teal-blue jacket was becoming soaked. Needing someone to talk to, I reached for the phone and called my best friend to tell her the news.

"Tia, my mom just called me and said that my dad died."

"You okay?"

"Yeah." Sniffling, I stood up and closed my office door.

"You want me to go to the funeral with you?"

"No, I'm not going," I said as a few more tears trickled down my cheek. A tap on my office door signaled me to pull it together. I was still at work and had to keep it professional.

"Nicole, a guest would like to speak to you," Maritza said.

I sighed. I really didn't feel like talking to anyone.

"Get Ryan, I'm in the middle of something."

"He told me to get you." Maritza sounded frustrated.

"Okay, give me the room number and tell the guest I'll call in a few minutes." *I hate hotel guests!* I thought. They got on my damn nerves. I didn't have time for that shit today.

Maritza said she'd relay my message. She left, but a few minutes later she was right back in my office. "He said it is very important and needs to speak with you now," Maritza said, sounding distressed.

"I'll call you back, Tia." I hung up the phone and then walked down the hall to my manager, Ryan Greene's, office. He was online, playing poker. Ryan's from the West Coast and is very laid back—too laid back to be a manager of a hotel. With curly brown hair and light ocean-blue eyes, Ryan was cute, but being that he was such an asshole, he might as well have been ugly.

"Why do you try to make me deal with all the crazy, disgruntled guests? It's your turn," I yelled.

"Because you are better at it than I am. Plus, all the time and effort it took you to come in here, you could already have solved the guest problem. Right?" He turned back to playing poker.

At that moment, Maritza rushed into Ryan's office. "Please, will one of you come out and deal with this? They are really angry."

"Okay, I'll be right there," I said with a sigh. I walked back to my office and got some more tissues and blew my nose.

As I went to the lobby and approached the front desk, an upset Pakistani man asked with a heavy accent, "Are you the manager?"

"I'm the assistant manager. What seems to be the problem, sir?"

"I just checked into room 309 and the room . . . Never mind, just explain something, please. I can't quite understand why there is a used condom in my bed."

I was just as shocked as he was. "A used condom?" I repeated, dumbfounded. I shook my head. I really didn't have an answer for him, so I just jumped on the computer and began searching for another room.

He continued to ramble on, saying, "Very disgusting, no one cleaned my room. My wife and my child can't sleep in a dirty bed."

I looked over at his wife, who had a gold earring in her nose. Her hair was parted on the side and pulled back into a bun. She was wearing traditional blue-and-gold garb and had a baby hoisted on her hip. Seeing her and the baby made me feel even worse. I kept trying to see if there were any other rooms available, but every room in the hotel was filled.

The Pakistani man and his wife started going back and forth, speaking in their language. I couldn't understand a word they were saying, but judging by the tone of their conversation, I could tell they were becoming very upset.

"Sir! Listen, just give me one more moment," I said, hoping to calm them down. Finally, I found a room and quickly made a key. I came from behind the desk, apologized, and offered to walk the couple upstairs to inspect their room.

"Has this room been cleaned? I don't want another dirty room."

"Yes, sir. It's clean and I upgraded you to a suite," I said and apologized again.

He spoke again with his wife in their native language, and then began to pick up their luggage, indicating that they would accept their new room. With a walkie-talkie in hand, I escorted the couple to the room and we inspected it together.

He was a little calmer and thanked me. After I exited his room, I got on the walkie-talkie and asked the head of housekeeping to meet me in the laundry room.

This was another day at Choice Springs Hotel. I'm the operations manager and have been on the verge of quitting for the last two years. The hotel is located at the Philadelphia International Airport and we get a lot of convention traffic as well as people coming into town for business meetings.

Choice Springs is a franchise that's owned by a mega-rich family from Dallas, Texas. We don't report to a corporate headquarters, and most problems are handled internally, which means, we don't handle anything. Most days are easy, but boring at the same time. I like to keep my door half-closed so I can play around online, forwarding e-mails to my friends, watching video clips and Googling anything and everything that pops into my mind.

I do work from time to time. Every now and then I respond to a complaint or two. I come to work every day, but I do as little as possible. I don't get paid enough to work myself into a sweat. On the flip side, there are not many jobs at places that are open twenty-four hours a day, seven days a week, and even open on holidays. I need to find a better job.

I entered the laundry room in the housekeeping

department. Rows and rows of white sheets and towels were everywhere, and the loud dryer was making the entire room hot. Ms. Annette was on the phone as I entered her cramped office. I waited as she gave me the *one minute* sign with her big chunky finger. After she completed her call, she turned and said, "What's the dilmo?"

I held back from correcting her and saying dilemma, because she would just shrug and say *Whatever . . . you know what I mean.* She was the kind of person who would argue you down even when she was wrong.

"Ms. Annette, who cleaned room 309 yesterday?"

"I have to check. Why? What's wrong?"

"I just had a guest complain about finding a used condom in the bed."

Ms. Annette looked down at her clipboard and said, "Oh, Crystal cleaned that room. She needs to get fired because this is the third time she didn't properly clean one of her rooms. Plus, she smokes weed during her break with her purple-lipped self."

"I need you to pull Crystal's file," I said, before Ms. Annette went on any further about Crystal. "And tell Crystal to come to the front desk."

There was no union at the hotel. We were at-will property and Crystal was about to be fired. But first I had to hear what she had to say. She was called down from the third floor.

I told Ryan what happened. He didn't like doing any other work, but when it was time to fire somebody he was ready and willing. He clapped his hands twice. "I'll handle Crystal," he said. I handed him her record and watched him swiveling back and forth in his chair as he practiced how he was going to fire her. Firing someone was the worst part of my job, and Ryan's favorite.

Crystal strolled into Ryan's office. Her hair was in long braids and she was swinging her hair off her neck. She had various colored tattoos from her neck to her fingertips. Her eyes were going from my face to Ryan's, and I could tell she was trying to read our expressions to see what we were going to say.

"Crystal, you cleaned room 309 yesterday and it wasn't up to the hotel's standards and—"

Before I could complete my sentence she stuttered, "I wanted to say I like this hotel, it is nice, and I want to stay here and I shouldn't be fired because I'm not the only one popping sheets. Everybody is doing it."

"What exactly is popping sheets?" I asked.

"You know, like you take the ends of the sheet and hold it up and flip twice and everything like hair and stuff falls off the sheet. But everybody is really doing it."

"Well, Crystal, you got caught and everybody else will be warned about following policy in this hotel, but I'm sorry to say, we are going to have to let you go. Today is your last day." Ryan spoke with such authority and conviction, you would have thought he was Donald Trump yelling *You're fired.*

"Okay," Crystal responded and then started crying. I handed her a few tissues. Ryan walked out of the office to hold a meeting with the rest of the housekeeping department. I felt bad as I walked Crystal to the back to empty out her locker, but there was nothing I could do. I felt her pain. I was going through a lot of shit, too.

After that episode I went back to my office and closed the door. My mind started racing again. I swear, when it rains it really pours. That's the only thing that could explain what was going on in my life recently. I wasn't having any luck lately in love, I hated my job, and my family life sucked. My last two long-term relationships were with men who were already taken. And neither situation was my fault entirely. I met the first unavailable man on a dating Web site. We'd been dating for a year before I found out about his wife. She worked at night, and one day decided to play detective and followed him to my house. Needless to say, that relationship was over. I don't know why I didn't see the signs. He never took me to his house. I knew where he lived, but he always said he liked it better at my apartment.

I met the second no-good liar at a singles club. He was there with his single friends. I started dating Malcolm Walker, only to find out he was separated. He said he was getting a divorce, but during the course of us falling in love, he went back to his wife because she was pregnant. I was so upset with him, but not angry enough to leave him alone. My selfish side wouldn't allow me to stop loving him. However, three months ago I came to the conclusion that I could no longer be his side piece. I dated him for three of his five years of marriage. Leaving him alone has been one of the hardest things I ever had to do in my life. Just imagine . . .

you meet your soul mate . . . you have long talks and walks and you come to the realization that he is the man you want to spend your life with . . . you find out that he is already married.

Yes, he had to go. I was tired of singing Whitney Houston's "Saving All My Love For You." The hell with that. Besides, it wasn't like I was living the mistress life—set up nice and living good. I hate to admit it, but I paid for most of our dates. At one point, I was even putting gas in his car, trying to help him out because he had to pay his car note and his son's day-care bill. Most of the time Malcolm's bank account read *insufficient funds.* It didn't matter though, because I loved him. I would even get us discounted rooms at hotels. Initially, I didn't feel like I was getting used. I thought I was helping out a friend. But with all I was doing for him, he couldn't do the one thing I wanted him to do for me, which was leave his wife and marry me. And things haven't always been this way. When we first met he was so good to me. I think that is part of the reason I was staying around, because I thought one day, when he left her, he would go back to being the man I met and fell in love with.

Since I left Malcolm alone, it seems like karma is punishing me for messing with another woman's husband for all those years. Because since I have been a "real single girl," I haven't been able to find anyone. Not one good prospect for a boyfriend. It's hard trying to do the right thing, because at any point I could be vulnerable and go back to Malcolm. He calls me every few days and tells me how much he still loves me, on my answering machine. He says he knows I deserve better and that he didn't expect me to wait forever. He also said he knows he is being selfish, but he can't let me go even though he understands how I feel, and wishes I would be a little more patient with him.

It's sad because I want to be there for him—I want to be his everything, but I just can't take being number two, anymore.

On the morning of the funeral, I decided an hour before that I wanted to go. I just felt like I needed to be there. I had to see him one last time and say good-bye. I threw on a black shirt and black jeans, and barely brushed my hair. I put on my big black down coat, hat, gloves and drove straight to the church. I didn't care how I looked, I had to say good-bye. I felt that if I said good-bye, it might heal all the pain and sadness I had trapped inside of me ever since I was a little girl.

The big church sat at the corner of a large intersection. There were several black Town Car limos and a hearse in front of the door. An older man opened the door to the church and handed me an obituary. He told me I could stand in the back because all the seats were filled. There were people of all ages dressed in variations of black. A woman's voice bellowed from the front row. I looked around and saw sad people in every direction. I was crying too, but not for the same reason as the others. My tears were not tears of sorrow. I was crying because I was mad. I was mad as hell because my father had never been here for me. I was mad because he gave me life, but was never a part of my life. *I hate you! I hate you! I hate you!* I screamed internally. If it were possible, I would have brought him back to life just so I could kill him again. But at the age of fifty, he'd had a heart attack before I could get to him.

The preacher read the eulogy and then the funeral was over. Feeling really nervous, I got in the line to view the body. I didn't know what I was going to do when I got up there.

The line moved closer to the casket. I had so many thoughts running through my head. I stopped feeling angry and started to feel sad. Very sad. I saw his wife on the front row out of the corner of my eye. She was heavier than I remembered, but still had those freckles. She had on a big black hat over her reddish-brown colored spiral curls. Her chest was heaving up and down as she cried. For a millisecond, I felt sorry for her. Then she looked over at me and stared like she was trying to figure out where she knew me from. She must have figured it out because she suddenly gave me this wicked look and I turned away. Her evil-ass look invoked old memories and fears.

Finally, I was next up to the coffin and I told myself I wasn't going to break down, but the closer I came to the casket, the harder it became to hold back my tears. I approached the white-and-silver casket and saw Raymond Hawk. He was wearing a black suit and a white shirt. I touched his cold hand and began crying harder. I mean real hard. I don't know what it was, but something about that organ playing made me lose it. I was making the line stand still by crying uncontrollably. It was my last glimpse of him and my last conversation with him. I started talking to him, quietly asking, "Why? Why, Dad? Why didn't you love me?" I asked "Why?" so many times, like he could hear me and was going to give me an answer. People behind me patted me to move forward. I got myself together enough to leave his side. I wanted to run, but I couldn't. I had to walk out of that church with dignity. But while I was walking, my legs began wobbling. Luckily, they didn't give out. I made it to the bathroom door and bent over crying by the radiator. I could not stop crying.

An older woman walked over to me and said, "Baby, it's okay." She hugged me close, trying to comfort me. "It's okay," she said again. "He is one of God's angels now." I almost laughed in her face as I thanked her and ran out of the church.

CHAPTER 2

After the funeral I went home. I felt so empty, so alone. While everyone was holding one another and consoling each other I had no one. I made it home and sat in my car in front of my house. I didn't want to go in. I looked down at the obituary. *Raymond Hawk was a loving father and teacher. He will be mourned by his wife Elaine and two children, Candice and Ray.* My name was not even mentioned. In his life and in his death, I didn't exist.

The UPS driver was pulling up to my house at the same time. I sighed and walked to the door and signed for the huge box the driver was pulling up the steps. My mother came out and she looked me over one time and then said through the permanent grimace on her face, "Where you coming from?"

"I went to the funeral."

"You did?" she said as she sucked her teeth and told the driver where to place the box. "I can't believe you went to the funeral looking like that. You could have at least did something with your hair."

"I curled my hair, Mom."

"It doesn't look like it. And you wore jeans! You should have wore a dress, a suit, something. You should have told me you were going. I could have brought some gasoline and a match and told that bastard to burn in hell."

"Mom, please."

"What? That was a joke. I don't know why you're all upset. You didn't know that man. Fuck him. He ain't shit. He ain't never do a thing for you. The person you need to cry about is me. I bought you everything you ever had in your life." She inhaled deeply, as if to draw strength to continue her rant. But I changed the subject. As the driver walked out I asked my mother about her latest purchase inside the big box. Her face lit up. "It's a television. I ordered it last week. That other TV was only forty inches and that wasn't big enough. This one has a fifty-two-inch screen and a lot of extra features. Isn't that nice?" She pointed at the box. "Now Ernest can watch his games in high definition. The technician is going to come and mount the TV on the wall on Friday."

"What did you do with the other television?"

"I put it in the basement. I was thinking when you finally move out, you can buy it from me. Uhm, Nikki, do me a favor? When Ernest gets here, tell him I'm going to a sales meeting. Oh! Another thing . . . me and Ernest have been talking, and we think it's time for you to move out."

My mouth dropped open. "I've only been here six months, Mom. You said you were going to give me a year."

"I changed my mind. So, you need to be out of here in three months." She looked at me and said,

"What? You're grown and I'm going to convert that back room into a closet. I need the space." She put on her coat and walked out of the door like she hadn't said anything wrong. My mom was just evil. Some people are mean because they are ugly and use their meanness as a defense mechanism, but my mother is privileged in life. She's always been beautiful. Lolo has beautiful honey-toned skin and soft, light brown eyes and highlighted sandy-brown, cropped curly hair. She always had what she wanted in life, but she still finds reasons to be nasty. Ever since I was young, I just learned to do the right thing and to stay out of her way. I made sure my room was clean, I got good grades, and the dishes were done. Because if there was so much as one dirty spoon in her sink, she would go off. I don't know what to say about my mom. She is just not like a regular mom. I'm her only child and I think she just never learned how to be a mother, wife, or a friend. She shows hardly any emotions and she thinks the whole world is jealous of her. She lives to make herself happy. She is just someone who will say anything she wants. Sometimes she thinks about what she said, and then apologizes after she hurts your feelings, or she'll tell you to get over yourself. My stepfather, Ernest, deals with her mess. I don't know why.

She cusses him out every other day. It's been many days, over the years, that I've wondered if my stepfather was really a man. My mother has made countless insults toward him and assassinates his manhood whenever she has a chance. He is not allowed to bring any of his fishing equipment or tools out of the basement, yet she has Avon and Mary K products that she thinks she sells, workout equipment that is halfway put together, and a bunch of other bullshit stacked up to the ceiling in the dining room, all from the Home Shopping Network and QVC. My mom knows all the delivery drivers on a first-name basis and gets excited about her daily surprises.

Two minutes after my mom pulled off, Ernest came in. He is a tall, bald, stocky man with light olive skin. He works for Amtrak and works overtime almost every day. So he can pay for everything my mother buys.

"Hey, Nikki. Where is your mom?" he asked, limping in the door.

"She said she had to go to a sales meeting."

"So, your mom ordered some more stuff?" he said, shaking his head, looking at the big box in the living room. "I'm going to cut her credit cards off. She is out of control with her shopping."

It always amazed me how Ernest would act surprised by my mother's purchases when he was her sponsor. Every time he told her not to charge anything else, they would start arguing and she would cuss him out. He would have to sleep on the sofa. A few days later, he would apologize and then give her more money to make up for upsetting her. He showed his love by spoiling her. He spoiled me, too, but he spoiled me from a distance—like an uncle—and didn't discipline me at all. He was there for all my milestones, but he didn't really treat me like his daughter, and I didn't think of him as a father. I thought of Ernest as just my mother's husband. Plus, whatever my mom said, he generally went along with. As he pulled the television out of the box to examine it, I asked him if my mom was really kicking me out in three months.

"No, don't listen to Lois. She ain't really kicking you out. She is just trying to scare you. You still got your year, but you better get to fixing up that house."

"I know. I just don't know where to begin."

"Nicole, the best thing and only way to handle that house is a little at a time."

"You're right, Ernest, I'm just so scared."

"You just got to get you a better job and find you a good man to help you."

"Yeah, I guess."

As I walked up the stairs, the only thing I could think of was that I needed to get out of this crazy house. I walked into the only room I had any peace in. My tiny bedroom. I could only fit in one dresser and a full-size bed. I had moved back home with my mother after I was ripped off by this home remodeling company. I bought a fixer-upper house and got scammed out of thirty-one thousand dollars.

One of the hotel guests was a real estate investor named Warren Lieblich. He would come in from Palm Springs, Florida, every month and would go to the sheriff's sale and buy houses. He would tip the front desk a hundred dollars just for calling a cab for him. He was always pulling out wads of hundreds. So, I asked him how could I get started. He gave me a little information and I bought a house for a couple of thousand dollars and then I got a loan against it. I was ready to buy cheap property all over the city. I really thought I was on my way to being a real estate mogul. I had it all planned out. I was going to convert the house into a duplex. I was going to have the people on the first floor paying off my loan and I would live rent-free on the second floor. But the contractors had another plan. They went in my house and began fixing it up, for two days. Then the next day they never showed up, and I had already paid them.

The next day I went up to their office, but it was empty and the phone was disconnected. I felt so violated and taken advantage of. I sued them and filed a complaint, but I'm probably never going to see any of my money, because I heard that hundreds of other people are suing them, too. I didn't get none of my money back yet, and doubt if I ever will.

Chapter 3

Every weekend someone thought it would be a good idea to have a party at our hotel. Today it was a pool party. Usually I would turn my head the other way, but as I was making my rounds I saw dozens of kids running down the hall and a trail of water followed them. I walked to the pool area and saw a cake and food near the pool. It was all these children doing cannonballs in our shallow pool. They were running and sliding all over the hard concrete that surrounded the pool. Every time they ran I cringed. I knew it was only a matter of time before someone got hurt. There were kids playing in the hot tub. It was pure chaos. I walked over to a few parents sitting nearby. "Who is in charge of this party?"

"I am," a heavyset blonde said, raising her hand.

"Miss, you can't let your children run and jump in the pool."

"What's wrong? We're not doing anything wrong. I paid for my hotel room, so they can get in the pool."

"I know you did, ma'am. But the kids shouldn't be running up and down the hall."

"They're not running up and down the hall. They're fine, they're kids."

As soon as she said that, a little boy slid and hit his head on the side of the pool. The blonde ran over to him. He was bleeding profusely from a big gash on the back of his head. I dialed 911, as all the children ran over to see if he was all right. The party was over. The little boy that slipped was her son, the birthday boy. She took him to the hospital and the rest of the party packed up and left, leaving a path of destruction.

I called our maintenance man over the walkie-talkie and told him to meet me at the pool. Curtis came up in blue Dickie pants and a white-and-blue striped shirt with his nametag on it. He worked at the hotel before I got there, but I didn't care for him because he was always staring real hard, like he had X-ray vision and could see through clothes. He was just a crusty-looking, perverted-looking man. His nickname in the hotel was Smokebreak, because he was always bumming a cigarette and smoking outside, and his dark complexion.

"Curtis, close the pool, please. And have this area cleaned."

He looked around at all the mess and said, "Don't worry about it. I have it, but please stop calling me Curtis. Miss lady, the only time I'm Curtis is when I cash my check. I'm always Smokebreak."

"Right, Smoke break," I repeated after him.

"No, one word. It's a compound word—Smokebreak." I was thinking, *Whatever, just please get this pool area looking back to normal.* My day could not end soon enough.

* * *

After a long day of work I needed a drink. I was meeting up with my friends for drinks at the legendary Copa. The Copa was known for making great margaritas. I waited for Tia and the unofficial member of our team, Reshaun. Reshaun was a little older than us and had a son. She was my girl, but we weren't as close as me and Tia.

I noticed the Copa was filled with women on girlfriend dates. I hoped that the women were just taking a night off from the kids and husbands and not actually out here trying to scope like I was. If so, that meant the thirty-to-one ratio was not just a myth, because there were about sixty women and only two guys sitting at the bar and there was not enough testosterone to go around. I looked around, and texted Tia and told her to hurry up.

I love Tia like the sister I never had. It's been me and her since fourth grade. We got in trouble together all through grade school and high school. In our senior year at Martin Luther King High School, we were bored one day and began pulling the fire alarms just to have a little fun. Needless to say, we got suspended and as soon as we were reinstated we got kicked out for inciting a riot. At least that's what the records say. We didn't start a riot. We just both were in the middle of a big free-for-all fight. We were the Thelma and Louise of Mount Airy just because we didn't have anything else to do. It was so boring in our neighborhood. To this day, my mom has never forgiven Tia for getting me kicked out of our high school. We were so damn bad for no reason at all.

My former partner in crime is now a police officer. I love her, but I told her if I dialed 911, I would not want to see her show up and help me. Because Tia got some mean ways, like if she thinks you think you're cute, she will give you a ticket. And she is not the least bit diplomatic—everything has to be her way. But it works for her, because she loves her job. Though she's a cop, she's been dating this d-boy/con artist for the last six years, on and off. Her man's name is Lamar, and he's the kind of guy who just doesn't want to do anything right. Instead of working, he'd rather find a quick hustle. And when he is not scamming or getting lawsuits, he tries to sell weed. I think he smokes more than he sells. He's such a con artist, he always got a slip-and-fall case pending. At one point, he even had a three-card molly ring going on downtown. So, being Tia's best friend, I'm all for her dumping that loser, Lamar, and upgrading to someone who at least earns a legitimate income.

Tia walked in the bar smiling. "You okay?" she asked. She knows me like the back of her hand, and just one look at me told her that something was wrong. She's tall, thin, with almond-colored skin and a boy shape. She was dressed in black, dirty-wash jeans and a cream, oversize sweater. She walked in and hugged me.

"What the married man do now?" she said as she scrunched my shoulder.

I removed her hand and said, "It's not the married man this time." I pushed the obituary over to her. "Look, that's my dad," I said.

"Wow, you went? Why'd you go by yourself? I told you I would go with you."

"Yeah, I know. I decided to go at the last minute. I just felt like I had to be there. I wanted to see him for the last time, you know?" I felt tears building up and I tried to hold them back. They were starting to cloud my vision, but as I spoke I just couldn't stop them. "It's just not fair, Tia. Like . . ." I paused for a second. "You don't understand. All I ever wanted to do was have a conversation with him." I picked up a napkin and started dabbing at my eyes.

"It's okay," Tia said as she took a seat and patted my back.

I didn't think I would break down in the busy restaurant. I tried to wipe my tears away with the small white paper napkin. "I'm tripping, right? I just think my dad could have helped me. Look at the types of men I've dealt with. If my dad had been in my life, he would have warned me not to get involved with married men or he would have made sure that I went to college. If he'd acted like a father, I wouldn't be stuck in a dead-end job. I just wish I knew him. You don't know how that feels to not know your own father."

"You're right. But I do know having family is a lot of drama," Tia said, trying to make me feel better.

Of course, she could say that—she was the baby girl of four, her parents were still happily married, and her whole family spoiled her and gave her whatever she wanted.

"You know, I just wonder what my mom did to make him leave. She had to do something horrible to make him not even want to be around me."

"What makes you think it's your mom's fault?" Tia asked.

"Come on, you know my mom is mean. Look at how she treats Ernest. It had to be her, because the one and only time I met my dad, he really seemed like he had it together. He had two other kids and took care of them. My father was a teacher—that meant he was around children all day. He must have liked kids."

"I don't know and it doesn't matter. Don't worry about him or that stupid family. Look at you and all you've accomplished without your father or his family. But then again, Lolo might have something to do with it," she agreed. We both laughed and our waitress approached us and took our margarita orders.

"I didn't come out to spend the night talking about Lolo, but guess what? She told me I have to move in three months."

"Yo, your mother is so crazy. Remember when she made you wear the same clothes to school for a month as a punishment and everyone was laughing at you?"

"Yes, I remember that shit. I'm still traumatized. That was on some abusive *Mommy Dearest* bullshit. But, forget Lolo, I really feel like a piece of me has been missing my whole life," I said as I tried to hold back more tears.

"Nikki, knowing your dad would not have made your life perfect. If that was the case, then what's my excuse? I have both my parents and I still make bad decisions about men. Shit, look who I've been with for the past six years!"

"I know what you are saying, but I just think it would be different if he'd been a part of my life."

"No, it wouldn't have. You grew up with Ernest. He is a good stepdad."

"It's not the same," I said, shaking my head in disagreement.

"Come on, Nicole, daddies don't solve everything in life. I got a lot of shit wrong in my life, too. One thing I've learned in life is that you don't get everything you want. Everybody is missing something. Nobody gets five out of five. And everything happens for a reason."

"I feel like I got zero out of five. I just wish I knew him before he died."

"I know. I know, but you can't change what's already done."

For the next twenty minutes me and Tia were going back and forth, and she couldn't change my opinion or how I felt. The waitress placed our drinks on the table and Tia began defending her argument again.

"Who do you know who got both their parents and are smart, look good, have a good relationship, a banging body, and just got it all? Seriously, think about everybody you know. Everybody is longing for or missing out on something. Take me for example . . . I'm cute, I got a man, I have both my parents, I have a good job, but I got a flat butt."

I looked at Tia and we both started laughing again. She was so damn silly.

"You right. So nobody gets five out of five?"

"I don't think so. I think it rarely happens that way," she said, as she flagged our waitress down and ordered another round. She sipped on her drink some more and then she turned her attention back to me and said, "Listen, may he rest in peace, but forget that man. Seriously, life goes on." I took a deep breath and tried to agree with her.

Tia's phone rang. I took another sip of my margarita and looked over at the entrance. I hoped some men would show up so I could have some eye candy to look at, because all these other girlfriends on dates wasn't what I wanted to see. The same two men were at the bar and I think they were more interested in each other than in any of the women in the place.

"Oh, my God! She is crazy!" Tia said as she placed her phone in her bag.

"Who was that?"

"It was Reshaun. She is on her way and she really is marrying that African. Soon as she gets here, we both need to get in her ear."

"What? He trying to stay in the country?" I asked.

"No, I think she just wants a free ride and she sees this as her opportunity to sit back and not have to work so hard. You know James hasn't been helping her with Briggy since they broke up. So she can be marrying him for so many reasons."

Mid-conversation, Reshaun came in. She was all smiles. I felt bad that we were about to ruin her smile. She was always so happy and always had something nice to say. But something had to be said. How do you marry a man that you've only known for thirty days?

"Did y'all order my drink?" Reshaun asked.

"Yeah, get your drink 'cause we coming for you," Tia joked as Reshaun ordered an apple martini.

"What are you talking about?" she asked, as she took off her colorful scarf and hung her gray wool jacket on the back of her chair. Reshaun was cute, with a curvy, size twelve shape. She wore her hair back in a clip with curls hanging out of the clip. She was wearing chunky black-and-silver earrings, dark jeans, and a sheer black shirt.

"Reshaun, why are you marrying that man just so he can get a green card? Do you love him?" Tia blurted out.

"A little. Well, I'm not exactly in love yet. But I like him. I just got to dress him up some."

"What if he runs back to his country or something?" I asked.

"Oh, God! Y'all sound like my mother," she laughed.

"No, this is for real," I said, hoping we could get through to her.

"Reshaun, sweetie. I know it is hard out here being single, but you don't have to marry any ol' body," Tia said.

"That's what y'all think I'm doing?" Reshaun asked as she turned to me and then to Tia.

"Yeah, pretty much. Don't throw in the towel yet. You're still young. Wait until you're about forty-five or fifty at least, before you to decide to settle down with some African you don't even know," Tia chimed in as she grabbed Reshaun's hand to offer her support.

"Listen, his name is Michael. He is not some African. He doesn't need a green card. He is a citizen and was born and raised in London. Secondly, he's educated. He has a college degree and he loves me." She snatched her hand away from Tia's. The waitress arrived and placed her martini in front of her.

"I do kind of feel like you're settling and you didn't even introduce us to him yet," I added.

"I'm not settling and y'all can meet him. We are getting married next week, so I'm not sure if you will get a chance to meet him before then."

"So, Reshaun . . . in only one month, you know he is the one."

"Yes!"

"Why? Because you don't like your job or your apartment, and you want a new car and a new home with somebody else handling the payments?"

"He is a good guy. He has done more for my son, Briggy, than his father has done in seven years."

"There are a lot of guys out here who will help you with your son," I said.

"I don't think so. He is a good role model for Briggy."

"You want Briggy around anyone? For all you know, that man could be a child molester or a serial killer. One month is not enough time to get to know someone," Tia said, getting more upset.

"It is hard out here. I know enough about Michael to let him put a ring on it." Reshaun looked around at all the lonely women sipping on drinks. "I've had about enough of this female bonding bullshit."

"But you just met him. Why can't you just date him a little longer and see how it works out?" I asked.

"No, I'm getting married. He wants to marry me. I'm done with all that princess stuff . . . sitting around wasting time, waiting for Mr. Right. Y'all can keep waiting for your soul mate. 'Cause I'm done waiting."

"It can happen," Tia said.

"Well, how come it didn't happen to none of us yet?" Reshaun asked. Me and Tia looked at each other, curled our lips up, and got quiet. She did raise a good point and she continued her testimony.

"Since I broke up with James, all I have had is a stream of forty-eight-hour boyfriends. It seems like you need three men to make up one good one. And I'm tired of this shit. I'm tired of y'all being my dinner dates every weekend. This is how I feel . . . I'm thirty years old and at this point in my life, I think that if you meet somebody who loves you more than you love him, you marry him and go on with your life. Since I've been with Michael, I've had a sense of peace. He makes me feel like someone else is in this fight with me. Everything has changed. No, I don't love him with the kind of passion I'd like to feel, but knowing that he loves me and would do whatever for me, makes me appreciate him and love him in my own way. So y'all can be my friends and accept it or not," Reshaun lashed out as she got up from the table. With tears falling, she walked toward the bathroom. I gave Tia a look that said *Now, look what you did.* She shrugged her shoulders and took another sip of her drink.

I got up and followed Reshaun to the bathroom. I walked into the two-stall, cramped, and dimly lit bathroom.

"You okay, girl?"

"Yeah, I'm all right," she said as she flushed the toilet and exited the stall. She went over to the sink and washed her hands and splashed a little water on her face.

"Listen, if you like him, I love him. Sorry if I sounded like I was hatin'. Okay?" I gave Reshaun a big smile and said, "Congratulations!"

"I hate Tia sometimes. She thinks she knows everything, but her life is not together, either."

"She doesn't mean to act like a know-it-all," I said.

"Yes, she does. But before she starts pointing her fingers at other people, she needs to get rid of her boyfriend. How she sound, talking about me? At least I found someone who can hold it down. Her man don't do shit for her."

I knew Reshaun was right, but I didn't say anything. The funniest thing was that we all had answers for each other's problems, but couldn't solve our own issues.

We walked back to the table and Tia apologized, too. After three more rounds of drinks, all was forgotten. We both congratulated Reshaun again, even though we still didn't agree with her decision.

As I left to drive home from the restaurant my only thought was that I just wished we could all find good men. Then I wondered what Malcolm was doing and I thought about calling him. I fought the urge to give in. I couldn't. It was time for me to find a love of my own.

On the way home, I started feeling those margaritas. I almost fell asleep at every red light. I only had four blocks to go and hoped I could make it. When I finally made it to my block, I was so happy. I looked over at my house. The downstairs lights were still on, and that meant Ernest was still on the sofa, watching television. I didn't want him to see me stumbling in the house, so I decided the trek from my car to the front door was too far to go. I was sleepy and it was warm in the car. I figured I would just close my eyes for a few minutes. I made sure my doors were locked and leaned my seat all the way back.

A loud knock awoke me. Damn, it was now morning and I was still in my car and the engine was still running. My mom was looking at me through the thick glass window. The morning sun rays were shining directly in the car. I squinted up at her and rolled the window down.

"You slept in this car. You know somebody could have stole you and this car. Are you crazy? Something's wrong with you. Were you drinking?" My mom looked at me with disgust. "Why are you so damn irresponsible?"

She was asking too many questions at once and her voice, along with the glaring sun, was making my head hurt. My mouth felt dry, and the rest of my body was being taken over by dizziness and nausea. I lied and said, "I just pulled up."

"Nikki, I'm not stupid. You look like shit. You better slow down on all that drinking. It is a problem when you can't even make it inside the house."

I continued to try to convince her that I didn't sleep in the car all night and I had just pulled up a few minutes ago. She finally left me alone and got in her car and pulled off. As I turned my car off, I saw the Check Engine light on. I made a mental note to take the car to my mechanic on Monday morning. I went in the house and slept off my hangover. Saturday came and went. I slept the whole day away.

CHAPTER 4

It has been three months since I declared that I was not dealing with Married Man Malcolm anymore. Every time I saw his number appear on my phone screen I ignored the call, but I couldn't help but wonder what he really wants. Was he calling to say that he was really ready this time? If so, was I missing my chance to be with him? I would love to hear *Nikki, I'm getting a divorce.* That would be music to my ears. That was the only way I would take him back. And he can't just say it. He would have to have some proof that he had really filed for a divorce. I wanted to see the divorce decree and the judge's signature. Or at least that's what I thought it would take. I knew Malcolm was married, but I also knew he was so unhappy. I just wished he could get the strength to leave her.

I was debating if I should just pick up the phone or send it to voice mail. A little voice kept telling me not to answer the telephone each time he called. And I was doing good being strong, until Malcolm left me a message on the answering machine. He was practically crying on there. And as soon as I heard his voice I lost it. My rock-hard exterior turned right back into a soft pillow. After listening to his tearful apology on my voice mail, I did something I hadn't done in three months. I called him. Malcolm didn't have to provide me with anything but an *I really miss you,* an invitation to meet up with him, and I was all his again.

"I miss you so much, Nikki. I got a few hours. Can I please see you?"

I wanted to tell him I didn't want a few of his hours, I wanted all twenty-four or nothing at all. But I didn't have the strength to play hard-to-get anymore. So, I called my hotel's sister property that's located downtown, and reserved us a hotel room, using my associate discount rate. *I'm so damn dumb,* I thought as I made the reservation. But, I think every woman has one man she will never give up hope on, who she dreams one day will change.

After I reserved our room, I showered and unwrapped my hair. I put on a lavender bra and thong set. I threw on a pair of blue jeans and a pink sweater, and gold-and-pink earrings. I couldn't wait to meet up with him. I told him to meet me at the hotel on Walnut Street. I was ready in less than fifteen minutes, because I didn't want to waste any of our time together.

"Mom, you going back out?" I asked my mother.

"No, why?"

"Can I hold your car? My Check Engine light is on in my car."

"I don't care, as long as you fill up my tank. The keys are on the kitchen counter."

* * *

I made it downtown in ten minutes. I pulled into the parking lot, and I saw Malcolm flashing his lights at me. I parked, locked my mom's car up, and walked over to his red Dodge Intrepid. He got out of the car and gave me the warmest hug, like he really missed me. I looked up at him and he turned me around and leaned me against his car door and planted kisses all over my neck and right cheek. My entire body warmed up. Oh, I missed him so much too. I loved him. I couldn't wait to get upstairs in the hotel room and let him fuck me nonstop.

"You look so beautiful." He pulled away from me, smoothed his hands over my hair. He took another look at me and then kissed me again. And said, "Please don't stay away from me. I need you. You know that, Nikki." He actually had me feeling guilty and emotional, like I was wrong for staying away from him.

"Come on, let's go inside." I grabbed his hand to lead him inside the hotel.

"Hold up, let me grab Tyler."

"Tyler? You didn't tell me you had your son with you."

"I had to pick him up. She is at a baby shower."

My excitement gauge went down from a ten to a minus two. How could he fuck me nonstop with his son sharing a room with us? I looked in the car. Tyler was asleep with his coat on him. Malcolm's wife probably thought if he had the baby with him, he wouldn't cheat. I knew that's what her stupid ass was probably thinking. She was trying to ruin our evening, but I wasn't about to let her do that.

As he got Tyler out the car, I went to the front desk and began checking in. Malcolm had a seat on the lobby sofa and began unbuttoning Tyler's coat.

"Do you need a crib?" the front-desk clerk asked, looking over at Malcolm and the baby.

"No, but do you have any suites at the associate rate?"

"We have suites, but not available at the associate rate."

"How much is the regular rate?" I asked.

"With tax included, it is two hundred and fifteen per night." I pulled out my cash and handed eleven twenties over to her. She made me a room key and said, "I hope you and your family have a great stay. The elevators are to your right."

"Thank you," I said as I got my change. Malcolm and Tyler followed me to our suite. I was a little mad that the baby was there, but I wanted to make the best out of the situation. I wasn't mad at his son, but I was mad at his stupid mother.

We went into the suite, where there was a queen-size bed and two night stands in one room and a living room with a pull-out sofa-bed in the other. I turned the television and light on in the bedroom. Malcolm took Tyler's clothes off and laid him on the sofa. Then he came in the bedroom with me and shut the door.

"I still feel bad with Tyler being in here," I murmured.

"He is asleep, he can't hear or see us. You're wasting time. I missed you. Why have you been neglecting me for all these months?"

"I don't know. It's just that I need to know how long we're going to be playing this game. I've been patient for three years, Malcolm. Come on," I said as I turned and walked a few steps away from him.

He grabbed me and turned my body around to face him. He put his finger up to my lips and said "Shhh" because he knew where I was going and he didn't want to hear it. He tilted my chin and kissed me. As soon as I tasted his lips, all my defenses were gone—once again.

He knew how to work me. Very softly, he stroked the side of my face. My entire insides began to warm up. Malcolm had the blueprint and the key that opened every door on my body and there was nothing I could do about it. He quickly undressed and then seductively peeled down my jeans and then pulled my pink top over my head. His naked six-foot-two, dark brown, wood-grain-colored skin stood in front of me. *I love you so so much,* I thought. I couldn't help the way I felt. Malcolm was perfect and I wanted to kiss every centimeter of his gorgeous, sculpted body.

His legs, chest, and stomach were full of ripped muscles. I kissed him as he slowly removed my bra and then began to let his tongue wrestle with the hardened tips of my nipples. His tongue won as I squirmed and tried to enjoy the moment and not scream out his name. I didn't want to make too much noise with Tyler in the other room.

He then left my breasts alone to go and play with other parts of my body. He shimmied my panties down, inch by inch, until they were hanging around my ankles. I flung them off. Malcolm kneeled down in front of me and took his thick, moist tongue and began wagging on my clitoris like he was thirsty and my insides held the water he desperately needed. With every lick, I could feel my knees getting weak. The sensation of his tongue had me winding my hips. I was now ready for him to enter me, but before he placed his hardness inside me I had to return the favor. He had done such a good job pleasing me, he deserved it. I began sweeping my lips back and forth, covering what I missed with soft kisses. I licked his shaft up and down, and then started making little circles around the head of his dick with my tongue. Then I pulled him inside my mouth. I couldn't help from moaning as I felt his manhood grow in size and power. I stopped midway because I wanted him to release inside my body.

Malcolm threw me on the bed and turned me over so my ass could point directly up at him. I was on top of the bed with my legs spread apart, each foot touching the opposite side of the bed. Forcefully, he entered me. And once again I wanted to scream from pleasure. But I was forced to control myself and hold it in. I grabbed the white bed sheets as my tightness bench-pressed him, pulling it in and out. He twisted his pelvis from one side to the other, trying to knock out each wall with his stroke. He worked it from side to side, and then switched to a straight stroke, hitting my G-spot each time. I could feel that his body was about to climax and it felt so good, I didn't want it to end.

"You want this?" I asked him.

"Yeah, baby," he mumbled.

"Does it feel good?"

"Yes, your pussy is so fucking good and you know it."

"Then don't cum yet. Try this time to hold back," I said. I really wanted to say, *Is it good enough to leave that bitch? Is it good enough to be with me, every day?* But of course, I kept those thoughts to myself.

"I can't hold it, Nikki, it's too good," he groaned as his body jerked back and forth into mine until he couldn't move anymore. And that's when I clenched together my insides and wrung every ounce of fluid from his body.

"Baby, don't do that. Stop! For real. I love you, Nikki. You about to make me cry," he said as he collapsed on top of me and panted in my ears, telling me over and over how much he loved me.

When his heart rate calmed down, he put on his underwear, went to the bathroom, and checked on Tyler. Then he came back and we just lay in the bed and held each other. The sex was always so good, so beautiful and great. But being held by Malcolm afterward was my favorite part. I loved resting my head on his chest and hearing our heartbeats playing drums back and forth, together. This was true heaven and it always ended too soon.

We took a brief nap before Tyler awoke. Malcolm gave him a snack and turned the Cartoon Network on and came and got back in bed with me. He left the door open and Tyler sipped on his juice cup and ate Cheerios from his container. We both dozed off again until Tyler began crying. When I opened my eyes I saw my pocketbook, keys, credit cards, and makeup scattered all around the room.

Malcolm jumped up and said, "What are you doing, Tyler? Stop crying." Then he stared at his cell phone. "She called me nine times!" he yelled. Suddenly, he jumped up and began dressing Tyler.

His phone started ringing again. He answered and I walked in the bathroom to give him some privacy. I hated hearing his conversation with her. She must have asked him where he was, because I could hear him say, "Getting something to eat." Then he said, "He's fine. He took a nap. Yeah, we went to the movies. I'll be home shortly."

His last words made my heart hurt, and that familiar feeling of being all by myself crept up on me once again. Before I finished washing my face, he came inside the bathroom and said, "Let me get in here real quick." I turned off the faucets. My feelings were hurt, but I didn't say anything. I tried not to let my emotions show. I left the bathroom with my game face on, trying to act like there was nothing wrong.

Tyler knew me. He smiled as I played with him while his father showered, washing away what we just did.

"You a daddy's boy. You love daddy?" I asked him as he smiled and playfully slapped my cheek.

Malcolm came out of the shower smelling of soap and cologne. He dressed quickly. I couldn't help feeling sad as I walked him and his son to his car. He hadn't even pulled off yet and I was missing him like crazy. I watched sadly as he put the baby bag and Tyler in the car. Next, he threw his duffel bag in the trunk. I gave him a hug. "I don't want you to go," I whispered, holding on to him with all my might.

"I don't wanna leave you, Nikki. But you know what it is. I have to go."

"When am I going to see you again?" I asked as he got in the car. I hated that I had allowed myself to be pulled right back into the same messed-up situation.

"I don't know, but I got to go, I don't want her tripping." He saw I was about to tear up so he said, "It is not going to be that much longer. I promise you."

I managed to hold back my tears and said "Bye," as he pulled off. I waved at the car as it traveled out of sight. I couldn't help being upset. It's just that I wanted him so bad. I wanted him to get a divorce and marry me. We could buy a house and his son could come and live with us. I would be a good stepmom. I just wished we could wake up together every morning and he would be at my beck and call.

I went back to the suite, showered, and then threw my clothes back on. I knew he was going to have to leave me, but I didn't expect him to leave this early. It was only seven and it was still early, so I decided to stop by Tia's. I hadn't been able to reach her for a couple of days.

CHAPTER 5

Tia lived in a big house that her parents gave her and her brother. Her brother got married, so now the house belonged to Tia. She had so much space and was so lucky. If she didn't have Lamar's bum-ass around all the time, I would be trying to stay with her instead of living with my mother.

"You look cute. Where you coming from?" Tia asked.

"The hotel with Malcolm and his son."

She didn't say anything right way, but I knew what was on her mind. She wanted to say something, like I was wrong, but I knew that already.

"You a bold bitch," she said, shaking her head.

"Whatever, you going to stop disappearing? Who you creeping with?"

"Nobody, Lamar just be on some ish. Every few days he wants all of my time and I got to give it to him."

"Damn, you could at least send me a text message or something."

"I know," she said.

"What was you about to do?"

"Nothing. How about I'm pregnant again. And Lamar going to tell me to get rid of the baby," she said as she sucked her teeth.

"He got a lot of damn nerve. Tell his ass that his mom should have got rid of him."

"I don't know what I'm going to do. It is a miracle I'm pregnant again. He told me ever since I peed on a stick that I'm acting crazy."

"What?"

"He being a little ignorant. He'll get over it. I hope he will, anyway."

"Can you get desk duty?"

"Maybe. I will if I make it to my second trimester. I'm going to have to figure it out."

This was Tia's third pregnancy in the last five years. She had one ectopic pregnancy the year before last, and a miscarriage last summer. It was wrong to think, but I thought maybe she wasn't supposed to have a baby by Lamar and God was trying to tell her that.

"Reshaun got married," Tia said.

"I didn't think she would really do it."

"They went down to Maryland. It only takes forty-eight hours to get a marriage license down there. Let's see what she doing," she said as she dialed Reshaun's number.

"Can you come out, girl? Why not? Okay, bye."

"What she say?" I asked.

"She said she is not leaving her husband, but we could come over there. Let's go meet this guy."

* * *

We drove over to the new apartment Reshaun shared with Michael on City Avenue. All we knew about Michael was he was from Liberia, he was thirty-five, and was an engineer for Lockheed Martin. Their condo was spacious and decorated with abstract paintings and modern leather furniture.

In one week Reshaun didn't even look like my friend anymore. She had on eyeglasses that she never wore, and was wearing flat shoes. Though she didn't look like herself, she looked like she was so happy. As soon as we entered, Reshaun took us on a tour of the condo. She was in the middle of cooking something and the smell was flooding the condo.

"Where is Briggy at?" Tia asked.

"Him and Michael went to play basketball, while I finish dinner."

"You only knew him a month and you're leaving your son with him already? I am happy for you, but I still would watch him," Tia said, scrunching her nose up and shaking her head.

"I'm not stupid, Tia. I checked his criminal and child abuse records. He is not wanted. I know all his previous addresses. I ran his credit. I have his social security number and he put my name on this condo. We took our HIV test. I took all the precautions, but I'm not going to start looking for something to be wrong. When you look for stuff you find it. Michael is everything I prayed for. I have faith. I'm going back to school. He told me if I don't want to work anymore I didn't have to and I can go to school full-time."

"What are you going back to school for?" I asked.

"I'm not sure yet." Reshaun shrugged. "I was

thinking about getting a degree in pharmacy, maybe. Or something like that, maybe physical therapy. First I'm going to take the rest of my prerequisites and then I'll decide on my major. Michael's going to help me. I just feel so comfortable. I just never had this feeling before. It feels so good to have a good man in my life."

"I think you should try to help yourself," I pointed out.

"I am, but I just think somewhere along the line somebody got to wake up and realize that they have a good person and stop trying to find all the wrong. We do it all the time . . . finding flaws in everyone we meet. I just feel like I gave a good guy a chance," she said, folding her arms defensively.

"And what is that supposed to mean?" Tia asked.

"It means I'm accepting him the way he is and I'm not looking for his flaws or any reasons not to love him."

"So this is it?" I asked, as I surveyed her new home.

"Yes, and he will be here in a few minutes and you can both meet him. You don't know how happy I am that I looked outside of the box. I could have really let this wonderful man pass me by because he doesn't match what I thought I wanted."

I felt bad because I was tempted to ask her if she was really happy. People usually don't get this happy this fast without strings. It just doesn't happen. I gave Tia a look and she looked back at me, nodding. We both agreed Reshaun was settling and if that was all right with her, we would have to go along.

Moments later, Michael came in. He kissed Reshaun's cheek and handed her flowers. We all smiled as she opened the cabinet beneath her sink and grabbed a vase. I don't know what I was expecting, but he looked surprisingly Americanized. I think I was looking for a tall, royal, dark-skinned man with high cheekbones to enter the condo. But Michael was a medium shade of brown and was an average height and just looked like any ordinary black man. His clothes gave him away just a little bit. He had his shirt tucked into his old stone-washed blue jeans with his cell phone on his hip inside a holster, and an earpiece wrapped around his lobe.

He was very pleasant, and he had the cutest British accent. He spoke with us for a few minutes and then went into his office. We talked a little bit more and then me and Tia got up to leave.

"Love ya, be safe, and have fun. We all going to go out in a few weeks and have dinner," Reshaun said as she walked us to the door.

"All right, girl. See you," I said. We walked to the car and I looked at Tia and said, "So, what you think?"

"I don't know, I'm just saying," she said as we got in the car. Tia and I had our own little language. I could look at her and she knew what I was thinking.

"What are you saying?"

"I dunno. He is a little funny-looking and a little short."

"He's not funny-looking, and I think he's mildly handsome," I said as I began laughing, unable to contain myself. "Maybe we are wrong," I said.

"Maybe. But I doubt it."

* * *

After leaving Reshaun and Michael's condo, I wondered what real love might feel like. I'd never seen Reshaun so content and happy in her life, about anything or anybody, since I'd known her. Granted, it had only been a month, but for some reason, her happiness seemed real. I was a little more convinced.

"How long before that is one of us, wearing glasses and staying in on a Saturday night?"

"What do you mean?" I asked.

"I mean, will we ever just enjoy making dinner, going to work, and never having fun?"

"Hell, no. We going to be old and still hanging out. I want our husbands to go out and still meet for dinner dates. We are going to party until we are both wearing Depends."

"You right, but she is out of the club," Tia said.

"Yeah, her membership has been officially revoked." I laughed hysterically as I drove back downtown.

We went from Reshaun's condo to a little place call Bobby's Crab House to have some dinner and drinks. Tia asked me if I was dealing with my dad's stuff. I didn't really want to talk about it, but she kept asking.

"I'm doing okay. I'm still having thoughts here and there, but I'm dealing with it. I cried a few times."

"You think you should see a counselor or something? If it really is bothering you like that, maybe you should."

"I don't need to see a counselor, I'm fine. I'll get

over it. I don't really want to talk about it. Damn, I wish you could drink with me. Why you got to be pregnant?" I laughed as I looked over the menu.

"I'm still going to get a drink. One won't hurt. I really need one."

"No, you can't have a drink. It might hurt the baby," I said, looking up from the menu.

"Trust me, I need one. Internal Affairs is investigating me."

"Why?" I asked, alarmed.

"Last week, Lamar got locked up while he was driving my car. He had stolen televisions and hundreds of bootleg DVDs and CDs in the trunk and I'm stressing bad. I really might lose my job."

"Is he out yet? What is Lamar saying?"

"He is out, but he is not saying too much. But really, what can he say, but sorry. The bad thing is that Internal Affairs is going around talking to people on my block. My neighbors told me that they are asking about my character and what type of activities go on at my house."

"Really? That's crazy."

"Lamar said he is not going to let anything happen to me, but this shit is just coming at the wrong time. I'm pregnant and I might be getting fired. If I get fired then I won't have any benefits. I don't know what I am going to do without my job. If I get fired I'm probably just going to move to South Carolina with my family."

"Don't worry, you are not going to get fired." I tried to reassure Tia, but in my head I was thinking *damn.* That was some crushing news and a drink was needed. I ordered us double mango margaritas with sugar rims. We drank and talked about our crazy lives. We got off her events and got back on mine, which was Malcolm. I had a million reasons why I should leave him again. And ten million reasons why I wanted to stay. It didn't make a difference that I had just come from having passionate sex with him. I still wasn't satisfied. I wanted more from him and he wouldn't or couldn't give it to me and that made me furious.

"Tia, I hate the way I don't have total control over him. And I feel like I'm not ever going to get him the way I want him. I feel like I'm wasting my time. Like even today, we had this great afternoon together. Then it seems like as soon as it began, he had to hurry home. I just feel like cutting him off forever. Staying away from him for three months obviously wasn't long enough."

"Yeah, leave him alone. I don't think he is ever going to leave his wife."

"You are probably right," I said, sounding sad and defeated as my margarita was starting to take effect of my movement and speech. I found myself becoming emotional to the point of being on the verge of tears. "Tia, I love him so much. I just want him to be there for me and love me more. It's like he stopped trying. Like I'm never going to have his heart. Like he is happy with the way things are."

"You are never going to have him the way you want him, as long as he is married."

"I know you are right." I continued spilling my heart out again about my dad, Malcolm, and my job. It wasn't until last call that we got up from the stools and got ready to go home. All we did for the last few hours was have the same conversation over and over again. Why couldn't men act right? Why did they cheat? Why couldn't they be satisfied with one woman? I felt like we were going in circles but, at the same time, it was therapeutic to be able to get it all out. Through all the alcohol, I realized I really needed to do something about Malcolm and I could clearly see that Tia should really get rid of Lamar, also. Maybe Reshaun was right about giving a good guy a chance. I was giving a married man a chance and Tia was giving a thug a chance. Would Tia or I give good guys all the chances we'd given Lamar and Malcolm? Probably not, at least not yet.

"You okay to drive?" Tia asked as we approached my mother's car.

"Yeah, I'm all right," I said as I staggered slightly. Tia put on her seat belt and announced that she was going to Lamar's house. I became instantly mad. All that shit she just talked about Lamar—*He ain't no good* and *I'm ready to leave his ass*—and now she wants me to take her to his house in Willingboro, New Jersey. I really didn't feel like it. Everything in my body was telling me to drop her off where I picked her up. Instead of going with my first instinct, I drove across the Benjamin Franklin Bridge into New Jersey. I felt okay, but felt myself dozing off a little. I swerved into another lane, but I caught myself before I hit the car in the next lane. I checked in my rearview mirror and noticed a police cruiser do a quick U-turn. Seeing the cop car following behind me made me perk up. My back got stiff and I placed both my arms at three and nine o'clock on the steering wheel. I wasn't trying to get pulled over. I came to the next light and it was turning yellow. I wanted to speed through it so bad, but I didn't want to give the cop any reason to pull me over.

Tia was half asleep and I had to wake her up without making a lot of motion. So, I slightly tapped her.

"Tia, there's a cop behind us," I said as I tried to get myself together.

"Okay, you're fine, right?" she asked as she turned around and looked at the cop car.

"No, I'm not all right. I'm so damn drunk."

"Okay, just play it cool. Drive regular. You know if we get pulled over I can't show my badge. I told you I'm under investigation. Stop looking in your mirror and just drive normal." I took her advice, but I just kept thinking about the cop pulling me over. I went four more blocks before I looked in the rearview mirror again. Luckily, I didn't see him. He had turned off, thank God.

I was in the clear, or so I thought. I was a few blocks away from Lamar's house when this little red sports car came out of nowhere. I think he ran the red light, but all I know is I tried to swerve into the other lane to avoid hitting him. Trying to get out of his way made me lose control of the car. And as much as I tried, the car would not stop spinning from side to side. The car whipped back and forth, even though I was struggling to keep it going straight. There was nothing I could do. I knew we were about to crash. I put my hands up in front of me and waited for the impact. Then we did a full circle and slammed into the guardrail and I hit my head against the windshield. By the time it was over, the car was facing the opposite direction of traffic. Smoke was everywhere, the airbags had burst open, and my mom's car alarm started going off. The dust from both air bags was making me gag. Tia was coughing too. I asked if she was okay and she nodded her head but looked like she was in a state of shock. I looked out of the window and down at the street. There were pieces of the car on the ground. The driver of the sports car came over and asked if we were okay.

"Yeah," I said, shaking my head yes while imagining my mother having a fit over her car.

He pulled out a cell phone. "I'm dialing 911."

I was still feeling a little bit of the effects of drinking and didn't want to appear drunk, so I reached in my glove compartment and sprayed perfume on my clothes and then looked through my bag and put a few pieces of chewing gum in my mouth.

"Do I look drunk?" I asked Tia as I turned to her. She inspected my face.

"A little, but just play it off." She dug in her bag and handed me lotion to put on my face, and some lip gloss.

What looked like the same police cruiser from earlier pulled up behind us, his red and blue lights flashing. I could see the officer approaching through my side mirror. He had a big black ranger hat, navy blue uniform, and big black combat boots. He stomped his way up to the car.

"You guys okay?" the officer asked as he bent over to look into the car.

"Yeah, uhm, we're fine," I said.

"Do you ladies need medical attention?" he asked as he shined his flashlight in our faces. We both said no, but he still told us to stay put, until the ambulance got there. As we waited, a red truck pulled up with flashing yellow lights. The tow-truck driver got out and began talking to the police officer. I wanted to get out the car. I was wondering if I should call my mom. Tia had called Lamar and he was on his way to pick her up. All I wanted was to just have the car towed to the shop and then call my mom and have her and Ernest come and get me. Yeah, I knew she was going to go off over me wrecking her car, but I'd deal with that later. I touched the side of my head, and could feel a little bump coming up and it hurt. I wished I could call Malcolm, so he could be by my side, but I couldn't. I began massaging the growing knot on my head. I felt so sad, so scared, and didn't know what to do.

Minutes later the ambulance pulled up and two EMTs came over to the car and helped us out and began evaluating us. I didn't feel great, but I didn't want to go to the hospital. I had to get this car home and get it fixed. As I walked with Tia to the ambulance, one of the EMTs noticed the bump on the right side of my head. They wanted to take me in, but I said no. I had to sign a form that stated that I was refusing medical attention. However, Tia said her neck and back were hurting and she wanted to go to the hospital. I told her to call me later. The tow-truck driver started putting the car on the tow. The only thing that was on my mind was getting this car fixed. I looked at the front grill that was hanging off and the tire that was busted. I knew I was looking at at least four thousand dollars' worth of damages. I had no choice but to call Lolo, tell her what happened, and ask her to come and get me.

After Tia left in the ambulance and the car was on the tow truck, the officer began asking me questions about the accident. I was still trying to keep my distance as he wrote up his report. I didn't know if he could smell the alcohol or not. I sat on the curb and kept trying to appear as normal as possible, as I waited for my mom to get there. I thought I was acting pretty normal, but he kept having me repeat myself. I was beginning to feel a little nervous. Then he asked me, would I mind walking a straight line for him and take a Breathalyzer test. I knew I wasn't really drunk, so I took it. I must have passed because the police officer continued on like everything was fine. At least I thought it was fine, until two female cops pulled up in another car and walked over to me. They asked me to stand up and to place my hands on the police car. As soon as I did as they asked, they cuffed me and put me in the back of their car. On the way to the station they informed me I was under arrest for driving under the influence and that I was going to jail.

At the police station I felt like the dumbest loser. I wished my day would have ended at the hotel, with Malcolm. Something had been telling me to go home and I didn't. Now I was stuck in a dirty cell with crazy people and roaches. It was hot, and people were sleeping on the floor, oblivious to the stench and filth inside the cell. There was an old woman with matted gray hair and no teeth. She smelled like urine and looked like shit. There were a few young prostitutes. They looked like meth addicts with horrible red, crater-like blemishes on their pink skin. They kept scratching and I began to itch. I was disgusted and wanted out of that cell. This other lady was arguing with herself and I couldn't tell who was winning. Then she would stop and yell to the guard that she needed her insulin. I wanted out of this place, immediately.

I am not a drunk. How did I end up sitting in a jail cell? I kept asking myself over and over. *Dumb ass!* All I could think about was if I'd followed my first instincts and hadn't crossed that bridge to take Tia to Lamar's, I would be home in my bed right now. Now, because I didn't say no, I was going to have to miss a day of work. I might even get a criminal record for this bullshit.

I used my one phone call to call Lolo. I told her what happened and where I was, and without saying one word, she hung up on me. I didn't know if she was on her way or not. But when I was released from the jail, she was there with Ernest. I was given a notice to appear in court in thirty days. During the car ride home, I was waiting for my mom to lecture me about how she told me about drinking and driving and I should have called a cab. But she didn't say anything. My head was still spinning. I felt like a teenager who got caught being out late and my parents were picking me up from the party. Every time she would look at me, I felt like I was going to get slapped or popped upside the head. I wanted my mom to calm down before I attempted to explain what happened. I knew that it was very unlikely. Lolo couldn't go without saying something to me.

"So are you an alcoholic now? Let me know if I have to send you to rehab so I can start saving up," she blurted out.

"Lolo, leave her alone. She don't have to go to rehab, she just had one too many and got caught,"

Ernest said as he looked at me through the rearview mirror.

"You shut up. I'm talking to my daughter, not you. Nicole, you could have killed somebody." I didn't bother responding to her. I knew everything she was saying was true and I didn't feel like discussing it.

As soon as I got in the house, I showered—and tried to get my thoughts together. Then I called my job and lied to them about the seriousness of my car accident. After I got that out the way, I called Tia to make sure she was okay. Her phone rang like eight times. I was about to hang up when she finally answered.

"Tia, you okay?"

"Yeah, girl, I'm fine and the baby is fine."

"Well, I got locked up," I sighed.

"You are lying."

"No, I'm for real. I got a court date."

"Shut the fuck up."

"When you left, that cop made me walk a straight line and take a Breathalyzer and I failed the test."

Chapter 6

Last week taught me so much. One, I would not drive at all after I've been drinking. Two, I wouldn't drink for a long-ass while. I had to get my mom's car fixed after I just got mine fixed. I had to hire an attorney, and pay all kinds of fines. If I got found guilty, I could get points on my license. I just wished it had never happened. My mom hadn't said too much, and that meant she is like a ticking time bomb, waiting to explode on me. Even though I knew it was coming, I just didn't know how and when. I came in from work and I tried to rush upstairs to my room, but my mom caught me.

"Uhm, did Tia say anything to you about the accident?"

"No, why? Mom, I'm really busy," I said, trying to avoid a confrontation with her.

"That bad-shaped, flat-assed hefa is suing me. I received a certified letter today. She ain't getting a dollar out of me."

"Mom, what? Who is suing you?"

"Your so-called friend, Tia."

"Tia is not suing you. There must be a mistake. I'm going to call her now and get it straightened out."

"Ain't shit to straighten out—she ain't getting shit out of me. Then, she got that real big injury attorney off the television commercial, Ed Tolamge, like she really got a case. I hope she don't think she is going to get paid. I thought you said she wasn't hurt, Nicole?"

"She wasn't hurt. She went to the hospital as a precaution, 'cause she's pregnant. I'll talk to her, Mom."

"You better before I do. I don't need this shit right now. This girl trying to sue me. Ernest got problems with his prostate and he's sick! I got enough damn shit on my plate."

"Wait a minute, Ernest got prostate problems—like cancer?"

"Yeah. He got an appointment to go to the doctors again tomorrow. They gonna run some more tests."

"Why didn't you tell me?"

"I don't know. You was looking all sad lately, you know, since you went to that funeral and everything. Plus, Ernest ain't really want anybody to know."

"But Ernest is like my dad. I still want to know what's going on with him." Oh, my goodness, this is horrible, was all I could think as I went to my room.

After work I went straight to Tia's house. I knocked on her door and she didn't answer, but her car was there. From outside her house, I called her phone.

"Where you at, Tia?"

"I'm at Lamar's house."

"I'm at your house. I need to talk to you. Why did my mom just get a letter from your attorney saying that she is being sued by you?"

"Oh, yeah, I've been meaning to tell you about that. Lamar thought I should sue the insurance company because I am having a little back pain."

What Tia was saying didn't register with me. Was she serious? I should have known shady-ass Lamar was behind this bullshit.

"Okay, listen, Tia, when you sue the insurance company, you know you are suing my mom, right?"

"No, I'm not suing your mom. I'm suing the insurance company."

"You're suing my mom. You are not even hurt. I see you got that con artist in your ear, again."

"No, it's not like that at all. I'm suing the insurance company. The way my attorney explained it to me, that's what insurance is for. You are supposed to use it. Your mom won't have to come out of her pocket. When I settle, I will throw your mom a little something."

"My mom don't need you to throw her anything. What she needs is for you not to sue her."

"Uhm, Nikki, I got to go. I'll talk to you later," she said as she hurried off the phone.

The first day I wasn't that mad at Tia. The second day after my stepfather said something to me, I still wasn't really that upset. But when my mom burst into my room on my day off and said I had to go to the insurance office with her, I became fuming mad. Her agent said she needed to come down and discuss everything with him. I so didn't need this shit.

We walked into the insurance office nestled in the busy strip mall. My mom's agent, Rick Sarento, told us to have a seat. I tried not to make eye contact with my mom. I knew she was about to say something to me, so I turned the other way. I couldn't take her mouth right now. But she wouldn't be Lolo if she didn't criticize me.

"You not going to let yourself go, are you?"

"Mom, I threw this on to come down here with you."

"But still, nobody could ever catch me outside looking the way you do. Nicole, you always look a mess. You never listen to anything I say. We could have avoided all of this if you would have listened. I warned you about that girl like thirteen years ago—she ain't right, but you will learn."

"Ladies, are you guys ready?" Mr. Sarento asked as he pulled out all this paperwork and placed it all over his sloppy desk.

"Now, here's the deal, Mrs. Edwards. It is not going to be my decision, but it is very likely the adjuster may deny the claim."

"Why?" my mother asked, surprised.

"How can they do that?" I jumped in.

"Well, first, you were not on your mother's policy. Secondly, when there is alcohol involved it is pretty much a shut case. The blame is pretty much on the driver."

"I wasn't that drunk. I was more tired than drunk."

"It doesn't matter, but don't get all excited.

They haven't denied the claim yet. But I wanted to give you the worst-case scenario, because there are a lot of variables," he said as he looked up something on his computer screen and then printed out something else.

"So, that's what you think is going to happen?" I asked.

"Yes," he said as he looked at my mom, and then at me. "The adjuster is going to make a determination based on the investigation. So, Miss Edwards, if we deny the claim you will be responsible for damages to your own car and any civil case or injury cases."

"She is not even hurt," my mother said, shaking her head.

"Well, good. Maybe you can talk to this friend of yours," he said as he strained to read the police report.

"So, she does have a case?" my mother asked.

"Not really, but she can definitely sue for medical bills, but anything above that, such as pain and suffering, she doesn't have enough evidence to make a case. It is going to take a lot of rehab and extensive treatment and a bunch of doctor visits to convince a judge that she deserves compensation. Something like that would take, at the very least, six months to two years. But if she follows through and is successful, she can put a lien on your house."

Hearing the words "lien on your house" was all my mom needed to hear. On the way home she called me every type of retarded, stupid bitch there was in the world. I was so mad at Tia, and even madder at myself.

* * *

I tried to reach Tia for about two weeks. She didn't answer my texts or calls. My mom had even left a few messages for her. I even did a few drive-bys past her house and she was never there. I really couldn't believe she was acting like this. This was not the Tia that I knew. That dumb-ass man must have been all in her ear all kinds of ways. First, he got her to want to sue my mom and now she is not speaking to me. Something is definitely up. And even though I had promised Reshaun weeks ago that I would go to dinner with her and Michael, now I didn't want to go. I didn't know what I was liable to do when I finally saw Tia's ass. I knew she was going to be there, but a promise was a promise. However, I couldn't be sure that I wouldn't kill Tia.

Michael and Reshaun were already seated in a private room in Maggiano's Italian restaurant. The table was white, with candles and place settings for five. Michael stood up and gave me a fast hug and thanked me for coming. Reshaun hugged me and was still rocking her married look. She looked cute, though. She was wearing her glasses, a blue button-down shirt, and black slacks. Our waitress was pleasant and came around and took orders for our appetizers and wine. As I ordered my calamari and a red wine, Tia and Lamar took their seats. I looked across the table and rolled my eyes. I didn't acknowledge either of them. Tia spoke to me anyway, but I ignored her. I picked up my phone and began checking my messages and acting like I was sending a text. As far as I was concerned, Tia and her man didn't exist.

Halfway through dinner, Tia was still trying her best to make conversation with me. It was so obvious I was still not speaking to her, but for some reason she still kept trying to make idle conversation. I looked over at her, sighed, and shook my head. Then she looked at me and asked what was wrong with me. I twisted my lips and was ready to get up from the table. The more I stayed in their presence, the more and more pissed off I became. Here it is, I've been calling and leaving her messages and she didn't even bother to call me back and now that she was in my face, she couldn't stop talking. I rolled my eyes again, letting her know . . . *I don't think so, you slimy bitch!* Then she had the nerve to ask me what was wrong with me. So since she asked, I leaned forward and said, "Tia, I don't believe you are going to sit across the table from me and act like nothing happened."

"What you talking about?" She looked around at everybody like I was talking crazy.

"You got a lot of damn nerve acting like nothing is going on. Me and my mother have been calling you and leaving messages every day for you. And you didn't have the decency to return any of our calls. You know my mom can lose her house if you go through with this lawsuit," I screamed across the table.

"Listen, I told you what it was. I gotta protect myself," she yelled back.

"You not even hurt. What's wrong with you? You not going to get anything. You wasting your time and putting my mom through unnecessary stress."

"I don't know what you are talking about."

"You know exactly what I'm talking about. How

you let this part-time con artist and full-time loser, come between us?"

"Who you calling a loser?" Lamar asked, looking over at me.

"Thirty-four-year-old d-boy, sit down," I said. He acted like he wanted to hit me and I gave him a look that said, *Do it, so I can whup your ass.*

As we argued, I heard Michael ask Reshaun what a d-boy was. She whispered, "A drug dealer." Then Reshaun said, "Please y'all, come on, we are here to celebrate. Let's relax and discuss this later."

"I can't relax. My mother's house can get taken. I'm not playing with you, Tia. You better do something."

"You not playing with me? Please," Tia said.

"No, I'm not. I'm serious. You need to call your attorney and tell him that you want to drop the case. 'Cause if you don't, Tia, I swear, you going to make me fuck you up," I said as I balled up my napkin and sat with my arms crossed.

She stretched across the table. "Fuck me up! Please! Don't tell me what to do, Nikki," she said as her voice elevated.

"Tia, for real? Really? Wow, I can't believe you going through all this. Times aren't that hard. I can't believe you. You're a dumb-ass bitch," I said as I stood up and Michael tried to get me to sit back in my seat.

"Don't call me out of my name, bitch," she shouted.

"Fuck you, bitch, and the nothing-ass you got sitting beside you." I was so mad I wanted to reach across the table and choke her for being so dumb. I couldn't, so I picked up my glass and threw red wine in her face. It splattered everywhere, all over Tia and the table. By now, the restaurant manager came to the table and asked us to leave. I was on my way out anyway. I got up and walked out of the restaurant. Reshaun and Michael followed me as Tia tried to wipe the wine off of her clothes.

"You okay?" Reshaun asked.

"Yeah. I'm fine. How much do I owe you?" I asked as I opened my wallet and tried to hand Michael some money.

"No, no, please. I'm so sorry to see you fight. I'm taking care of the bill," he said. I thanked Michael and told Reshaun I would call her. I was about to get in my car when I heard footsteps coming toward us. It was Tia and Lamar. Tia was really trying to test me because she was still mouthing off. I was trying not to hurt her silly ass. I knew her drinking always made her think she was invincible, but I was about to show her she wasn't. She ran over to me, still talking shit. So I had no choice but to pop her right in the middle of her nose. Her nose began to bleed and then Reshaun and Michael grabbed me, instead of grabbing her. This gave Tia enough time to punch and scratch me in my face. After they pulled her off of me, she then ran back to her car. I chased her, and then she grabbed a crowbar out of her trunk and began swinging it at me. I backed up and tried to take it away from her. While all this was going on, Lamar wasn't doing nothing. Finally, Reshaun and Michael got to her and made her drop the crowbar, and began holding her back. Tia couldn't get to me physically, so she just started yelling insults.

"Kiss my ass, Tia!" I screamed and began walking back to my car.

"No, you kiss my ass. You stupid drunk-ass bitch. Nicole, that's why you got a DUI."

"Your mom! You stupid bitch!" That was the only thing I could think to say.

"At least I got a mom and dad, you fucking bastard child. How about that?"

Those words pierced my heart, hurting me worse than any other low blows she could have come up with. I looked over at Tia in disbelief. I knew she just didn't go there. I began to rush toward Tia again, but was stopped by Reshaun, who kept screaming, "Y'all better than that. Y'all two grown women fighting. Come on, we all grew up together, we are like sisters. Cut it out before somebody gets hurt."

Realizing that I couldn't get past Reshaun, I yelled, "Tia you're a loser-ass bitch, and you are never going to be anything as long as you keep a nothing-ass man in your life." Lamar was just standing there looking dumb, because he knew I was talking about him.

"Whatever, at least I got a man. How about this, Nikki? How about you go get your own man and keep other people's men's dicks out of your throat, you dumb-ass whore."

Whoaa. Tia was taking it too far. First she wanted to call me a bastard child, and now I got other people's dicks in my mouth. If she thought I was going to let that comment go, she was mistaken. I climbed over the Honda Civic parked next to my car to get to her. She was talking mad shit and I wasn't the one. This time, Reshaun and Michael couldn't keep us apart. I grabbed her hair and started dragging and pulling that bitch around the parking lot. I just kept hitting her in her head and punching her all in her face. I could hear them screaming for me to let her go, but I wouldn't. At the same time, Lamar grabbed her, and Michael and Reshaun got to me. I still had pieces of her hair in my hand. I came back to my senses when Reshaun said the cops were coming. I was not for sitting in a jail cell again. I picked up my handbag and got in my car. My phone started ringing instantly, but I didn't bother answering it. I pulled out of the parking garage as fast as I could, mad as hell. If I had a gun I would have gone to Tia's house right then and shot her ass without a bit of remorse. I tried to calm myself down until I caught a glimpse of myself in the mirror. There were scratches all on my neck and she had put a big one across my forehead. The entire ride home, the words *bastard child* kept ringing in my head. How could Tia sue my mom and then talk about me like that? She had really crossed the line. Some things you just don't say unless you mean them. Over the years, me and Tia have been through a lot of things. But nothing ever this bad.

I went to Walgreens and bought cocoa butter for my scratches. My phone began ringing again, and I looked down to see that it was Reshaun. I knew I owed her an apology for embarrassing her in front of her new husband and acting crazy in the restaurant.

"Yeah," I answered.

"Are you crazy, Nicole? What is wrong with you? I can't believe you were acting like that. You pulled out big clumps of Tia's hair. I really can't believe this."

"Reshaun, she shouldn't be suing my mom. When I see Tia again, I'm going to kill her. That bitch crossed the line."

Reshaun interrupted me and said, "Hold on, somebody's on the other line. Don't hang up."

"No, I'm hanging up." I knew it was Tia on the other line. As soon as she answered her other line, I disconnected the call. Seconds later, Reshaun called back again.

"I can't believe y'all tripping like this," she said.

"Reshaun, I'm not tripping. My stepdad might have cancer. So my mom don't need nothing else on her plate. I've been trying to call Tia for two weeks to try to get her to come to her senses. You know that bitch ain't even answer the phone. But at dinner she wants to keep talking to me like everything is okay. No, that's not going to happen." I was getting worked up and had to take a deep breath. "Did you hear what she said about me? She called me a bastard child and said all that stuff about I need to get another woman's man's dick out of my mouth. That shit hurt. That hurt me more than any punches she could throw, because now I know how she really feels about me. She can't take the words back, Reshaun. Not ever."

"She didn't mean it. Y'all both were just mad. She doesn't feel that way about you."

"Whatever, I got to go."

"Nikki, she is tripping and y'all both upset. She got fired from her job and you still upset about your dad."

"She got fired over that nigga. That's exactly what I'm talking about. He got her fired from her job, she knocked up, and she still don't see what's happening with her life. Lamar is destroying her. Like I said, Tia is a dumb-ass bitch."

CHAPTER 7

I was in my office goofing around. I was supposed to be making rounds at the hotel, making sure everybody was doing their job. Instead, I was too busy planning my weekend with Malcolm. His wife was going out of town and I would have the whole entire weekend with him, and I couldn't wait. He was saying how much he missed me and I definitely needed my fix from him. I was more than overdue. Plus, I knew he could take my mind off all this Tia stuff. I was going to get with him and forget about everything. I couldn't wait to be in his arms. Because if I didn't get with him, I might go find Tia and finish beating her ass. Every time I looked in the mirror I got madder at that bitch.

Ryan walked in my office. "What's up?" I asked.

"We need to have a meeting today. Heads up—start looking for a job."

"What's going on?" I asked, stunned.

"The home office is selling this property to Clearview Parker Hotels."

"And what does that mean?"

"When they take over a property, the new team comes in and changes everything. They clean house, fire all of management, and totally rebuild."

"You are joking, right?" I said, standing up.

"No, I wish I was. Clearview is real strict, with extremely high standards, and the hotel and staff get inspected all the time. There will be a lot of surprise inspections. Just a whole lot of bullshit. The new company is just too detail-oriented."

"Are you serious?"

"Very! I need everyone in the break room at five today."

As much as I hated this job, I needed it. I didn't know what the hell I was going to do without any income. I would never be able to fix up my house or move out of my mom's house. I frantically began to type up a letter about the mandatory meeting that was going to happen. As I handed out the letter, everyone was asking questions. I didn't really have a clue, either. It is not that I don't like to work. Well, I really don't like working, who does? It is just I had got so accustomed to doing nothing and calling it work, that I couldn't imagine my cushy lifestyle changing. Doing nothing and getting paid was officially about to come to an end.

At five, all the staff members met in our break room. The front desk staff, the housekeeping and laundry departments, were all in attendance. Ryan stood up with his dramatic self and said, "Everyone, I have some news to announce. This hotel is getting bought by another chain. There are going to be a lot of changes." There were a bunch of sighs and murmurs. Unhappy employees complained that it wasn't fair and conversed with each other, ignoring the fact that Ryan wasn't finished speaking yet. Ryan cleared his throat and got everyone's attention again.

"Everyone here is an at-will employee. When you started working for the company, you signed a page from the employee handbook, agreeing to the company rules," he said as he held up a copy of the light blue booklet.

"So are we all getting fired?" Ms. Annette asked. Ryan looked at her and answered, "For the time being, everyone will keep their job, but I cannot guarantee what the next management team is going to do."

"I can see people like Smokebreak losing their job, 'cause all he do is smoke outside, but the rest of us shouldn't be fired. We work too hard."

Ryan couldn't get another word in before everyone began to complain. He tried unsuccessfully to answer all the questions.

As soon as the meeting was over, I went online to look for jobs. I couldn't afford to get fired. I applied for positions everywhere, from hospitals to day-care centers. I would be a security guard if I had to. I just had to keep money coming in.

CHAPTER 8

I got a few callbacks from jobs I applied for, but most of them were not paying enough. I thought I would work anywhere, but that's a negative. Only one job seemed promising. It was for a daytime manager at this small hotel in Plymouth Meeting. It was about thirty minutes outside of Philadelphia. That was a little farther than I would like, but it was a small property and I would get to chill on the job again. Nothing ever happens at small properties in that area.

I had an interview and gave myself an hour to get there. I left my house at nine so I could fill up my gas tank and give myself a little delay time. I knew with traffic, it might take me about forty-five minutes. I pulled into the station, and ran in to pay for my gas. I was surprised by the long line. Some people were standing at the register waiting to pay for coffee, and others were playing the lottery. There was this lady in front of me with a long list of lottery numbers she was going to play. *Come on, lady, I got to go,* I thought as she yelled, "And box my triple threes for a dollar." The computer was spitting out her lottery tickets and she played like twenty more numbers that seemed to randomly pop in her mind. The woman finally left and the cashier asked me which pump I was using. The lady playing the lottery had taken so long, I had forgotten the number of my pump, so I squinted through the window so I could see the number. I gave her the number, handed her the money, and ran out to pump the gas. I opened up my gas tank and pressed the Start button on the pump and nothing happened. I hung the nozzle up and tried again. Nothing. The gas pump wasn't working. *Damn, I don't have time for this.* Furious, I stomped back into the convenience store and told the attendant that the pump wasn't working.

"What number you on?" she asked as she looked down at her computer screen.

"Six."

"Six is working. Pull the lever up." I stood there for a second, giving her a look like, *you dumb bitch, don't you think I did that?*

"I did that. It is still not working," I said, trying to stay calm as I cussed her out under my breath again. I went back out to the pump and tried to make it work. I clicked the pump, lifted the lever a few more times, and it set to zero, but still no gas.

"Do you need help pumping your gas?" a male voice asked.

"No," I said without bothering to look up. I was becoming more frustrated by the minute. I looked down at my watch. It was now nine-twenty, and I was still wasting time. I looked at the window of the store to see if the dumb cashier could see that the pump was still not working. She was waiting on another customer and wasn't paying me the least bit of attention. *Damn, damn, damn!* It just wasn't my day.

Finally, I looked over at the man who had offered to help me. He was wearing a brown vest, jeans, a vanilla long-john top and brown work boots. He said, "You sure you know what you doing?" He was nice-looking but he was being smart, so I ignored him. He took me not responding as an invitation to come and assist me. He walked over to me, took the nozzle out of my tank, put it back on the lever for a few seconds, and then lifted the handle like I just did, but this time it worked. The gas started flowing. I was happy it was finally working, but mad that I was appearing to be a moron.

"You're welcome. Anytime," he said sarcastically as he walked back over to his black Toyota Tundra four-door pickup truck. I didn't want to say thank you, and I didn't, because I was a little embarrassed. The pump stopped at thirty dollars and I put my gas cap on and got back in my car. Before I pulled off, the man tapped my window, handed me his card, and said something corny, like if I needed help with pumping my gas again, I should call him. I tossed his card in my bag. I wasn't thinking about a man right now. All I was trying to do was get to my interview on time.

I flew up Interstate 76—luckily there wasn't that much traffic. It was twenty minutes before ten and I was making good time. According to my directions, I was only five minutes away. That would give me enough time to walk into the interview early and make a good first impression. I got off the exit, made a right after .8 miles and then made a left after .5 miles, but I did not see the office building I was looking for. I went into the business plaza and searched up and down, looking for the building.

I was lost for the next fifteen minutes. I kept circling tall buildings that all looked the same. For the life of me, I couldn't find building 745. I started to get scared when the clock read ten o'clock. I was late. They would never hire me, after being late. Oh, my God, I was frustrated. I pulled over and asked for directions and got even more lost. I wanted to turn around and go home, but I needed this job. I kept looking for the damn building and finally I found it. I parked in a handicap parking space and ran inside the office building.

"Hi, I'm here for an interview with Claudia Mitchell-Smith." The receptionist looked at the round white clock on the wall and said, "What time was your interview?"

"It was for ten." I glanced at the clock, too. It was ten twenty-five.

"You can have a seat, but she has another appointment. I'll see if she can still see you. For now, you can start filling out this application." I pulled out a pen and she handed me the application and clipboard.

The woman who was going to interview me came out and greeted me. She was wearing a fitted, tailored taupe suit. From her handshake, she seemed really nice. As soon as we entered her oversized corner office I acknowledged that I was late. I figured I should get the elephant out of the room and then start emphasizing my positives.

"This is a hard place to find. I am so sorry I was late."

"Don't worry about it. It was hard for me to find it the first week I worked here." She sat down behind her desk and began asking me about my background and my current job responsibilities. I answered all her questions. Then she went on to ask me what I thought were my best and my worst traits. I told her my best quality was that I worked hard and I was a team player. Then she asked me what was my worst trait, and I lied again and said sometimes I didn't know how to stop working at the end of the day. She nodded her head with approval.

"So what is your ideal work environment?" she asked. I looked her directly in her eyes and repeated her question back to her and then said my ideal work environment was somewhere I could grow on a professional and personal level. She smiled a little and then said, "That's great to hear, because we believe in promoting from within. As a matter of fact, let's take a tour. I want you to see some of our renovations."

She told her secretary she would be back and she took me down the road to the actual hotel. She introduced me to the manager and then we toured the property. They had a new fitness center, a nice restaurant, and everything was sparkling clean and so organized. Throughout the entire interview, Ms. Smith said everything I wanted to hear. They had a great benefits program that included tuition reimbursement after ninety days of employment. She also said seventy percent of their management was hired from within their company and they had hotels all around the world and there was always room for growth in their organization.

After the tour we went back to her office. I knew I had the job. She said I was the last to interview for the position and she mentioned that she was really impressed and that I should be hearing back from her by the end of the week.

I walked out of that interview feeling so good. I was ready to call Choice Springs and tell them I quit. Claudia said if she hired me, she'd want me to start in the position in two weeks. I needed that little break in between so I could be all energized and ready to go. But I was not going to quit, because I wanted to keep my paychecks consistent so I could keep paying my mom for the damages to her car. I decided to just wait for Claudia to call me on Monday. After I heard the words, *You're hired,* Choice Springs could go to hell. Maybe instead of taking two weeks off, I'd take only one.

When I arrived at work, I went into my office and, of course, I really wasn't doing anything now that I was sure I was leaving. Ryan hadn't been doing too much, either. Since getting the bad news, everybody was in laid-back mode. I logged online and checked my messages. There was a sale at Bebe's and Reshaun had forwarded me some junk about ghetto prom pictures. But the e-mail that captured my attention was the one where the subject read, YOU AND MY HUSBAND.

I looked at the name of the sender. It had the initial T and the last name Walker. I opened it immediately. It had to be a mistake. During all the years of me dealing with Malcolm, his wife had never contacted me. I was shocked. My mouth was wide open as I read:

We have never met, but I know about you and I KNOW YOU KNOW ALL ABOUT ME! I am Malcolm's wife of five years. I've known you have existed for at least the last year. So I know you are aware of our marital problems. REAL WOMAN to WOMAN, I would like to ask you to leave my husband alone. I am writing this letter as an alternative to confronting you. Let's just say you don't want that. Because I am aware of all the hotel stays and I know which one you work for at the airport. I would hate to come to your job and cause a scene. So that's why I am writing you a letter instead. I am fighting for my marriage and I would hope that as a woman, you can respect that and won't try to be the "clean up woman" waiting on the sideline.

At the bottom of the letter she put *P.S. Again, I would hate to come to your job and ask you this in person.*

After reading the letter I was pissed the hell off. How did she get my job e-mail address? How did she know where I worked and did she call herself threatening me? I was so mad. I never contacted her in three years, and how dare she deem it necessary to reach out to me? I been had her number and address, but I never used it. I wanted to but I didn't. I always imagined how she looked every time I hung up on her when I was looking for Malcolm. From the sound of her voice she seemed perfect. Her "hello" was like she had her life together. But obviously her life was falling apart—anytime you got to reach out to the mistress, you have definitely lost control. She must have felt them papers were about to be mailed to her. I reread the letter again and started laughing. I looked at the time she sent it—it was at five twenty-nine in the morning. *Wow,* I thought. It showed her weakness—she couldn't sleep because she was thinking about me. She was practically begging me, the other woman, to leave her man alone. How pathetic.

Even though I had just come into the office, I went to lunch anyway. I got in my car and dialed the number she left at the end of her e-mail. Yes, I was dealing with her husband and I loved him. And I was about to cuss her ass out for having the audacity to threaten me by e-mail. She felt like she knew so much about me, I felt compelled to call her and tell her everything I knew about her.

"Is this Theresa?" I asked arrogantly.

"Yes, this is. Who's speaking?"

"You sent me an e-mail this morning at five twenty-nine." I think she was surprised I called her back. I had to let her know my position and that I was not scared of her.

"I did and I meant what I said."

"I don't care what you meant, but let me tell you something. Don't you ever in your life e-mail me again. If you want to stop your husband from cheating, e-mail him or tell him to his face 'cause I'm never going to leave him alone."

"Oh, really!"

"Yes, really, and don't try to blame me as the reason why your marriage is having problems. You were having problems before I met him. He's leaving you because you're boring in bed, because you nag him, and because you never have time for him. You put your trips to Toledo to visit your family, school, baby, and your job before Malcolm. You never have enough time for your man."

She was silent and I was trying to think of anything else I wanted to get off my chest before I hung up on her.

"Oh, and another thing, come to my job and I'll get you arrested so fast for trespassing, harassment, and anything else I can think of."

"You're nothing but a home-wrecking slut," she said. I laughed. Was that the best she could come up with?

"I'm a home-wrecking slut? You need to learn how to be a slut and then maybe your husband wouldn't be all in my face all the time, telling me how good I make him feel, begging me for more." I was being spiteful. But so what, she deserved it. She shouldn't have come at me the way she did.

"You're nothing more than his whore. That's the only reason he is with you."

"Please, it is more than sex with us. The only reason he is with you is for Tyler. If he didn't love his son, he would have left you a long time ago." I could hear her pause, like how did I know her son's name. I continued on and said, "Tell your husband to leave me alone. I don't have his hands tied behind his back—he keeps coming back to me," I said angrily and ended the call. She kept calling my cell phone and I forwarded her to my voice mail each time.

That was at one this afternoon and now it was five and I was scared to answer my phone. I felt like I had got a lot off my chest, but I wasn't considering the repercussions while I was going at it with wifey. I left no doubt in her mind that me and her husband were fucking. By the time Malcolm called my office line, I was petrified. I answered my phone and Malcolm screamed in my ear, "Nikki, did you talk to my wife?" I could lie and say no, but I didn't feel like I had to lie.

"Yeah, she sent me this crazy, threatening e-mail, saying how she was going to come up to my job and beat me up and fight me. I got scared when I saw that bullshit in my in-box this morning, so she left her number and I called her back."

"You actually called my house, Nicole? Oh, my God, Nikki . . . what is wrong with you? I don't believe you. You don't ever call my house. I mean not ever! And don't you never, ever disrespect my wife." *Don't ever disrespect his wife? Excuse me.* He wouldn't let me get a word in at all. He just kept yelling at me like I was his child. "You shouldn't have picked up a phone to call my wife. You know I'm going through something with her. All you did was give her more ammunition. I really can't believe you would do something so stupid."

"You should have told her not to contact me," I said, taking up for myself.

"I don't care what she does. You should have respect for her; she is the woman I am married to and the mother of my son. How about if she kicks me out or don't let me see my son? You don't have anywhere for me to stay if she kicks me out. Oh, my God. I am really disappointed in you. How could you be so stupid? Damn, Nikki. Shit!" After his lecture I did begin to feel a bit remorseful.

"I'm sorry," I cried.

"Nikki, don't be sorry. Be smarter. It's done now. Don't worry about it. I got to fix this. I am sorry. I am sorry you got to go through this with me—it's not fair to you. You deserve better, Nic.

You are a beautiful woman, and you deserve so much better. I don't know what I am going to do. I am sorry for calling you all crazy. Let me handle her and I will call you later."

"Can you get away later on?"

"I'm going to try. I'm going to try. I'll call you in a few," he said as I shut my office door and broke down.

After work I went straight home and took a shower and began to get dressed to meet Malcolm. I didn't want to waste any time. I wanted to be ready when he called. Judging by today's event, she was going to kick him out and he was going to need somewhere to stay. I packed my overnight bag and made reservations for us at a hotel around the corner from where I worked. They were set up like little apartments, with small kitchens and living rooms. He could stay there until we found him an apartment.

By ten at night, Malcolm still hadn't called me. I really was beginning to be upset with myself for arguing with Theresa. What was I thinking? Why did I get smart with that lady? I probably got him in all types of trouble—I should have known better. At midnight I took off my clothes and lay across the bed. I was surprised he hadn't called yet and really surprised that his wife hadn't kicked him out yet.

CHAPTER 9

I didn't have my best friend, and neither the dream job nor Malcolm had called me in weeks. I felt like everything was going wrong at the same time. Reshaun wanted to get me and Tia on a conference call to work everything out, but I was not interested at all. I was still so mad at her. I didn't know if I would ever get over it. Me and Tia have had arguments before, but never this big. I still couldn't believe she screamed all my business to the world and that she had no hesitation about suing my mom. Luckily, my mother's insurance company paid for the damage to her car. I just had to pay her deductible. I think somehow my mom's agent got it pushed through. I don't know how it happened, but I was so grateful. But Tia didn't know that, and I hated her for trying to come up on my mom. I never thought there would be a day that me and her would not be in each other's life, but when money comes into play anything is possible. I was leaning on Reshaun a lot more since I wasn't fucking with Tia. She really was settled in her life. At first I was like, she was crazy for marrying Michael. Now I have had a change of heart. I wished I could find someone like Michael. I needed a man of my own. I didn't think me and Malcolm were going to be together. He still had not bothered to call me or return any of my calls. I so regreted calling his wife. I knew he was about to leave her and I should have just waited. I called him again in hopes that he answered this time. I knew she had probably been playing him so close and he couldn't get away from her. I guessed I would just have to give him a little more time.

At work, I wasn't beginning to feel so stuck. I thought about quitting every day, but without another job lined up that wasn't really an option. I had no other choice but to be on my best behavior. Clearview Parker had taken over Choice Springs about two weeks ago and already put the smack down on everything and everybody. No one was safe. No one! Ryan had already quit; he was out and left us to fend for ourselves. I didn't have my own office anymore. I was forced out into a common area with no privacy. The new management actually expected me to do work. They kept finding things that needed improvement. There was so much wrong with our hotel, even I was in shock. We had a lot of abuse of overtime and people had been clocking in for other workers who didn't come to work. Our staff was stealing toilet paper, soap, paper towels, and trash bags. Just anything that could fit in their bags. There were rumors swirling all around the hotel.

Maritza, Smokebreak, and Ms. Annette were looking for me to answer their questions about the changes and I didn't have any answers. They were firing people left and right. Some people deserved it and others didn't. The Clearview team consisted of three people: the regional manager, the district manager, and the national compliance manager. The main bitch of the whole operation was this woman named Kathy. She was the national compliance manager. She was an army of one. She was extremely intimidating. Short, brunette, and mean. Kathy wore glasses and almost looked like her second job could be a dominatrix. Because underneath all that mean exterior, she was moderately attractive, and I could tell she wouldn't mind beating someone for pleasure. But what really made me dislike her was her age. She was only twenty-nine. Who was that mean, that put-together, and that intimidating at twenty-nine? I was embarrassed that I was afraid of her, being that we were so close in age.

Kathy made me manually go through all the employees' files and review attendance and pay records. It was crazy. They changed our logo, gave us new uniforms, new bedding, stationery, and refurnished our lobby. Then they drained the swimming pool, because the pH level of the water was off and had traces of E coli. The non-management employees were no longer allowed to enter the hotel through the front doors. They all had to come through the rear entrance. It seemed wrong, like it was the slave entrance. Every day there was some new change, and all the changes and having to work in a tense work environment was driving me crazy. But the worst thing for me was losing my office. Kathy thought I should be out on the floor more. I felt like I had been drafted into hotel boot camp and I wanted out immediately.

* * *

It was only ten o'clock and I was already working hard. They had me stooped over a toilet, shining a blue light inside the bowl, looking for bacteria of any kind. If I found any, I had to have the housekeeper come redo the room. If a room was unsatisfactory three times, the housekeeper was fired. After my random room inspection, I had to make sure that all the hotel rooms were sold out. Then at the end of the day, I had to do a report, listing everything I had done throughout the course of the workday. I was tired and completely drained. When I left work, I would be so tired I would just come home and go to bed. But tonight I had a little energy so I dialed Malcolm again. His phone just rang and rang, and then his voice mail came on. I was tired of leaving him messages, but I left him another one anyway. It was like my tenth message, saying how I know I was out of line and I would never do it again. In my heart, I knew I'd probably lost him forever. I was coming to the conclusion that he was done with me, even though I didn't want it to be over. But what was making me so angry was that I'd been trying to break up with him, but he wouldn't have it. But now that I was the one pleading, he was not giving in and didn't seem to care. I honestly thought that Malcolm was eventually going to be all mine. I don't know what the big deal was—so what, I called her. It's not like she didn't already know I existed. I just confirmed her assumption. I wished I was her. I wished I was someone's wife and somebody's everything. I felt like I deserved a good man of my own like Malcolm, and a nice house. I didn't know if I'd ever have a man of my own. Out of millions and millions of men out there, there had to be one man that's for me. I was praying one would come my way. At this point, all I wanted was just one average-to-handsome, tall, good provider, with one-to-two children. I wanted him to be an honest, decent, and educated man. My dream man should be a law-abiding citizen who had never been to jail nor was in danger of going. I could cross some of those qualities off if I had to. I just hoped I wasn't in my thirties before I found the person I was really supposed to be with. I knew one thing: I was not a runner-up. Not at all, I was too good to be. I was never dating another man who was already taken. Because in the end, it never works out and you are all alone.

Chapter 10

I was so sad. I loved Malcolm, and for him to just drop me so easily was devastating. He was a rotten, good-for-nothing bastard. As I stared at my cell phone I began to think about how much I hated Malcolm. I hated him. I hated him. Malcolm got me feeling like I was nothing. He robbed me of my self-confidence and all my self-esteem. I felt like I didn't have anyone on my side. I was sitting here feeling like I wasn't good enough. But I had to stop thinking about him because he was not thinking about me. If he was thinking about me he would have called me by now. He could have snuck and called me on his way to work, while he was on his lunch break, or during the drive home. Shit, if he really was feeling me, he'd sneak and call me after his wife went to sleep. I was never dating a married man ever again. I got out of my bed and walked over to my closet and pulled out all of the pictures I had with Malcolm. In each picture he had the same sly grin. Just looking at his picture upset me. I was so upset I sat and I tore each picture in half, one by one. *I got to get out of this damn house,* I thought. I swear it felt like those four walls were closing in on me. I felt like a child, like I was on indefinite punishment. I hoped I'd get out of this back room soon and move. I had to, because every night I kept having visions of still being in this room thirty years from now. No kids, no man, just stuck taking care of my mom and Ernest. I didn't want to be stuck. That shit scared the fuck out of me. I wanted to be in love. I wanted to have somebody. I was done with the single part of my life, the going out every weekend shit. I wanted to get married, like Reshaun. No. Hold up. Maybe not marriage so soon. I just needed a friend. I really needed to hear that everything was going to work out and that I was a good person and was just going through a rough patch. I wanted somebody who just wanted to do the world for me. I was tired of waiting. They say don't look and you will find, but I got a question for those who say that. What the hell do you do in the meantime? Sit in the house? Who would I meet if I didn't leave the house? Maybe the FedEx driver would change routes, because that's about the only man that came past 6257 Stanton Drive. What was I supposed to do—get a hobby or something? I was clueless. Why did I have to love someone who was already taken?

Before I went crazy, I made a call to this guy named Charles, who I had met a few months ago. He seemed like a real nice guy and always wanted to go out, but I never took him up on his offer. I didn't really feel like going to the movies or dinner, but what else was there to do? His phone rang twice and then it went to voice mail. I called him right back, but still no answer. I didn't feel like leaving him a message. Instead I deleted his number. I thought some more of who I could call. Then I remembered the man I met at the gas station. I dug around in my pocketbook and tried to find his card. I scanned the card and found his name at the bottom. Dre. I shook my head. I was so desperate. I didn't know what I was going to say when I called him: *Hi, we met at the gas station!* That would sound a mess, but what else could I say?

I dialed his number, he answered, and I said, "Hey, this is Nikki, we met at the gas station."

"Yeah, hey, how you doing?" he said as I heard fumbling with his phone and someone talking loudly in the background.

"Did I catch you at a bad time?"

"Uhm, no, I got a minute." I usually waited a few phone calls before I felt comfortable allowing someone to take me on a date, but I went right in. No need to waste any time.

"So what are you doing the rest of the evening?" I asked.

"Uhm, not too much. Just finishing up some paperwork and getting ready for work tomorrow."

"You work on Sundays?"

"Sometimes. If I have a project that needs to be completed or if I'm behind on a job."

"What type of work do you do?"

"A little of this, a little of that."

That was a real vague answer. I knew he wanted me to ask him more questions about his job, but I refused. I didn't really care. I just wanted him to take me out. "So are you taking me out tonight?"

"Yeah, uhm, give me a few and I'll call you back."

* * *

Dre called me back and we met in Center City. He was half an hour late, but I was just happy to be out. Honestly, I forgot what he looked like. I knew he wasn't unattractive, but I still was surprised when he approached me at the bar. He was taller than me, but not exactly six feet. He had butter-pecan brown skin and a medium shade of brown eyes. He took a seat next to me and placed his coat on an empty stool. I told him the wait time for a table was thirty minutes.

"So you want to stay here or go somewhere else?"

It was cold outside and I didn't want to move. "We can wait."

"What are you drinking?"

"A Shirley Temple." I noticed his reaction as he laughed at me.

"Isn't that like soda and cherry juice? Let me order you a real drink."

"I don't drink right now," I said as I stopped him from calling the bartender over to us.

"You are not pregnant, are you?" he asked, checking out my figure.

I almost spit my drink out and said, "What? No. Why would you ask that?"

"Well, I dated this girl for a couple of months and she was five months' pregnant. She would never drink around me and was always tired. So now I ask. So are you?"

"Hell, no. Trust me, it is nothing like that, it's just a long story." I didn't want to get into the whole DUI thing.

"So what's up? What took you so long to get with me?"

"I don't know," I said.

Dre went on to ask me more get-to-know-you questions. Before I could think about what I was going to say, his phone began vibrating on the table. He flipped his BlackBerry over and looked at it and then he answered it right in the middle of our conversation. *How rude,* I thought. He got three more phone calls and texts while we waited for a table to become available. We got to know each other briefly, between his calls. His conversation was kind of typical, nothing exciting, but at least I wasn't sitting alone in the house.

We were finally seated and our waiter was nice. He came right over as soon as we were seated and asked if we were ready to order. I was. I didn't know about Dre and really didn't care. "Yes, I'll just have the angel-hair pasta with shrimp."

Then Dre looked at the waiter and he turned the menu to the back and started ordering off the dessert menu. He said he wasn't hungry, and I didn't mind until our food arrived. The waiter brought out this humongous, mile-high, dark chocolate layer cake with vanilla ice cream. I was so disgusted, because Dre was so excited about the cake. I just looked around at the other dates. *Why me?* I thought. Everyone at all the other tables seemed like they were in love and having fun. And here I was with a man rubbing his hands together, happy about having dessert for dinner, like he was seven. Then he offered me some. I shook my head no. I didn't look up. His phone chirped again and he began texting and then he asked me if I said something. Between his phone and dessert, he was ignoring me.

"I didn't say anything. But I should have. Uhm,

you're being kind of rude. Are you going to talk on your phone and text our whole date?"

He looked up and said, "You know what, I'm sorry. I have this job that I need to get material for in the morning and I'm telling my brother to be ready early. My sisters and mom tell me about it all the time. It's just a bad habit." Then his phone rang again and he said, "Damn, I'm sorry, but I really have to take this call." And he got up and walked away from the table.

Now, he was just okay, nothing special. It was not like I wanted all his attention, but what he was doing was just downright disrespectful. It was crazy that I was dealing with all this just so I wouldn't have to stay in my room. I looked over at him standing a few feet away, and rolled my eyes. Nah, I don't think so. I waved the waiter over and asked for the bill and a container for my food. He came back and handed me the check.

While Dre was walking back to the table I was about to get up to leave. He had the wrong one. I wasn't with the disrespect. That was my new rule. No disrespect at all. As I walked past him, he grabbed my arm and asked where I was going. At first I looked at him like he better get his arm the fuck off of me, then I said, "Listen, it was nice meeting you, but I have to go."

"You can't sit and finish dinner with me?"

"No!"

"I'm sorry for being rude. That was a real important phone call. Listen, I'm really done with my phone. Let me make it up to you," he said as he nudged me back toward the table.

I reluctantly sat back down and we started our

date over. I didn't really want to leave, but I had to let him know what he was doing was not acceptable.

Dre grabbed my hand and said, "Let's start this date over. I apologize for being late and inattentive to you."

I laughed because he was cute and being corny at the same time. So now that he was on my time, I began probing him for information. "So, who keeps calling you? Your girlfriend? Or your wife?"

"I don't have one of them. It was my brother, and one of my sisters, and my children's mom."

"Why they calling you so much?"

"I would like to know the same thing. They all act like they can't function or make decisions without me. I'm going to turn this thing off." He sighed. Then, assuring me that he was being true to his word, he turned off his phone and then put it in his jacket pocket.

"Everybody calling you. You must be really important," I snickered, being sarcastic.

"By the way my phone is always ringing, it looks that way, don't it? But it is not like that. And my kids' mom is crazy. She calls me more now than she did when we were together. I think she does it to get on my nerves. She is still mad that we broke up."

"Why is she mad? Why did you break up with her?"

"I had to leave her because she couldn't get herself together. She didn't want to do anything with herself and wasn't supportive on anything I did. I'm running my businesses and she just wanted to sit home and be lazy. Plus, she never had anything positive to say. So I finally gave up on her."

"Really," I said, but I was thinking, *Here we go again.* Another man telling the no-good-woman story—I've heard it many times before. It usually goes, *My ex was this, she was that, but yet I stayed with her for all these years, even though she was a bad lover, horrible cook, and had no ambition.* Dre was just like any other lying man.

"Yeah, sometimes I feel like she's one of my kids. She calls me about every little problem—"

Oh, shut up! I definitely started tuning him out. I was now sorry I'd gotten him to open up about his baby mama drama because he wouldn't stop talking about his ex. I mentally went in and out of the conversation, adding murmurs that sounded like I was really listening, but I was actually thinking about what I had to do at home.

"She begged me not to move out, and as soon as I moved back in she cheated on me. I was playing my part and everything. She just didn't appreciate me. I don't know what her problem was. I think she wasn't raised right. I was taking care of my kids, her, and her other daughter that's not even mine. Then her brother needed a job and I had him working with me, so he could stop stealing cars. I feel like I just wasted six years of my life. You know?"

"Wow, that's a whole lot to walk away from, two kids and six years," I piped in, not really caring about his situation.

"I know, right? But it was time to leave. She wasn't trying to do her part and it just wasn't working. You feel me? She was just real childish. She was into a lot of dumb shit. Her and her girlfriends always want to sit back and get high. And she could never keep a job. I'm the type of man who doesn't mind paying all the bills, but do something. She wouldn't even clean the house. I be at work all day and when I got home . . . no dinner . . . .house a mess . . . and the same dishes would still be in the sink from the morning."

"So, she never had a job?"

"No, I sent her to a bunch of schools. She went to hair and culinary school and she never finished either one."

"So, what does that say about you?"

What you mean? he asked, by his expression. I could tell he didn't have a clue, that he didn't think that he contributed to his baby mother's behavior. He was doing so much talking he was becoming flustered and I guess rehashing old memories got him upset. He stopped talking enough to ask me if I wanted to have a drink. I said no, even though I needed a drink real bad if I was going to continue to listen to his tale of the "good for nothing woman."

"So, what you meant by what does that say about me?"

"You stayed with her all those years, you might as well have stayed some more. Why leave now?"

"No way. I had enough. Besides, the trust was gone."

"I'm just saying you were together for all those years. That's a long time to be with someone you're not even married to."

"I was going to marry her. But she was on some other shit."

"How long have y'all been broken up?"

"A little over a year."

"That's kind of long for you to still be this mad."

"I'm not mad. No, not at all. So, what's your situation, Miss Nicole?" he asked, finally turning the focus on me.

"I'm single."

"Nobody in your life? Not even a special friend? I'm asking you this for a reason. It may come back up later, and I'm going to come back to this conversation. So, again, are you positive?"

"Yeah, I'm sure." I felt like I should tell him about Malcolm. But what for? Me and Malcolm were over. My past relationships didn't matter. So, I repeated my status. "I'm definitely single."

"So, who you say you live with, again?"

"I live at home with my mom and stepdad. I do have my own house, but it's just not livable." I started getting mad thinking about my situation. "I bought a house and I got burnt by the contractors. I signed a thirty-one-thousand-dollar check over to them before they finished the work. At the time, I didn't know any better."

"Damn, so they got you like that? You never pay anyone before they complete the job."

I nodded in agreement. "Well, yeah. I know that now. So, now I'm paying for a house that I can't live in because it has no plumbing or heating system. This is the first time I've lived back at home in years. I had my last apartment for six years." I told him so I didn't seem like a loser who lived at home.

"Where is the house at?"

"West Oak Lane."

"Maybe I can take a look at it for you. That's what my company does. We remodel homes and rehab houses."

"That would be good, but I don't have any more money," I said, laughing.

"Don't worry, we'll work out a good price for you."

"All right. We'll see, Dre. What's your real name? Andre?"

"No, Dondre."

"That's different," I chuckled.

"Are you laughing at my name? My dad named me. He just passed two years ago. He was eighty years old, but he was still working and running around like he was younger."

"Eighty! How old was he when he had you?"

"He was in his fifties and my mom was only twenty-five. My dad liked young ladies. This was his problem. My mom was his third wife, and I'm the oldest of my dad's third set of kids. I got three sisters and a brother." He looked up in thought, counting in his head. "I think I got like . . . um, seven older brothers and sisters and they all are, like, in their fifties and sixties. They ain't never really dealt with us, though. They was mad at him because he kept having kids, even while he was getting up in his years. Yeah, he was a player for real."

"That is too funny. I'm the only child."

"Are your parents still together?"

Dre had hit a subject I didn't want to talk about. My eyes blinked as I gathered my words. "No. Actually, they were never together and my dad passed away a couple of months ago."

"Damn. Sorry to hear that. Were you and your dad close?"

"No, not at all."

"Yeah, I was close with my dad. My whole family

is close. We do everything together. We go to plays, bowling, and restaurants all the time. Maybe one day you can meet them."

"Yeah, maybe," I said as we finished the second part of our date.

Over the next hour, Dre didn't look at his cell phone. I learned that he was thirty and had a construction and a remodeling business with his best friend Syeed. Our conversation was a lot more serious and interesting than earlier. Dre talked a lot about his business goals and how he wanted to expand his company. I listened as he became more and more interesting. He paid for our meal, and he began walking me toward my car.

"You not ready to go in, are you? Let's go to this lounge that I like, not too far from here."

I looked down at my watch—it was only ten-thirty. "I guess I can stay out a little longer." We turned around and began walking toward his car. We walked about three blocks and still didn't reach his car. I was tired and the heels I was wearing weren't meant to be worn for long walks. "How far did you park?"

"Right up here. It's only a few more blocks. Come on," Dre said as we approached an intersection. He attempted to be romantic and hold my hand as we crossed the street. I snatched my hand away and the moment I did, I almost got hit by a car. Dre pulled me out of the street and said, "See, you being mean and look . . . you were about to get hit." He grabbed my hand again and raised it up to his mouth and gave it a kiss. I didn't want to get hit by a car, so I let him hold my hand until we reached his car.

We drove a few miles and parked in the garage adjacent to the lounge. We walked across the street to the Red Sky Lounge. It was a nice place I had heard about but had never been to. It had art deco décor, with a half-circle bar, zigzag mirrors, and a red twinkling-star ceiling. We had a seat at a little table surrounding the small dance floor. It was semi-packed. There was a mixture of people, and the live band was playing Sade songs. Dre went to the bar and ordered two cranberry and Belvederes. He came back to the table looking better than when he walked away. I could see myself starting to like him. And though I shouldn't have been drinking after what I'd been through, I figured, what the hell.

"So, Nicole, what are you looking for now? Are you dating to date, or trying to settle down?"

I was a little taken aback by his directness and I really didn't know how to answer him. "I don't know. How about you?" I asked as I flipped the question back at him.

"You know what? I do want to be in a relationship. I like having someone special in my life. So, again . . . how about you?"

"I don't know. I'm just living. Whatever happens, happens. I feel like if I meet somebody I like and it is meant to be, it will be."

"So, do you like me?"

"A little." I smiled as the Belvedere crept up on me. I had taken only a few sips of my drink, but I guess it was affecting me because I didn't eat that much and I hadn't drunk in awhile. I was a little tipsy, but I didn't let him see it.

At the end of our date I didn't want it to be over. We did a one-eighty. He had already asked me to go out next weekend. He opened my door and helped me step into the truck. I reached over and opened his door for him. He started the truck and turned on his radio.

"So, did you have a good time?" he asked as he leaned into me.

"Yeah, I really did," I said, and then he tenderly pulled my face closer to his. Our lips connected and he began kissing me. His lips were moist and supple, but I still tried to pull away. Dre wouldn't allow me to budge. Every time I moved away, he moved in closer. He continued to passionately kiss me all over my face and neck. With each kiss I went from doubt to certainty. Then I remembered we were sitting in his car in the middle of a public parking lot. I'm a grown woman and didn't like the idea of kissing outside. "We have to stop. Can't people see in here?"

"No, relax, my windows are tinted. Nobody can see us in this truck," he said as he kissed my neck, and his hands were exploring my breasts. I couldn't stop him. I didn't really want to. He lifted me up and scooted me to the backseat of his Crew Max truck. I felt moisture beginning to flow from my insides, and at that exact moment, I felt his fingers working to unzip my zipper. Before I knew it, he glided my pants off and his head was in my lap. He began kissing me on my stomach and hips. Then his kisses came closer to my feminine region. I squirmed a little as his lips landed softly between my legs. He slowly glided his tongue in and out of my pulsating interior. If it didn't feel so good, I would have told him to stop. I still couldn't get over the fact that we were in his truck. I looked at him as he gave me pleasure. He was in a semi-crouched position.

"Please stop. You doing something to me," I said as he continuously did what he wanted to do with my body. We were in an erotic zone, but I couldn't help but think that somebody might see us. Out of the corner of my eye I saw a group of people walking past. I pushed him up. "Can't they see in here?"

"No." He proved it by waving his hand at the people walking past. Oblivious to the sex show taking place inside the truck, they went on about their business without so much as turning their heads in our direction.

Dre went back to pleasuring me, and this time I didn't stop him. He gave every fragment of my body an orgasmic eruption. It was the longest, strongest climax I ever had. I sat back, dazed and a little confused when it was over. Dre grabbed a condom out of the glove compartment. He ripped the package open with his mouth, and threw the wrapper on the floor. He took off his jeans, boxers, and shirt. Then he placed his erection into my center, as I lay flat, with my legs open and welcoming. His body plunged inside me, thrusting hard and deep, forcing my head to bump up and down, banging against his camel-colored, soft leather interior. I felt like

I couldn't breathe. All I could do was moan with excitement until he exploded.

How do you go from *I hate you* to *I think I love you?* We both were quiet as we slipped our clothes back on and climbed back to the front seats. Dre dropped me off at my car and walked me to my door. I kissed him good night and watched him drive away. I had no regrets—he gave me exactly what I needed.

CHAPTER 11

Ernest didn't have cancer, but just the thought that he might have, scared my mom some. She had been trying to be more compassionate. But it was just not working for her very well. Her compassion came off as her acting strange. She was trying to be extra nice. She'd been calling me throughout the day to tell me she loves me. She even asked me if I wanted to go to the movies and have a girls' day out. I told her no, I was too busy working, I didn't have time.

She was downstairs cleaning out the dining room, preparing to make another trip to the Goodwill. It was her fourth trip this week. She read somewhere that you can't receive unless you give, and since she always wanted more, she was doing her part by giving away all the stuff she didn't want or need.

"You sure you don't have anything else?" Lolo yelled up the steps.

"No, that's it, Mom," I said as I examined my closet.

As soon as my mother left, Ernest called my name. I ran to the top of the steps to see what he wanted. "You need something, Ernest?"

"No, somebody's at the door for you," he said, coughing.

"Who?"

"Some woman. She said she had something important to talk to you about."

What woman? I thought. Then it dawned on me. *Oh shit, Theresa. How did she find me? I'm not dating Malcolm anymore, so what does she want with me?* Irritated, I came down the stairs and peeped out the window. All I could see was a woman with a lot of hair, dressed in a black leather jacket. I couldn't get a good look at her face. I didn't want to go to the door. But I knew she wouldn't go away if I didn't. I nervously opened the door. She stared up at me. She kind of favored me, just a little chunkier. That's why Malcolm loved me so much, because I was a skinnier version of his wife.

"Are you Nicole Edwards?" she asked. *Should I answer her?* I wondered. She was clutching this green leather bag. That's where she probably was storing her gun or whatever she was going to use to hurt me. *As soon as she pulls out the gun I am going to duck and then run in the house and call the police.*

"Yes, I am Nicole Edwards. Who wants to know?"

"Candice Hawk. I think I am your sister. Is Raymond Hawk your father?"

"My sister! My sister," I repeated as my heart pounded fast. I held my chest. She had no idea. "Yes, Raymond was my father."

"I saw you at the funeral and I told myself that it just can't be, but when you broke down I knew it was you. I tried to find you that day, but I couldn't. You must have left."

"I did. I went into the bathroom."

"Oh, well I didn't see you anywhere outside. But I just had this feeling after I saw you. When we were growing up, Ray always used to tell me we had a sister—he said that you had another mother. And when we were little y'all came to our old house in south Philly. I never believed him, because I had asked my mom about it and she acted like she didn't know what I was talking about. Then about a week ago, she finally admitted it and gave me your name."

"She did?"

"But you were so hard to find. You weren't on Facebook or MySpace. So, I hired a private investigator. It was hard to do all this because I don't live in Philly anymore. But I found you." As she spoke, tears streamed down my face. I couldn't believe she had gone through so much to find me. She started crying and then I started crying even harder. She reached out and hugged me. "I'm sorry if I upset you."

"No, it's just that I am so surprised."

"Me, too. I was shocked when the private investigator gave me the information. As soon as I found out where you lived, I drove right over here. That's my boyfriend in the car. He thought I was crazy," she said as she pointed to a car parked several doors down. "He looks like he is getting antsy. We have a long drive home, so I'm going to leave. But I just had to meet you. Is it okay if I call you and keep in touch?"

"Of course. I'll give you my number and my e-mail address. Where do you live?"

"In Connecticut," she said as we exchanged our information.

Candice left, and I was still in shock. I went back in the house and pulled out my father's obituary and stared at it. I couldn't believe she had found me. I had thought about looking for them, but I didn't know if they would accept me, so I didn't bother.

When my mother came back home I shared the good news with her. I told her the entire story and all she could say was, "That's nice, Nikki, but I need to talk to you." I couldn't believe she wasn't sharing in my excitement. She called Ernest into the dining room and they both took a seat. My mother gave a long sigh and then said, "We have something very important we need to discuss with you. Nicole, I am saying this because I love you. We have been talking this over and we think it's time for you to get married."

"What?" I had to stop myself from laughing; they couldn't be serious.

"Don't laugh. This is not a joke. You are twenty-eight and it is time to get yourself together. You are not getting any younger and you can't live here with us forever."

"You know what, you are so right," I agreed, still trying not to laugh in their faces.

My mom was still taking herself very seriously. "You don't have to tell me. I know I am right."

"And Nikki, there are a few guys at my job I can introduce you to. One just got a divorce a few weeks ago. He is a nice guy," Ernest joined in.

"Are you two finished? I'm going to sleep," I yawned. Did they really think there were all these eligible men and I just wasn't ready? They both were crazy. I was still giggling to myself at Lolo and Ernest's marriage intervention as I watched television.

My phone rang. I answered it and a voice called out, "So you just going to take advantage of me and not call me anymore?"

"Who is this?"

"It's Dre."

"What's up?"

"So you just going to take advantage of me and not call me anymore?"

"I took advantage of you? That's not how I recall it."

"Yeah, you did. Were you sleeping or do you have company?"

"No, I'm not asleep. I wouldn't answer the phone if I had company."

He laughed a little and said, "I guess not. Well, I was on my way in the house and I just wanted to check in on you. You haven't called me in a couple of days."

"I know, I've been a little busy."

"So, when am I seeing you again?"

"I don't know. Soon."

"You know I got some free time to look at your house. If you not too busy, I want to go and check on your house tomorrow."

"Maybe. I'll call you when I get off," I said as I ended the call. I wasn't sure how I felt about Dre. He was nice, but I wasn't in a rush to be involved—but if he wanted to look at my house I would let him.

* * *

I didn't have to call Dre because he called me and asked for the address and met me at the house after I got off work. I took the padlock off the front door and we walked in. I didn't have the electric turned on, so he pulled out his flashlight and looked around. We walked into the kitchen and he hit the wall a few times. Then we went upstairs and toured the second floor. Dre shined his flashlight on the ceilings and floors of each room. We inspected the back room last. He jumped up and down on the floor a little bit and said, "Your floor is good in here. All you need in this room is to tear down the wallpaper and paint. That middle-room ceiling is going to have to be replaced and your front room and downstairs all need new Sheetrock. This house is not that bad, though."

"It's not?" I asked, surprised, as we came back down the stairs.

"No, it won't even take that long to fix. I can have my brother on it as soon as we finish up this other job."

"How much is it going to be?"

"It is probably going to take less than fifteen thousand to fix this place up."

"I don't have any money. Can you put me on a payment plan?" I joked.

"We'll see about that," he laughed, as his phone started chiming. He looked down at it briefly and said, "So, I'm gonna call you later. Okay? A matter of fact, take a ride with me real quick."

I got in his truck and then we drove a few blocks to a house that was getting remodeled. There was a big Dumpster outside. When Dre got out of the car, everybody stopped what they were doing. I couldn't even hear what he was saying. But Dre looked real good talking to his workers. They were respecting him and listening intently to his every word. I liked the way he was the one who delegated shit to others. After he finished talking to his work crew, he jumped back in the car with his cell in its usual position—attached to the side of his head. One of the workers ran up to the truck. Dre rolled down the window. The man said hello to me and then he asked Dre to call him, stating they needed to talk as soon as possible. Dre told him he would call him.

"That's my little brother, Brandon. He trying to get me to pay him and he is not done. I put up with him because I'm trying to keep him out of the streets."

"Really?"

"Yeah, he just had to do six months in the county. He had to figure out the hard way that he's not built for jail. Anyway, I'm going to have him start your house as soon as they get done with this one."

"So, is he going to take a long time on my house?"

"No, I'm not going to let him. I'm going to make sure of that." Dre drove me back to my car and gave me a kiss on my forehead and told me he would call me later.

Chapter 12

I have been going back and forth with my sister through e-mail. She lives in Hartford, Connecticut, with her boyfriend, and she just graduated from the University of Connecticut. She is twenty-two and has already been accepted to medical school. She seems so nice. I have a brother, Ray, who's in the army. He's stationed in Germany and married with three kids. She gave him my number and he has called me a few times. Our conversations were very awkward, but we are going to have dinner when he comes back to the States.

Initially, I was so happy and flattered Candice found me. But now she is calling me every day, bugging me like a real little sister. One day I had four messages on my voice mail just from her. It was a little uncomfortable. She was trying to make up for years in a few weeks. We can't jump right into being sisters—to me, she's still practically a stranger. I didn't want to be mean, but she was moving too fast. Every e-mail she wrote was addressed *Hey, Big Sister.* I knew we were sisters, but still we didn't grow up with one another. I don't think that sister bond forms instantly. I was still trying to come to terms with everything. I needed time and she was rushing me. She was in town and wanted to meet me for lunch and I was going to tell her to slow down when we met up.

I met Candice at Cosi, this little coffee house on Walnut Street. It was very crowded. People were typing on their laptops and reading newspapers. She was sitting at a small, two-seat wooden table. When she saw me she jumped up and hugged me. Her thick hair was pulled into a sloppy ponytail and she was dressed in khakis and a long black T-shirt.

"Hi, big sis. I ordered you a mint tea. You got to try it. It's so good and I didn't know if you wanted a salad or sandwich."

"I'm not hungry. I'll probably just drink this tea. How long are you here for?" I asked.

"Just for a few days. And I wanted to apologize if I've been coming on a little strong and bugging you. It's just . . ." she blushed. "Well, I always wanted a sister."

"Me, too. Don't worry about it. You're not bugging me." I lied to her because I didn't want to hurt her feelings.

"Oh, here, before I forget," she said as she handed me an envelope. I opened it and was stunned to see all these pictures of our father. There were pictures of him from different stages of his life: army pictures, his high school graduation, and family vacation pictures. In a lot of the pictures he had big hair, and in one he even had a Jheri curl. I held up the picture with the Jheri curl. "This one gotta be from the eighties."

"Right, yes, Daddy had his curl for a long time."

"It looked like y'all had a good time. Where were y'all here?" I asked as I admired a picture of her, Ray, and their parents in front of a roller coaster, all making silly faces.

"Oh, I think we were in Busch Gardens in Virginia."

"That's nice. So nice. So how was Daddy? Was he like real nice? Or what? He seems like he was just a really good dad. You are doing so good and you're so smart. You are so lucky you got to grow up with him," I said, staring down at the pictures.

"It was okay. It was regular."

"You don't know how I wish I could have just known him, just a little. Thank you for these pictures."

"It's nothing. I got more."

"This really means a lot. I never had any pictures of him. When I was growing up, and even today, if I am in a mall and see a father with his children, I get a little sad. You know, watching the fathers look after their kids and making sure they are okay. They would be holding their hands, making sure their children were safe—that used to really get to me. And I don't know why, but sometimes I found myself getting jealous . . . even angry. I couldn't help feeling that way because I never had a father to look out for me like that. You know? Like one time I was in my car and I was flipping through radio stations and there was some song playing by some singer . . . John Mayer or somebody. Anyway, the lyrics went something like fathers being good to daughters, and girls turning into mothers or something like that. All I know is I just broke down and started crying. You ever hear that song?"

"Yeah, I know what song you are talking about. I like it."

"That song is so deep, when I was hearing it, it made me so sad. Like I used to always tell my old best friend, if I would have known my dad, I wouldn't have made some of the bad choices I've made."

Candice cleared her throat and said, "Uhm, Daddy was okay. He wasn't like the best dad ever. Like, you know, we didn't live with my father or mother growing up."

"No, I didn't know that. Who did y'all live with? They stayed together, right?"

"They were together, but they both had habits and my grandmother raised us. They were both in and out of rehab. One would get clean and then the other would go back out there."

"Really?" I asked. I couldn't believe it. She just showed me all those nice family pictures. They didn't look like they could have been a family affected by drugs. People who did drugs didn't go on vacation or take pictures and make sure their kids went to school.

"Like what kind of drugs?" I asked.

"They both were on crack. It isn't easy for me to say this, but you didn't really miss anything with Daddy. He was there with us, but he wasn't. My mother and father loved each other—I guess. But they loved drugs more than their kids. See, my mom was functioning. She hid her habit real good for years. She got up, went to work, and paid some of our bills, but Daddy didn't have the same control. When he was using, he would get skinny and even used to ask me and my brother for money. Then he would be so mean to us when he was getting high."

"But I thought he was a teacher for all those years?"

"He was a teacher in the district. That's who kept paying for him to go to rehab. I think the longest he was ever clean was like a year. My mother held it together for as long as she could. She was the kind . . . actually, she still is the kind who tried to make everything seem perfect even when it wasn't." Candice looked at her watch and then said, "I have to go. I really wanted to give the pictures to you. I'm about to go visit Daddy's mom. My nana is seventy-seven. Do you want to go with me?"

"Where does she live?"

"In a retirement home in Lansdowne. It is about thirty minutes from here. Come on. You should go with me and meet your grandmother."

"Okay, I'll go," I said softly. I was still in somewhat of a shock to learn that my daddy was an addict and that he wasn't this perfect parent I had imagined him to be. Even more shocking was the fact that my brother and sister didn't have the easy life that I thought they'd had. Candice had given me a lot to think about.

* * *

That retirement home was full of seniors with walkers and wheelchairs. Nurses wearing an array of colorful uniforms whisked back and forth; some were busy passing out meds from a medical cart, and others could be seen inside patients' rooms, making beds or feeding sickly patients. And then there were the lazy ones, huddled by the nurses' station, kicking it like they didn't have shit to do.

We walked inside our grandmother's bedroom. Her room was just a step up from being an actual hospital room. There was an electric bed with a metal guardrail and a call bell attached. A small three-drawer wooden dresser sat by the window.

"Nana," Candice called out to a very skinny, diminutive brown woman with silver hair in cornrows. She was sitting on the bed watching television.

"You're here, finally," she said as she got off her bed. She was getting around good for a woman of seventy-seven. "Where is your brother? He said he was coming to see me. Y'all starting to forget about me?"

"No, we can't forget you, Nana. He is still overseas, you know that. I brought someone for you to meet."

"Who?" she said, looking around.

"Raymond's oldest daughter."

"Raymond got another daughter?"

"Yeah, and she came with me. Nana, this is my dad's daughter, Nicole."

"Hi," I said as I waved from the doorway.

"Why she standing out there? Ask her to come on in this room." I took her direction and came on in.

"Well, how come he ain't never say anything? Come here, girl, let me see you."

I walked in front of her and she examined me with her eyes. She reached out and grabbed my hands and turned them over and then looked me in my eyes. I had no idea what she was looking for, but she turned to Candice and said, "Yup, she that boy's girl. I wonder why he ain't never say nothing." Then she looked at me and said, "Well, I don't have much for you, but here you go, sweetie, get yourself something." I looked over at Candice as Nana tried to hand me money. I couldn't accept her money.

"Now, go ahead, girl, take it. Don't be rude. Somebody give you something you say thank you and be appreciative." She turned her attention from me back to Candice. "Candy girl, you going to do my hair before you leave?"

"Yes, Nana, I always braid your hair for you."

" 'Cause I don't know the next time I'm going to see you. Everybody always say how nice of a job you do to my hair. I say that my baby girl do my hair. The one who is going to be a doctor."

I sat quietly as Candice braided Nana's hair into two silver braids going around her head in a crown. Nana went on and on talking, telling so many stories out of sequence that I can't remember what she said. At the end of our visit we hugged her and said good-bye. I opened my hand and there was a five-dollar bill folded in a square. "She probably needs this. I'm going to give it back to her."

"No, please take it. She feels like she is helping you. She is getting up there and sometimes she doesn't really know what's going on anymore. She gave you five dollars. You lucky," Candice laughed. "She used to give me and Ray a nickel each year."

Me and Candice both broke up laughing. And she was slowly starting to feel like a sister.

CHAPTER 13

I love the springtime. It's a time to take the layers off. It was March, and people were everywhere enjoying the warmth. The temperature was only seventy degrees, but after months of thirty-two degrees and below, today felt like summer. Though I was trying not to rush things, I couldn't help it, and I was happy to hear from Dre. I answered the phone smiling. "Hey, Dre."

"Hey, where are you?"

"Driving. I'm on my way home."

"You have time to meet up real quick?"

I looked down at my clothes. I looked very business-like. Nothing about my pants suit read sexy. "I'm not really dressed. I still have on my work clothes."

"I know what you look like dressed up. When I met you, you were wearing a suit, remember? So, stop playing. I'm at John's on the corner of Fourth and South. Come meet me."

"Okay."

* * *

Dre was sitting at a circular table outside on the sidewalk. He looked so handsome. I watched as every woman who walked past our table was taking notice of him. His powder-blue sweater was hanging perfectly over his white button-down shirt and tie, and his dark blue jeans gave it a dressed-down effect.

"So I just wanted to hang out with you real quick. How was your day?"

"It was fine. The day is over, no need to harp on it. How about you?"

"I was just coming from bidding on this job, not too far from here. It's a new parking lot and condo on Delaware Avenue."

"Did you get it?"

"I'll know in a few days."

I munched on a salad and he had a steak and potatoes, which was surprising, but he still managed to eat a big slice of cheesecake by the end of the date. As the sun began to set, the temperature dropped a few degrees and it became a little chilly. He asked for the check and paid it. I set seven dollars down for the tip. Dre grabbed my hand and held it as we walked toward my car.

"So it was nice seeing you again, even if it was only for a minute."

"Yeah, good seeing you too." Dre smelled and looked so good. I wanted to just take him home with me. I was waiting for him to kiss me good night. He didn't make his move so I made mine. I tried not to, but I couldn't help myself. I pulled him into me and passionately kissed him for a few seconds, then I said good night and turned to get in my car.

Immediately, he grabbed me around my waist and said, "Good night? Whoa, you can't do that and then get in your car. You starting things. You must be coming home with me." I did feel a ball of energy between my legs and Dre's offer was very tempting. But I couldn't. Nope, for all I knew he had a wife or a girlfriend stashed somewhere.

"No, I have things to do at home. But maybe another time," I said as I got all the way in my car. Dre leaned in and kissed me on my cheek. I started my car and pulled my seat belt over myself.

"You think you might want to go to this play with me Friday?"

"Yeah, that sounds good."

"All right, be safe, I'll call you tomorrow."

I accepted Dre's invitation to go to the play *Almost Yesterday*. I read about it online at work. It was about an African-American family in the 1980s, during the Reagan era. All the reviews were good and it seemed very interesting. I couldn't wait to see Dre, or it. He never really saw me dolled up and I wanted him to see my girlie side. I bought a paradise-blue-and-black belted-waist dress. As I slipped on my dress my phone began to ring. I didn't answer it, but then it rang again. It was Reshaun. I really didn't have time to take her call, but I did anyway.

"Reshaun, hey girl."

"Why haven't you been calling me?" Reshaun sounded a little pissed.

"Because, I've been busy at work and I have a little friend."

"You got a friend? That's good. I was worried

about you after this Malcolm nonsense. Yes! I am so happy. What's his name? What he do?" she asked all in one breath.

"Calm down, let's not get excited. I've only been out with him twice. So I promise I'm going to tell you all about him. But right now I'm in the middle of getting dressed."

"You better call me and give me all the details."

"I will."

I was dressed and ready to go and so excited. If Ernest and Lolo were sitting on the sofa I would have danced out the door. I was counting down the minutes before I would get to see Dondre Hill again. I was at t minus fifteen minutes. I pulled out of my parking space, turned on my Beyoncé CD, and raced toward the expressway. I heard my phone and I turned the radio down.

It was Dre! "Hi!" I said, not bothering to put up any guards. I let him hear the happiness I was feeling.

"Nicole, you not going to be mad at me if I cancel, are you?"

Cancel, why did he have to cancel? Noooooo! "You need to cancel? Okay, I guess." I wanted to hide my disappointment, but it snuck out in my tone.

"Yeah, my kids' mom just dropped my children off on me unexpected, and I can't find anyone to watch them. But I'm going to make a few phone calls. I'm going to see if I can find someone to watch them. I'm going to call you back. Okay?"

I wanted to yell at him for canceling on me. But if I did that, I would come off as a crazy chick. Or I could tell him how cute I looked and he was missing out on all my sexiness. Or I could have said, *Don't call me until your kids are grown, because I don't have the time to deal with this foolishness.* But I didn't say any of that. All I got out was a faint, "Sure, no problem."

"Don't be upset with me."

"I'm not," I said as I ended the call. Are there any men left in the world who don't have a baby mom? I don't know why I thought Dre would be any different. Men are all the same. And why was he being honest all the time? Honesty is not the new black. I would have preferred if he just would have stood me up. Don't call me and tell me you are stuck with your children.

Once home, I took my clothes off and flopped on the bed. Oh, well, I guess instead of going out I'd get to catch up on my sleep. Yeah. Sleep sounded like a great idea. I snuggled under my covers and turned the television and TiVo box on. I watched a recorded episode of *The Tyra Banks Show* until I nodded off.

As soon as I was comfortable and content with staying in the house, Dre called back and said he found a sitter for his children and asked if I still wanted to go out. The play was over and I was not moving from the comfort of my bed.

"No, I took my clothes off. I'm staying in."

"Put your clothes on and I'll come pick you up."

"No."

"Why not?"

"Because I don't feel like it," I said with an attitude. *Fuck you,* I thought.

"You are a little spoiled, huh?"

"No, but I'm not for your games."

"Games? I told you I had my children. You tripping, you acting kind of crazy."

"Whatever. Don't call me crazy. I'm not crazy, I just have very low tolerance for people who aren't considerate."

"All right. Yeah . . . well, I'll keep that in mind. Good night."

"Bye." There was no way I was going to re-dress for him. I'd see him when I see him. After I hung up I realized two things. One, I was being too available too soon and two, I was starting to like Dre too much.

Monday morning at work, I was dragging around with the Monday morning blues. I had my resume out everywhere, and so far I hadn't gotten any callbacks. I was trying my best to just work it out, but each day it became harder. A lot of people were on a hiring freeze. I had to buy a Monster Energy drink every day before I went to work. That was the only thing that was able to keep me up and keep me sane and energized. I'd been working a fifty-to-sixty-hour week. I missed my thirty-five hour, extended-lunch-break work week. Most days, I couldn't even go out to lunch anymore. My diet now consisted of Oodles of Noodles, mixed nuts, and microwave popcorn out of the vending machine. I longed for the days when I could come in late and then just sit around doing a bunch of nothing. I understand that nobody really likes their job. People work to make money. But imagine hating every second of your day. I found no joy in what I did anymore. Kathy was always walking around the damn hotel with her clipboard, writing shit. I felt like I had a camera watching me and they even had me on call now. Yup, that meant any problems that happen at the hotel, they can call me. I felt like I should get off work at five and that's it. I'd be damned if they called my phone in the middle of the night and I answered. But other than that, I decided I was going to do the best job I could. If that was not good enough, then fuck it. If something didn't give, I was liable to go postal up in this hotel.

My phone ringing took me away momentarily from thinking about the crazy day I had at work. A smile crept on my face when I realized it was Dre. His call had come right on time.

"Where are you?" he asked.

"Home—I just got off of work."

"I miss you. Come see me."

"No," I said. Just because I was happy to hear from him didn't mean that he deserved to have his way.

"Why?"

"Because you stood me up the other night."

"Don't be like that. I called you right back. Come and see me."

"Maybe we can go out another night. I'm not coming to your house. I don't want to sit in your house. What I look like?"

"We can go out another night. I'm a little tired, and I just want to see you."

"No. I know what you up to," I said, very blasé.

"Nah, it's not even like that. I miss you."

"Yeah, right."

"What if I beg you?"

"I'm still going to say no."

"You don't want to see me even a little bit?"

I looked around my lonely, cluttered bedroom. My wanting to do something superceded my not wanting to see him. I needed to get out and have some fun. "Okay, I'll come over."

"You spending the night?"

"Now you are pushing it," I said. Little did he know I was already packing my bag.

I called Dre once I reached his cul de sac. He came to the door and motioned me toward his house. I parked in his driveway and entered. Dre's townhouse was basic, but nice. He had two brown leather sofas parallel to each other against each wall and a regular television in the corner by a big window with beige curtains. Everything was neat and calm, unlike him and his busy lifestyle.

"Take off your jacket." He came up behind me and whispered in my ear, "I missed you." He took my jacket off of me and hung it up in his closet. John Legend was playing on his iPod dock station.

"So, how long have you been living here?"

"A little under a year. I had tenants in here, but when their lease was up I moved in after I broke up with my ex."

"Who got married?" I asked as I noticed pictures on his mantle above his fake fireplace. There was a picture of him and his daughter at a wedding, and of him and his son at a football game.

"My sister, April, she lives in Maryland. My daughter was the flower girl."

"What's your children's names?"

"My daughter's name is Sabria and my boy's name is Mikel. Sabria's three and Mikel is five."

"It smells like you made real food tonight. What you cook?" I asked, smelling the aroma that wafted into the living room.

"Pizza pretzels."

"What is a pizza pretzel?"

"It's a soft pretzel, and you put tomato sauce, a little oregano, and cheese on it. You never had one?"

"No."

"Me and my sisters love it. That was our snack until my mom came home from work, every day after school."

"You always talking about your sisters and cooking and eating. They must be fat. All y'all seemed to do was make up food recipes and eat junk food."

"What? My sisters are in good shape. I'm going to tell them you was talking about them."

"Whatever, why don't you eat real food? You always eating junk, like a kid."

"I don't know. Something wrong with that?"

"No, it's just I know your teeth must be rotten and you going to have diabetes soon."

"No, I don't have any cavities. Look at my teeth." He stretched his lips into a big grin. "See, my teeth are prettier than yours."

"No, they not," I said as I glanced at his perfect pink gums and porcelain white teeth.

"Come on, I was upstairs," he said as he turned the lights off downstairs and I followed him up the steps. I looked into his extra rooms. He had an office and rooms for his children. The girl room had purple and pink pastel colors and the boy room was red and black.

The first thing I noticed in Dre's room was his black, four-poster iron bed that sat up high. Loose change, business cards, and receipts covered his big oak double dresser. A large oval mirror was hanging above it. His closet had rows of boots, shoes, and sneakers. Dre's television was a forty-something-inch screen mounted on the wall. After I looked around some, I sat on his bed. "This is comfortable. What kind of mattress is this?"

"I have memory foam cushions underneath. Sometimes I come home, and my body be aching. I need this." Dre fell back and stretched out, folding his arms behind his head and leaning on a pillow. I took my shoes off and scooted back next to him. We watched a little television as he smothered me in his arms and spoiled my neck and cheeks with kisses. I felt so good. So good, like I was supposed to rest my head next to his warm body each night. I was about to fall asleep in his arms, but his constant flicking through channels wouldn't allow it. Then something came over me. I felt a little scared. So scared I got up and asked him where his bathroom was. I didn't even have to go. I went into the bathroom and sighed. I didn't know if I was getting in too fast. I don't know what was wrong with me. But I just kept feeling like maybe I was moving too fast. Why was he so available and why did he want to spend so much time with me? He was so unlike Malcolm that it scared me. I kept thinking, why was he being so nice to me and what were his intentions? I stayed in the bathroom so long, Dre knocked on the door and asked was I okay. Damn it. Now he probably thinks I'm in his bathroom making it smell bad. I hurried up and came out the bathroom. I sat at the end of the bed, still feeling a little confused.

"Why you sitting there? You going to sit there all night?"

"No, I'm just relaxing."

"So, what's up, why you still acting so distant?"

I shrugged, unable to think of a good answer.

"Come back over here with me."

I scooted back again, and he rolled me over and began to kiss me, and a moment later we were both lying naked next to each other, our bodies about to connect to form one. Dre's strong arms just grasped my entire body, from head to toe. I didn't make any movement—his mere presence inside of me sent my pussy walls haywire. But then he began moving and I almost couldn't take it. He held his hand under my back and tilted me to the side so our bodies formed a slight arch. I lifted my leg slightly as he bit my neck and stroked my insides in every direction. After we were done, my body and mind were in another place until my ringing phone interrupted. I took his sheet and wrapped my body and searched for my phone. It was ringing louder and louder, and I couldn't find it anywhere in my bag.

"Your boyfriend keep calling you?" Dre asked as he looked over my shoulder as I answered my phone. I shushed him.

"No, it's my mom. She wants to make sure I'm okay. She is about twenty years late, but she is trying." I pushed the green button on my phone.

"Nicole, are you okay?"

"Hey, Mom, I'm okay. Yes. Okay. Talk to you in the morning."

"Are you coming home tonight? Because if you are I'm going to leave the lights on for you."

"No, Mom, I won't be home. Don't leave the lights on."

"Well, be safe, use a condom, and I love you."

"Mom, please. I'll talk to you in the morning." I placed my phone in my bag and returned to Dre's bed.

Chapter 14

I had been hanging out with Dre for a few weeks and I was enjoying every moment of it. So far, so good. There was a big difference in dating a single man and a married man. It was actually kind of strange. I wasn't used to being with a man who can give me all of his time. Another plus was that we didn't have to hide our feelings or constantly be on the creep. We could hold hands in public. I could call his phone and he would pick up, no matter what time it was. And it seemed like he really just wanted to spend time with me, and I loved it. And besides the attention, we got along so well as friends. Just talking about our lives growing up, family, just life. I told him about my dad and even about Tia suing my mom and our whole big fight. I really liked him. Though he was not perfect. He was always running late and always had to run and help somebody. His family was always going through something—he said it is the oldest-child burden he has. His family really relied on him, more than necessary, but that is not a bad thing.

My job was still in limbo. I felt like I had no one to talk to about it. I didn't want to tell my mom and I couldn't tell Dre that I might be jobless. I don't think any man would be excited to find out that his new girlfriend is unemployed. Especially since he said his ex couldn't keep a job. That is not sexy and would be a turn-off to any man.

Me and Maritza were in the back office telling jokes and reminiscing about the good-old days, when our job was sweet. I saw Kathy coming so I told Maritza to hurry up and act like she was doing some work. A guest came in and he pulled out his credit card and then asked to be checked in. I began searching for his reservation as Maritza looked to see what rooms we had available for an early arrival.

"I show that you are staying with us for one night, sir. You're staying in a nonsmoking room with double beds?"

"That is correct."

I smiled politely and then swiped his credit card and returned it to him. "You're going to be staying in room 417. Please enjoy your stay and join us tomorrow for a complimentary continental breakfast from six a.m. to nine a.m. And would you like a wake-up call, sir?"

"Yes, I would."

"What time?"

"Seven a.m. Thank you so very much." He seemed impressed by my professionalism and courtesy. So I continued, and said, "Thank you for staying with us and enjoy the rest of your day, sir."

Kathy wrote something down. I had to at least act like I wanted my job, even though I felt like I was acting like a yes woman.

It was Friday and TGIF. I needed a break. Though Ernest's cancer scare had changed some of Lolo's ways, it was impossible for her to change completely. She was still buying up everything on the shopping networks. I handed her the boxes that were left inside the screen door.

"Oh, what do we have here?" she exclaimed excitedly. She pulled out this amethyst bracelet and chain.

"This is nice," she said as she held it up and admired it. But as soon as she got a good look at the bracelet, she opened another box. "These are what I've been waiting for . . . my mother-of-pearls. They've been on back order for the longest. Aren't they beautiful?" she said, holding them up to the light to get a good view of the pearls' iridescent color.

All I could do was shake my head. I didn't have time to lecture her—I had a date with Dre and I had to get ready.

Dre told me to meet him at one of his rental properties at seven. It was now seven twenty-five and I was still waiting for him. The movie was beginning in another ten minutes. We definitely were about to miss it, I thought as I looked down at my cell phone. I called his phone again and he said he was around the corner. That was a lie. Ten more minutes went by. I was getting mad. Then a few seconds later, I saw gleaming headlights behind me. I shut my car off and grabbed my handbag and began to get out the car.

"What you doing? We taking your car," he said. Who told him I felt like driving? And he had a lot of nerve trying to call the shots, being that he was late. I sighed. "You got an attitude? I'm sorry. I'm letting my brother take my car."

"You always doing too much," I complained.

"The transmission in my brother's truck went, and he need to be able to get around, so I told him he could hold my car. Plus, my mom has to go to the market in the morning."

"Your mom don't drive?" I couldn't keep the annoyance out of my voice.

"I told you, she don't drive. So why are you mad?"

"'Cause you always saying ten minutes and take twenty-five. That's not cool. You need to be on time."

He apologized and kissed my cheek and said he was turning off his phone for the rest of the weekend and he was going to give me all his attention.

"The whole weekend," I said as I twisted my lips.

"Yeah, the whole weekend." He pressed down on the red button on his BlackBerry and his phone powered off.

Saturday morning we drove to the King of Prussia Mall. We were invited to Dre's friend Syeed's get-together. Dre wanted to get something to wear. Before we shopped for Dre we made our way into Frederick's of Hollywood. Inside the store I picked up some hot-pink crotchless panties that barely covered any of your ass. And I picked up cute boy-shorts. Dre slapped them out of my hand and hit me on the butt and whispered, "You shouldn't be hiding my sexy ass in cotton underwear."

"Your ass?"

"Yeah, it's mine," he said as he kissed me on my nose and gave me a hug.

We let go of one another when the salesgirl came up smiling. "Do you need any help?"

"I don't, but he does," I said, giggling.

"I'm jealous, y'all are such a cute couple. How long have you been together?"

Her asking that made us both burst into laughter. I shook my head a little and walked to the register. We bought three different crotchless panties and boy-shorts. We shopped the rest of the day. He bought a few jeans and he bought me a dress and these cute sandals.

We stopped at the beer distributor's to pick up cases of beer and coolers for Syeed's get-together.

"Dre, do we need to bring anything else besides liquor? Won't you call and see if they need us to pick up anything else?" I asked on the way home.

"No, I'm not buying anything else. Syeed's girlfriend is real particular. She doesn't eat a lot of things—she is a vegan. She is a little different, a real health nut. But if she start talking to you about you changing your eating habits, just grab me."

"Okay. How he meet her?"

"Through his sister, like a year ago. Sherrie is

very nice, but you'll see. She thinks Syeed doesn't eat meat. But he eats everything. I don't know why he lies to her."

Our plan was to get dressed and leave out for Syeed's get-together by ten. We had walked the mall all day and we both were drained. I didn't know his friend, and he said the girlfriend was a little nutty. So I wasn't in a rush to meet them. I saw Dre slow-walking getting dressed, so I did the same. By twelve I knew we weren't going anywhere, and I just went and took a steamy hot bath. Dre joined me. His tub was big enough for two. I sat between his legs and we just fell back. I sat so comfortable between his legs and the hot water calmed us both.

"So what are you going to tell Syeed?"

"I don't know, probably that I forgot. My phone been off all day. So he is going to think something was up with me. I'll think of something. Don't worry about it."

"Well, you should have turned that phone off."

"You right, but that thing is how I pay my bills. All my money comes through there. So you going to have to get used to it."

"I guess I'll get used to it."

"But I needed this break. Thank you," Dre said as he relaxed even more.

Sunday afternoon I was still at Dre's house. He had kept me hostage and I can't say that I minded at all. He made me breakfast, but not in bed. I came downstairs and he was putting our plates on his glass table. I sat down at the table and stared at my plate like there was a problem.

"I like my eggs sunny-side up. What's this?" I said as I frowned at the wheat toast, bacon, and scrambled eggs in front of me.

"What? You better eat my food that I slaved over," Dre said playfully.

"I'm only playing. I'm just happy you can make real food. I thought I was going to come downstairs to chocolate cookies and maple syrup."

Breakfast made me sleepy again. I got back in bed. Dre put on the Discovery Channel and began watching *Man vs. Wild.* It was a show about some crazy man encountering the elements. It was not that interesting to me. So, I nodded back off and napped.

I awoke groggy, and Dre wasn't in the bed with me. I got up and stretched and walked down the hall to find him. He was on the computer in his office. I didn't want to disturb him, so I tiptoed back to the bedroom. I began gathering all my clothes to get ready to take them home.

"Where are you going?" Dre asked as he entered the room.

"Home. I still have to wash clothes and get ready for the week."

"Why are you in a rush to go home?"

"I haven't been home since Friday night. It is time for me to leave."

"Get back in this bed. Just go home in the morning. Give me the entire weekend."

"Okay." I didn't want to leave Dre either. I was getting what I had desperately needed for years: undivided attention and lots of love.

* * *

By Monday morning, we had been together three days nonstop. The weekend went fast, and I had to hurry up and get out of there. As much as I hated to, I said good-bye to Dre. He walked me to the door. I walked out his house, down his driveway, and was shocked to see my car sitting lopsided, with broken windows. My driver-side window was smashed in. Pieces of broken glass were scattered all over the ground. I opened the door and I dropped my phone when I saw my radio missing and my steering column broken. Amongst all the glass on my seat, I saw wires hanging from what used to be my radio. I walked back to Dre's house and bammed on his door.

"What's wrong?"

"Look what somebody did to my car!" Dre came outside and gawked at my bashed-up car. "What the fuck is going on?" I asked him.

"Listen, I am so sorry. I know who did this," he said as he walked toward my car. "Don't worry, I'm going to get your car fixed."

"This is a mess. So who did this shit to my car?"

"My kids' mom probably got her brother to do it. She is into this. She is crazy. She is supposed to be moving. I wish she would so I can get rid of her drama. She is real crazy."

"Oh, she's crazy. She did all of this and you are not even together?" *Yeah right,* I thought.

"No. We're not together. I wouldn't lie about that."

"I have to get to work, Dre."

"I'll drive you, and don't worry, I'm going to get your car fixed." All I could think about was that my mom was going to be all in my business. She was going to want to know why I needed her car, and I couldn't go get a rental because I couldn't go to work late. My mind was elsewhere. Dre was still stuttering through his apology. "I am so sorry, you just don't understand how she thinks." He went into the house and came back out with a broom and dust pan. He swept up the glass and put a plastic trash bag over my window. He called, I guess, his baby mother. Because I heard him arguing and fussing with someone, saying, "Why did you do that? I don't care if I don't answer my phone or not. You don't do that. You are crazy, and why would you send him? You need to grow up. I talked to my children, I don't have to talk to you." I could hear her screaming through the telephone at him. He looked at me and said he was sorry again and I just looked the other way.

"Listen, I'm going to take you to your house to get your clothes and then I'll drop you off at work. Okay?" I didn't respond. I think steam was coming from my pores, literally. I just stood in silence. Dre, seeing he couldn't win, left me alone and he called his brother to get his car back. He then drove me home. I went in the house and showered. I hadn't washed my clothes, and had nothing to wear. I threw on an old black suit that I didn't wear anymore. It was a little faded, but I didn't care. I was so angry. I wanted to cry, but I couldn't.

I made it to work on time, but I was still too furious to look at Dre or say anything to him. He kept saying calm down, he was going to handle everything, but his car wasn't the one that was vandalized.

* * *

I couldn't concentrate at all. It was only a car, but technically that's all that I have. Who does something that malicious? By lunchtime, I was so confused and sad, I guess my bad mood was written all over my face.

"What's wrong with you?" Maritza asked.

"Nothing," I mumbled.

"You look like something's wrong."

I couldn't keep it in. I needed to confide in somebody and maybe get some advice. "Girl, the guy I'm dating . . . well, he got baby mama drama. His baby mom got some guy to come over Dre's house and break out all the windows of my car."

"Seriously?"

I nodded. "Ripped out my radio. Messed up my steering column and flattened a couple of tires."

Maritza reared back. "For real?"

I nodded. "What do you think I should do?"

"Make them pay for your shit. And press charges against that bitch."

"He's getting the car fixed for me. And I can't press charges against his kids' mother."

"Humph, please, I would."

The rest of my day moved in slow motion. As much as I was feeling Dre, I wasn't trying to get caught up in all that kind of madness. What was next? A bullet through my windshield?

By the time I was off of work Dre was at my job. His brother, Brandon, was in his car and Dre was standing next to mine. Blue tape was holding my new window in and I had all new tires. He handed me my keys and opened the door for me.

"Thank you," I said as I got in and noticed my new radio.

"Okay, so listen. Don't take that tape off that window for another twenty-four hours. The window has to set."

"Okay," I said, looking around for any other damage.

"Can we talk?"

"No. Thanks for getting my car fixed and I know it's not your fault, but I don't have time to deal with somebody who has unresolved issues."

"I don't have unresolved issues."

"Dre, listen. You are a nice guy, but I just don't think you and I should be together. You have drama that I don't need. I've been in a situation with drama before and it is not good."

"I told you what was going on."

"I know what you said, but I can't believe everything that comes out of your mouth. I'm done," I said as I pulled off. I left him standing in front of my work building. I really liked him and was having a wonderful time with him, but he was lying and I don't need that. I was tired of the same old story. Damn, now I was back to square one. All alone, again.

Chapter 15

Since Tia was out of my life and Reshaun was off to suburbia, I had to find a new BFF. I didn't have a boyfriend. Even though me and Maritza weren't super tight, we were starting to get close. All the madness that was going on in the hotel was pushing us together. She was my eyes and ears on the job, but she did like to hang out. We went out a few times, but it wasn't like being with my Tia and Reshaun. I missed laughing and joking with my real friends. Maritza was a little younger than me and didn't get all my jokes.

And then there was Dre. He wanted to keep calling my phone. I'm good. No thank you. Every time he dialed my phone, I didn't answer. If I called him the way he called me, I would be in jail and labeled as a psycho chick. He called all times of night, like we were cool or something. I guess he didn't understand what "I'm done" means. I didn't have no tears for anyone. Especially not Dre. He took me through too much, too soon. I felt like he was the new Malcolm and I couldn't get it right.

Me and my sister, Candice, were still keeping in touch. She was supposed to come down here for our father's birthday and we were going to go to his grave. I still felt funny saying "father," but it was good having her in my life.

Maritza invited me to her boyfriend Vincent's twenty-fifth birthday party. It was being held at some cabaret hall. She told me to get dressed up because it was going to be nice and sophisticated. I don't know how sophisticated it is when everyone has to bring their own bottle and food.

Maritza called me from in front of my door, letting me know she was outside. I triple-checked myself in the mirror. I still wasn't excited about going, but I didn't have anything else to do. She bought me a ticket and volunteered to come pick me up and take me home, so there really wasn't any excuse for me to not go. I got in her car and thanked her for coming to get me.

"Hey, I'm so glad you came. I thought you were going to tell me you couldn't make it at the last moment. As soon as we get to the party I want you to meet Vincent's cousin, Tony. He is an accountant and works downtown at the new Comcast building. And he doesn't have any kids."

"I don't need to meet anybody. See, if I knew you were bringing me to set me up, I wouldn't have come."

"Yes, you do. And he is good guy—y'all would be perfect for each other. All he do is go to work and come home."

* * *

We made it to the party in forty-five minutes—it was on the other side of the city. Twenty tables were spread out all around the room, with Happy Birthday balloons everywhere. Music was playing and everyone was dressed up and looked really nice.

"Is this an all-black party?" I asked, noticing all the girls dressed in black.

"No, but don't it look like it? Get something to drink and help yourself to the food. I have to find Vince." I poured a glass of Grey Goose and added a little pineapple juice. I wasn't driving, so I could drink as much as I wanted. Maritza came back shortly with her boyfriend, Vincent.

"Hi, Nicole. Nice to finally meet you. I'm going to find Tony for you," he said as he extended his hand. He left and came back with Tony.

Tony was nice-looking, but so very drunk. He stuttered, "How you doing?" And this is who Maritza thought would be a good match for me? No, ma'am. After they introduced us I walked away and went back to sit at the table. Maritza came back with some shots for us.

"What's this?" I asked as she handed me a shot glass.

"It's good, a shot of liquid cocaine." She wasn't used to drinking and after only a little bit of liquor, she was stumbling. The name of the drink sounded crazy, but I still threw it back. She went and grabbed more drinks and I sat, sipped, and enjoyed the atmosphere. Tony, the guy that Maritza thought would be a good match for me, was still stumbling around the party with a bottle of Moët in his hand. I looked over at him and shook my head. He began shaking up champagne like he'd just won a championship. Champagne was shooting out and spilling everywhere. He had the bottle in one hand, shaking it, and the other hand was going back and forth like he was rolling dice, doing some stupid dance. It was liquid everywhere. He kept screaming "Pop Champagne." It was funny at first, until it became contagious. His friends began joining in, jumping up and down in a huddle. They picked up bottles and began shaking up more champagne. Sudsy bubbles were splashing out and going in every direction. Maritza asked him to stop and then he sprayed her. It splattered on her black dress. For some reason, drinking champagne had made them think they were in a music video. Some of their champagne splashed on me, too. At first I didn't mind, but when it started getting in my hair, I knew it was time to go.

"Let's go, Maritza," I yelled as I yanked her up from the table.

"I'm not ready to leave," she said.

"I am. I need your keys—my cell phone and keys are in your car. I can call a cab."

"Vince took my car keys," she slurred. She was out of it. I couldn't believe I had champagne dripping down my face.

I had to go to the bathroom to wipe it out of my hair and off my clothes. By this time I was so mad, and I still couldn't find Vince. I was fuming, but what was I going to do? I was stuck at this ghetto celebration. I sat back at the table, disgusted. I wanted to leave. I noticed Tony and all his friends were out of champagne, but now were posing for the camera with empty bottles. Before long the celebration had ended. Tony was out of it, so they sat him at the table with me. Again, I thought, *And this is the guy they wanted me to talk to.* I was going to kill Maritza. His friends splashed water on him and then carried him out the party, because he had passed out.

Vincent came up to the table, asking me did I see Maritza. I told him no, and told him I needed Maritza's keys so I could leave.

"Come on, why you acting like that? Have some fun, mami." Once he saw I was serious about leaving he added, "Sorry about Tony being drunk. He doesn't usually act like that."

"It doesn't matter. I'm ready to go," I said as he continued to try to convince me to stay. I wasn't having it at all. Then he brought his other cousin, Emanuel, over to me and introduced us. I stood up and shook his cousin's hand. Vincent had to yell over the music, "This is my cousin Emanuel. We call him Manny. He is not acting like that fool Tony."

"Hello," I said pleasantly. Emanuel was so, so cute. I mean the kind of man who looks so good you would consider paying his bills. He could just walk around the house and do nothing except look good. He wasn't dressed right, though. He had on a bright red-and-white suit.

"How you doing?" he asked, eyeing me down.

"Good." I could feel myself blushing. His body was chiseled and he had a clean-shaven bald head. He was absolutely gorgeous.

"You have to have a drink with me, then you won't want to leave."

"Maybe, I might. What are you drinking?" I asked.

"These apple martinis and punch shots they

came up with. They taste good. You should try it," he said as he handed me a shot.

After three apple martini shots, I was feeling better. Emanuel asked me to dance. I lowered my guard and joined him on the dance floor. I was nervous because Lolo always said I couldn't dance. He pulled my hips close to his and we danced like a married couple in our own private space. I didn't know any of these people and I wouldn't see them ever again. The shots made me not have a care in the world.

At two a.m. the party was over and my feet were hurting. The back of my heel and my front toe felt like they were on fire. I was still trying to walk straight, but I wanted to take off my shoes. Maritza didn't care. She took off her heels and was walking around barefoot while Vincent was struggling to hold her drunk ass up.

She looked at me and I barely recognized her. Her eyes were blood-red and half shut. "You have fun? I told you we party hard and have lots of fun," she said in a slurred voice.

"You drive?" Vincent asked as we all made our way out of the hall.

"No, I came with Maritza. I'm okay, I can catch a cab. I just need to get my stuff out of Maritza's car." We walked out to her car and I retrieved my stuff and thanked Vincent.

"I'm not going to leave you out here. Just go to my house. I don't live too far and we can call you a cab."

* * *

Vincent got us to his apartment safely. We all walked into his dark apartment and he flicked on the lights. He handed me his house phone and the yellow pages. He and Maritza went into the bedroom and before closing the door, he said, "Just lock the front door when you leave." I turned to the taxi section and began calling cab companies. Some couldn't come out and another said it would be an hour wait. Moments later the jangling of keys made me jump. It was Emanuel coming through the door.

"You live here too!"

"Yeah, you cool?" Emanuel asked as he turned the television on for me.

"Yeah, I'm just trying to catch a cab home. It's going to be like a hour."

"That long? Well, if you get tired, you can lie down in my room. I don't bite."

"Okay, I'll keep that in mind."

Four a.m. and the cab hadn't arrived. All I wanted was to go home and get in my bed. I dialed the cab company back and a weary voice said, "We're still trying to send a taxi out to you." I said okay and hung up. I waited a little more for the cab and I drifted asleep. I was awakened by Emanuel tapping me on my shoulder and saying, "Come lie down."

My back was hurting on the small sofa, and I was so sleepy. I knew he wouldn't try anything with Vincent and Maritza in the next room. So I took his hand and he led me to his teenage-looking room. He had this old wooden bedroom set, and his bedsheets didn't match his pillowcases. I figured it was only for a few hours so it didn't matter, but it did. I awoke to cracks of sunshine coming through the window and Emanuel lusting over my feet. His mouth was wide open, tongue hanging out. He looked weird and perverted. I was so scared. It was like he was imagining himself doing things to my toes. That totally freaked me out.

"What are you doing?" I yelled.

"Nothing. I was about to give your pretty feet a massage."

"No, don't do me any favors." I sighed really loud and got up and walked out of the apartment. I walked until I saw a cab, then took it home.

Chapter 16

Sometimes people are gluttons for punishment. That would be me. I had to ride to New Jersey for my DUI court date. I couldn't believe I was still dealing with this mess. All of this because I had too much to drink and allowed Tia to talk me into driving her to Jersey. Emanuel had called and apologized for his weird appreciation of my feet. Maritza and Vincent said he was acting strange because he had a few drinks. I let it go and spoke to him when I was bored. I mentioned to him that I didn't want to go to court alone. He said he would ride with me. I didn't like him, but he was nice, and I was willing to be his friend. When I picked up Emanuel he was wearing his favorite color again, a bright-ass red sweatshirt and sagging jeans with untied construction boots. I thought he was dressed for the wrong decade. He looked so crazy I thought about pulling off as he reached for my car door. But then I didn't. It didn't really matter. He wasn't my man and would never be. But since he was nice enough to go with me to my court date, I figured I should be thankful.

"So, what's going on?" he said, tapping my leg as he entered my car.

"Nothing. Put your seat belt on." I exhaled and reminded myself that he was doing me a favor. Minutes later, we were crossing the Benjamin Franklin Bridge.

"We in New Jersey yet?" Emanuel asked, looking around.

"Yeah, why?"

"Oh, because this is my first time out of Philly."

"What do you mean?"

"I never been out of the city. This is what's up. I got to call my boys." He took his cell phone out and called somebody. "Guess where I'm at? I'm in New Jersey. Yup. I know. I just crossed the bridge. I will. Okay." He turned toward me and was like, "Do you do things like this all the time? I always wanted to start doing stuff like this. How far is the beach?"

In my mind, I was screaming, *You gotta be kidding!* But I kept my shock and disbelief to myself. "It's not close. It's like another forty-five minutes. You never been to the beach?"

"No, everything I need is in the city. I want to go to the beach one day, though, like maybe sometime in the next year or two. You been on a plane before?" he asked as he looked up in the sky, like a child popping his head in and out of the window, like the idea of traveling by plane was so amazing.

"Yeah." I answered without showing any emotion, but I was thinking, *What a loser!*

"That's fly. Wow, like I never knew nobody that's

been on a plane before. I would be so scared. I'm going to do that one day." He looked out the window again, grinning with excitement. I really thought he was making a joke until he continued on. "When you was on the plane how did it get gas in it? Like, does another plane meet them in the sky?"

Is this man for real or just slow? I asked myself. "Planes get filled up when they are on the ground at the airport," I explained, forcing patience into my tone. I really felt like yelling, *Shut the fuck up, stupid!* But I didn't because he was a nice guy. He couldn't help it if he was intellectually challenged.

"How you know?"

I couldn't believe he was even questioning what I was telling him. This time I ignored him. I turned up the volume on the radio and focused on driving.

I walked in the courthouse and we went through security, and I started having crazy ideas, like how about if they arrest me and make me stay in jail for like six months? Feeling nervous, I walked in and signed my name. I was told to have a seat. Once in the courtroom, I noticed my attorney. She came over and briefed me on my case. She began telling me that since it was my first offense, I was just going to plead guilty. With my guilty plea I could just get placed in a program.

"Your fine is going to be between three hundred and five hundred. Since your DUI resulted in an accident, and your blood alcohol level was just at .10 there is a possibility that you may be ordered to serve thirty days in jail."

"Thirty days in jail?" I felt a chill come over me. I stood up, feeling ready to run out of that courtroom. I couldn't do any time. Thirty days is a long time.

"You won't get thirty days in jail. Have a seat. They will be calling your name shortly." Twenty minutes later, my name was called and I followed my attorney to the front of the small courtroom.

The county clerk's office representative stood up. I didn't know what to expect. The woman said, "The county asked that the defendant, Nicole Edwards, be given a fine of five hundred dollars and twenty hours of community service."

"Counsel, do you agree with that?" the judge asked as he turned to my attorney.

"Yes, Your Honor. We do. We also ask that no points be added to the defendant's driving record and that she be allowed an intoxication class in lieu of community service."

"Yes, we agree, but the defendant will be on probation until the fine is paid." My attorney went back and forth a little more and then she came over to me and began trying to explain everything.

"What happened? Am I on probation?"

"You have to pay five hundred dollars and have to go to an Intoxicated Driver Resource program, and once you pay your fine and take your course—and as long as you don't get another DUI in the next six months—you will not receive points on your license or have a record. Just wait right here so I can get your paperwork."

Moments later my attorney came out with all the court documents I had to sign. I'd never been so happy to just pay a fine and take a class. It felt like a big weight had been lifted off my shoulders.

"Now, make sure you go and register for the class and take it as soon as you can."

"I'm going to mail them a check tomorrow and register for that class," I said and then thanked her. I wanted to give her a hug, but she was already walking away as she went to consult with her other clients who were waiting outside the courtroom.

Whew! That was a relief! I am never driving drunk again. I called home and told Lolo the good news. She didn't sound all that interested; she just said, "Okay, I'm on the other line. I'll see you when you get home."

Emanuel was sitting in the back of the courtroom. "So, you got off? That's what's up?"

"Yeah, I just got to pay a fine. Come on, let's go."

After we left the courthouse we stopped and got gas. After the attendant began pumping my gas, I noticed a handwritten sign that read, "Cash Only." What kind of place doesn't accept credit cards?

"All I have is a credit card," I told the attendant pumping gas.

"Only cash. Our machine is down, honey." The attendant gave me a sympathetic look. "You can go across the street to the ATM."

"I have money." Emanuel dug inside his pocket and said, "Here."

"Thank you."

"Don't worry about it. I got you," Emanuel said as he handed me his money. I thanked him, and then we were on our way back across the bridge to Philly.

Well, that drama was over. I really appreciated Emanuel's company. He'd paid for my gas and all the tolls and was my entertainment during the ride. He was a very nice guy, but there was absolutely no way I would ever go out with him again.

I was nearing his house and I couldn't wait to get him out of my car. I was exhausted from his dumbness and court.

"Thank you for taking this ride with me and thanks for paying the tolls and everything."

"You're welcome. Oh yeah, make sure you hit the ATM before I get out, 'cause I needs my money." The only thing that stood out was "I needs my money." *Huh,* I thought. I needed him to repeat hisself. I know this broke dude was not asking me to return the money he'd offered. I thought I heard him wrong until he said, "I really need that money you owe me."

"How much do I owe you?" I asked, confused and also a little angry. He'd said not to worry about the toll and gas and now he was asking for his money back.

He looked upward, like he was adding up figures. "I don't know, like forty dollars. I paid for the gas—that was like thirty, and then I paid for however much the tolls was." His cheerful expression had turned into an ugly frown. "I needs all my money, yo."

"Oh, my God. Are you serious?" I laughed.

"Yeah, I'm serious. I don't have it like that. I can't be giving no chick no forty dollar. What? You think somebody rich or something?" He gave a snort. "It ain't all sweet like that, baby."

"But you said don't worry about it," I said, confused.

"That don't mean don't give me my money back. It's hard out here."

I was steaming. I kept my eyes on the road. Wow, he wasn't so nice after all. I saw a Hess gas station and instantly pulled into the lot. Two things were going through my mind: I should burn him and not give him the money at all, or I should withdraw the money and then throw it in his face. But being the type of independent woman that I am, I was determined to let him know that I didn't even care about thirty-three lousy dollars. I got out of the car and slammed the door.

"Can you get me a Sprite?" he asked.

I laughed right in his face. He would be lucky if I took his ass all the way home. I bought a pack of Doublemint and a Cherry Pepsi. I took his measly forty dollars out of the ATM. I was still trying to decide whether or not I should throw the entire forty dollars at him, because technically I only owed him thirty-three dollars. Then I thought about it. I wasn't giving his broke ass an extra seven dollars. Cracking open my Cherry Pepsi, I got back in the car.

"You forgot my soda," he said, watching me take a huge swallow.

I didn't say anything. I knew I was on a date with a crazy, delusional person.

"You not mad, are you?"

"No, not at all," I said as I tried to hide my anger. I placed the money on the separator between the seats. I never looked at him or spoke to him for the rest of the ride. I pulled up to his house and as soon as I heard him shut the door, I pulled off at full speed. My tires must have left a burn mark, because I heard this loud screeching noise. I was mad at myself on the ride home. How could I have let this loser occupy a few days of my life? I couldn't wait to get to work tomorrow; I was going to cuss Maritza out for introducing us.

* * *

My phone vibrated on my dresser and then fell off, at one in the morning. My first thought was Dre. I wanted to pick up the phone and say *Stop calling me, you stalker.* But I'm glad I looked at the number before I answered. It was my job. Damn it. I didn't want to talk to them either. I knew I was on call and there was a strong possibility that I might get a call, but I never thought the call would come this late at night.

I answered sleepily. "Hello."

"Sorry to interrupt your sleep, but we have a major situation going on," the night auditor, Robin, said.

"What's wrong?"

"We are sold out and we have a guest here who has a guaranteed reservation and I gave her room away."

"Did you check to see if any other hotels in the area have any available rooms?"

"Yes, every hotel is sold out. It's a convention going on downtown. She said if we don't find her a room now, she is going to sleep in the conference room or lobby or call the police."

"The police? What are they going to do? Never mind. I'm on my way." I didn't want to go, but I had to. I dressed in jeans and a hooded pink sweatshirt and drove to the hotel.

I arrived and saw a tired brunette sitting on her suitcase right in the lobby. I walked over and introduced myself to the guest. I extended my hand. She looked up at me and stood up and said, "I'm not leaving this hotel, so you better find me a room."

I better? Who does she think she's talking to? For a moment, I thought about telling her to go sleep her ass on the damn floor.

"I have a meeting in the morning and my company is picking me up to take me to the building. It is now two a.m. and they will be here at seven. So tell me, what I am supposed to do? You reserve a room with a credit card for a reason. That's why it is called a guaranteed reservation. So tell me why I don't have a room."

"Please give me a moment and we will try to see what we can do."

"Don't try. Get me a damn room. This hotel had the nerve to charge my card when you can't even accommodate me with the room I've already paid for? I'm going to stay right here."

"Ma'am, I am very sorry we gave your room away. However, this is standard practice. Yes, you are correct . . . if you reserve your room with a major card we are supposed to hold your room. However, after twelve midnight, we assume that you may not be coming and we can sell your room to another guest. Now, if you give me a moment, I am going to find you accommodations elsewhere."

She stood stubbornly, with her arms crossed. "I am not going to any other hotel."

I was being extra nice because I felt extremely bad for her. But I was not going to let her keep telling me what I was going to do. I ignored her and went to the back office and began calling other hotels in the city. I was able to find her a room at the Holiday Inn in Olde City. I paid for her cab and gave her a voucher for her next visit. Then I scheduled a car to pick her up from that hotel and bring her to ours, so she could meet with her company in the morning. The whole process took about two hours. I was so sleepy, I wanted to cry. I still had to get up and come back here to the hotel to start my regular work day in three hours. This was just too much.

My alarm clock went off and I thought about staying in the bed. But I forced myself to get up anyway. I stopped at Wawa and bought two Monster Energy drinks. I was going to need something to keep me up all day. I sat outside in the car, looking at the front door of the hotel. I was still thinking hard about turning around, going home, and getting back in my bed and calling out sick. But then I saw Smokebreak. He waved to me as he swept up some cigarettes butts on the ground. Now that I'd been spotted, calling out was no longer an option. I tore myself from the car. Maritza saw me coming in the door and rushed over and pulled me to the back office.

"What's wrong?" I said, almost spilling my drink.

"I was here at seven this morning and I heard Kathy and that guy from corporate talking about you."

"What did they say?"

"They said that you were being let go."

"You sure?"

"Something about they were bringing someone from another property with more experience."

I knew I should have stayed home. It was shaping up to be one of those days. Now I had to decide whether I was going to get fired in person or by telephone. This was really unexpected. I was making improvements and thought they were going to keep me. How am I going to pay my bills? How am I going to move? *Shit*, I thought.

Right after I returned from lunch, Kathy said that she needed to meet with me in thirty minutes. It was official; I just had to hear the words come from her mouth. I came in the office and nodded. I was so happy I got the heads-up from Maritza. Knowing what was about to happen made me feel somewhat relaxed. Kathy was there with her boss and some other man I had never seen before. I sat down and waited to be told when my last day was.

"Well, I guess you're wondering what this meeting is all about?" Kathy said.

"I have an idea," I said.

"You do—okay. Well, as you know, we are at the last stages of our transition. It has been difficult. Though we wanted to keep everyone, we can't. However, we love the way you have been handling everything. Last night, the guest you handled was sent by corporate to test your management skills. You handled the situation in a professional manner. So, at this time we would like to offer you your current position with a salary increase as well as a place in our general management program."

I thought they were joking. Where were the cameras? But there weren't any. I was being given a job that I wasn't even sure I wanted. They were all smiles. I instantly accepted the position. It was something that I never really thought about, but too much of a great opportunity to pass up. I thanked Kathy and her boss. I was so happy I was getting promoted and not fired. I'll do my job as long as it came with a bigger paycheck.

Chapter 17

I met Candice at the cemetery that our father was buried in. It was his birthday and we were supposed to be saying Happy Birthday. I didn't feel exactly comfortable wishing him a happy birthday when he never wished me one. I knew he wasn't alive, but I hadn't had that close relationship that she'd had with him. But I took a deep breath anyway and followed her to Raymond Hawk's plot. There were gray, chalky headstones in every direction. I was careful not to step on any. I started tearing up as soon as I saw his headstone. Candice walked over and kneeled down and whispered, "Happy birthday, Daddy. Daddy, it's me, Candy," as she placed flowers on his tombstone. It seemed like she said a prayer or something and then she became more lively with her conversation with our father. She began speaking to him like he was really with us.

"I just wanted to let you know, Daddy, that Brandon is doing good. I'm doing good too! I'm starting medical school and I'm not going to let you down. I miss you, but I know you are in a better place. I know that and I forgive you. Look who I found, Daddy. My sister, Nicole. I know you didn't mean to keep her away from us." Candice tried to hold back tears, but she couldn't, and neither could I. She grabbed my hand and continued on. "I know you would want all your children to be together. Remember you would always say blood is thicker than water? I never forgot that. I miss you so much and I'm going to continue to make you proud. I promise. I promise and I'm going to take care of Mommy for you as soon as I get out of school. I love you, Daddy, and I miss you."

I stood there with my eyes closed. God, this was hard, I thought. Why did I agree to come? I couldn't do this. I couldn't. I tried to clear my throat, preparing to speak. Then she rubbed my back and said it was okay, and asked if I needed privacy. I told her no. I needed her there to hold me up. I couldn't muster any words to say. I just began crying uncontrollably and she kept saying, "It's okay. Let it out."

I closed my eyes and I gained strength and finally the words began to come out. I said the words I never thought I would say. "Daddy, I forgive you. I was mad at you for a very long time, but I'm okay now. There were points in my life where I hated you, Dad. But I don't hate you anymore. I don't. I forgive you, Dad. Candice is right. She found me and we are never going to lose touch. We lost a lot of time, but we are going to make up for it. And I can't wait to meet Ray. I heard he acts and looks just like you. So I'm going to get to know a piece of you. I'm not mad and I do forgive you. I finally forgive you. I'm not mad anymore. I love you." I opened my eyes and said, "Daddy, rest in peace." Then I stood there and said a silent prayer. We then both walked back to our cars and left.

As I drove out of that cemetery, a sense of peace overcame me. I felt like I had the conversation I'd always wanted to have with my father.

It's been days since I talked to Candice. She said she was going to be bogged down with her summer semester. At first the *big sis*'s were killing me, but now I suddenly miss her. She has had such an impact on my life. I think her knocking on my door was one of the best things that ever happened to me. All these years I've been feeling incomplete and now I feel whole. Since our last conversation, I've been constantly thinking about my life. I just want a change, I want better for myself. I need to get things moving. I have this new opportunity at my job and now I have to get moving on other aspects of my life. I've evaluated every misstep I've made and they all had one common factor. The one common denominator of all my problems, worries, and troubles can all be linked to a man. Not having a home, a stupid scamming man. I allowed a dumb man to dupe me into believing he was going to leave his wife. He didn't. I almost fell in love with another man, who was also fake. All men are the devil. They are stupid and I am done with them. Malcolm Walker can go to hell and so can Dondre Hill. I don't feel like adding another name to the list of all the men I hate, so I think I am going to be celibate from here on out. I'm going to get into myself. I feel like I have to move, and I have to have my own. I'm too old to be wondering and hoping and waiting for something or someone to rescue me. I'm done with believing in that knight-in-shining-armor fairy tale. I'm going to figure out a way to get my life together. I have to, I don't have a choice. What is my alternative . . . stay here and grow old in this back room? Hell, no. I'm going to have to save myself, because "Captain Save A Hoe" and his cavalry is not coming for me.

My plan to get on my feet was to borrow money from my 401k and get a second job somewhere. If I could fix up my house, room by room, I should be able to move in by the end of the year. I decided I was going to hire several contractors for different areas in the house. They could see each other working in there and be competition for one another and they would know I meant business. Plus, the odds were against getting scammed by all of the contractors. I went to the Home Depot to get paint. I knew I couldn't do anything major in the house, but I did know how to paint. It was a massive store. Like the size of an indoor football field. There were supplies and appliances everywhere, washers, dryers, fans, hammers, drills, saws, pesticides. I walked to the back of the store and saw plenty of handymen walking around. A few said hello. I ignored them all. I had enough with fix-it men.

I went to the paint aisle and picked up a can of white paint. I had no idea if I needed flat or glossy for my walls. As I sat there and read the Glidden paint can, I heard a familiar voice ask, "Miss Lady. What you about to paint?" I turned and saw dusty

Smokebreak from the job. He was standing, looking crazy as ever with a short friend.

"I have a house. I'm going to try to paint."

"Really? We do a little bit of painting on the side. Matter fact, we do it all," he said, smiling.

"You do? Do you think you can look at a job for me?"

"I could stop by and take a look at it for you. By the way, this my cousin and partner Pee Wee. He know how to do Sheetrock, electrical, and plumbing work and all of that."

"Really. How much you charge to put up some Sheetrock?"

"We would have to look at it and then give you a price. But nothing much. Just give us the address. And we will come through tomorrow."

After Home Depot, I went to a furniture store to price furniture. It would be a while before I could afford any. But I wanted to get an idea of what was available. If I saw what was out there then maybe I could envision it sitting in my living room. Then that would get me hyped up so I could get my second job to pay for it. But I didn't really care what was in there, because when that house was ready, I'd move in with an air mattress and a microwave and be ecstatic because it was mine.

The next day Smokebreak and his cousin came up to my house in a car that was being held together by a bungee cord. Once I opened the door they began looking all around. I wasn't going to say anything about a price. I knew they weren't capable of completing an entire house, but if I could get them to just do the minor things, I was sure I could save some money. Plus, I told them what happened to me before, so they might feel sorry for me.

As Smokebreak and his cousin walked around examining the place, I saw Dre's telephone number come across my screen again. He would not give up and that was not a good thing.

"Yes," I said, irritated.

"So, this is still your number?"

"Yes, it is."

"So, every time you saw my number come across the screen, you just ignored me and didn't pick up your phone?" I couldn't help but laugh. He knew exactly what I was doing.

"I told you I wasn't being bothered with you."

"That's not right. That really wasn't my fault."

I laughed a little more, then said, "Listen, it was good talking to you, but I'm in the middle of getting some work done to my house. So I'll try to call you."

"Oh, okay, well I don't want to hold you up," Dre said as I ended our conversation.

I turned my attention back to Smokebreak and his cousin. "So, when do you want to get started? I can give you a deposit now and the rest upon completion."

"No, since you said what happened to you before, just buy the material. We won't take payment until we complete the first half. We can start next week."

"Thanks, we'll talk." We walked out the house. I pulled the door closed and began putting the padlock back on. I came down the steps and as I was crossing the street to get to my car, a speeding car almost hit me. I jumped back on the pavement. Then the car stopped right in front of me and the window went down. It was Dre. He looked up at Smokebreak and his cousin walking down the steps.

"So, that's your boyfriend now?" Dre asked.

"No, does he look like my type?" I said, looking at how smokerish and raggedy Smokebreak looked.

Smokebreak looked back at me and asked was I okay. I told him I was and he said, "Good night, Miss Lady."

"You got a minute?" Dre asked.

"No, I have to get up early in the morning. And the last time I spent time with you, all my car windows were knocked out."

He pulled over and stepped out of his running car. "I said I was sorry, and now you going to hold it against me forever?" I looked straight ahead, my arms crossed. I couldn't look at him as he spoke because if I did I might start to believe everything he was saying. He placed his left hand on my right and began stroking it up and down. "I didn't know she would go off like that. Me and my children's mom made a clean break. Trust, there is not going to be any more breaking out windows. We broke up a long time ago, but she is still a little childish. But believe me, I had a serious conversation with her and it's not going to happen again. She's even moving out of the city and everything. I was really getting into you and I want to finish what we started."

I still wasn't convinced. "Let me think about it."

"Think about it? How about this, don't think about it. Just answer the phone the next time I call," he said.

I nodded yeah to him, and that was enough of an answer for him to get back in his car and pull off.

No sooner than I made it home, my phone chirped with a text message from Dre:

> I MEANT EVERY WORD I SAID. I WANT YOU. I NEED YOU AND WANT TO BE THE MAN YOU NEED. CALL ME ON YOUR WAY TO WORK TOMORROW.

I called Dre on my commute to work the next morning, as he asked. Once I dialed him, I regretted it. He would not stop begging me to meet him for dinner in Center City. He said he wanted to take me to this special place. I didn't know what to expect. So I agreed and needless to say, was a little disappointed when we pulled into the valet parking at the Hyatt hotel. Were we just getting a room? I didn't even say I liked him again and he was getting a room. Not good at all. It was going to take more than a hotel room to get me back.

We walked into the historic Bellevue Hyatt hotel. He smiled as he pressed the elevator up. I gave a half grin. I was about to call him out like, *how dare you?* But I waited, and I'm glad I did because I was pleasantly surprised when we landed on the nineteenth floor at this amazing restaurant. The place was shaped like a globe. The ceilings were high and in circular domes. From each table you had a perfect view of the city. It was very fancy, the kind of restaurant where dinner is presented to you as artwork, with green pieces of things you won't eat and with brown squiggly lines for decoration.

Dre gave the hostess our name and she picked up two menus and led us to a table. A white square candle softly illuminated the table. As soon as we were seated the waiter came over, dressed in a black-and-white suit. He introduced himself and read off the wine list. I sat across from Dre in awe. I hoped my face wasn't revealing how impressed I was.

"I missed you so much," Dre said when the waiter left. He reached across the table and grabbed my hand. He kissed it and then held on to it, caressing it. "You know, now that I got you back, I'm not going to let you go this time."

"Who says you have me back? I'm not back with you."

"Yes, you are. You know, I felt like I wasn't going to possibly get you back and that scared me."

"How you think I felt when I came to the door and saw my car? I can laugh now, but that was crazy." Now that like a month had passed, we were able to joke about my windows being smashed. The next two hours we were served a four-course meal and got caught up on one another's life. I told Dre about the promotion and he discussed trying to get full custody of his children.

After dinner we held hands and walked through the festive nightlife scene. As we walked, Dre began singing Al Green's "Let's Stay Together," off key. I put my hand over his mouth, giggling. His voice was offending my ears and disrespecting the song.

"I'm not amused."

"You didn't miss me a little?" he said, pulling me face-to-face.

"No."

"Nikki, I missed you so much it hurt."

"You missed me, yeah right. What you miss about me?"

"I missed your friendship. I missed hearing your voice, holding you and having you in my life."

"You did," I said, not knowing what else to say. Dre answered that perfectly. How could I respond to an answer like that? I stood silent as Dre looked me in the eyes and said, "Let's try it all again. Really try, no games." And I guess I said yes because I ended up at Dre's house after our long walk.

We both missed each other and didn't take any time undressing. I kissed him, nonstop, he was so energized. Before he had fully made his way into my body, I felt a little jerk and then heard him take one big gasp.

"You didn't!" I exclaimed softly.

"I did," he said, embarrassed. "Hold up, let me get myself together. It's just I'm so excited." Dre went and showered and we started all over. I kissed him softly on his navel. Then on his thigh. I let my next kiss land right in his warm groin area. My wet kisses began to revitalize him. From all my effort he rose in strength and size. My insides longed for him. He slowly placed himself in me. His first few movements inside me were a little rough. It was a friction that felt so good. Slowly he broke through my tight interior walls. After several minutes of pleasure, Dre flipped positions with me. I got on top of him and wrapped my legs around his body in a diamond shape. Then Dre picked me up off the bed and held my body against the wall. I kept sliding up and down, but I held on as tight as I could. Dre moaned. "I just might wife you. You hear me?" he asked as I acted like I didn't hear what he said. Then he said it again.

I whispered back, "You going to wife me? How about if I don't want to marry you?"

"I don't think you are going to have a choice. I'm serious. When we were apart I missed you so much." For the rest of the night our bodies got reacquainted and when it was over I looked up at his ceiling and prayed to God, *Please don't let him hurt me.*

Chapter 18

I read somewhere that when a man is ready, you will know it. He won't have to say anything—his actions will speak volumes. And now I knew exactly what that meant. By the following week, we were officially together, even though I wasn't sure if we were really together the first time. It felt so good, so happy, like every day was Dre-day and I was waking up in Loveland. When I looked in Dre's eyes, I just saw and felt love. He was all mine. He didn't hold back anything. Sometimes he would call me and say I was on his mind and he needed to hear my voice. I think the biggest thing was the R-E-S-P-E-C-T Dre had for me. I approached this relationship totally different from when I was with Malcolm. When I cut it off, Dre realized what he was missing. He cared about me and my needs. There were times when I caught him watching me when he thought I was asleep. And I just could tell he genuinely cared about my total well-being.

Dre told me all the time he was falling in love

with me. And I had feelings for him, too. As a matter of fact, I knew I was falling in love with him! It was hard not to. He said and did all the right things. He started on my house last week and I didn't have to do or say anything. He called me and said, "Meet me at Lowe's." Once I met up with him, he told me to pick out my cabinets for my kitchen. Then we both decided on Bella hardwood floors throughout the entire house and ceiling track lights. It was costly, but Dre was fixing it and he didn't ask me to give him any money toward anything.

Every day when we came in from work, we showered, talked about our day, ate dinner, and then just held each other all night, watching movies. In the morning I went home to change clothes and then we'd do it again. The *do it again* part was about to happen again. I looked over at the alarm clock that read five fifty-eight. The sun was about to rise and it was time for me to go home and get ready for work. I slipped out of Dre's arms because I didn't want to wake him up. He jumped up anyway and said, "What time is it?"

"Six."

"Hold up . . . before you leave," he said, sliding out of the bed.

"What, Dre? I got to get home and get dressed."

"Look in the closet." I looked in the closet. He had cleaned it—so what?

"What? You cleaned out your closet? That's nice." I was confused.

"I'm making space in my life. That other half is mine; this half is yours. It doesn't make sense for you to keep getting up early every morning and running home to change your clothes when you can bring a few things over."

"A few things?"

"Yes, just a few things. Don't try to take over my closet. I don't want to come home and see all your shoes."

"Okay, I'll bring a few things. Thanks, babe, but I really have to go."

"Oh, and here," he said as he followed me to the steps. "No more waiting outside until I get here." He placed a key in my hand. "I have to go out of town in a few days to look at some real estate in Douglasville—right outside of Atlanta, Georgia. Syeed said it's real nice and wants me to invest in it." I took Dre's keys and headed home.

Dre had only been gone two days and I was missing him. I decided I was going to stay at his house. I put the key in the lock and entered. I walked around and I could hear my own footsteps. I turned the television on so I could hear another voice. I dialed Dre to let him know I was at his house.

"Dre, I'm at your house."

"You okay?"

"Yeah, but I'm a little lonely. I have the television keeping me company, though. I'm not used to sleeping by myself anymore."

"Me neither, but I'm not going to stay here until Sunday. I saw the development—it's in the middle of nowhere and I don't like it. I shouldn't have even come. I know better than to listen to Syeed. Then you know they lost all my luggage at the airport?"

"Oh, no. What was in there?"

"My watch, a few pairs of shoes. I'm not going to worry about it. So I should be home first thing in the morning. I love you, and I'll see you then."

"I love you, too!" As soon as I hung up with Dre, another call came in. I knew I shouldn't answer it. It was Reshaun, and I knew all she was going to do was fuss me out about not keeping in touch. I clicked over without saying anything.

"You really shouldn't do your friends like this."

"Like what?" I laughed.

"Like not take their calls, don't call them back. I understand you have the new man and the new title at the job, but can I get a hello? Is that too much to ask for?"

"I know, I know. I have been doing so much. We have to get together."

"Come meet me tomorrow. While Briggy is at practice, we can sit down and talk outside at the park."

"Okay, I'm going to come."

I met up with Reshaun at the crowded park and we hugged briefly. She had a new short, edgy haircut. She looked more like the fly, sassy, cute Reshaun I was accustomed to.

"I love your hair, girl. You look like your old self."

"What are you trying to say?"

"Nothing, just your married look wasn't the best look for you."

"Whatever, my man like all my looks. But enough about me. Where have you been hiding?"

"I've been staying with Dre and just working all the time."

"That is so good. I told you that was your boyfriend."

"Yeah, you were right. I wish I would have met him years ago. I feel that peace . . . that love that you were talking about. I feel like he loves me unconditionally. I'm a little scared. I'm lying. I'm a lot scared. I just keep thinking that he is too good to be true."

"Don't feel that way, you got to live in the moment. How do you think I felt after marrying Michael so fast? But I didn't care, I dropped my guard, and it was the best decision I ever made. And I'm just trying new things and trying new things. Like why the other night did me and Michael go to a gentleman's club?"

I turned around with my hand over my mouth, shocked. "What?"

"Yes, and it was actually nice. It was very classy and the women weren't dressed all slutty. The whole club was erotic, but not sleazy. It was a place called The Venus Room. They serve dinner and the food was good. The entire atmosphere was nice."

"Dinner in a strip club. That sounds so disgusting."

"It's not a strip club. I know how it sounds, but I'm going to tell you I had so much fun. I actually am thinking about getting a pole for my bedroom."

"Shut up. Damn, maybe I should try to do something like that for Dre, when he get back."

"He will love it. Me and Michael came home

and had so much fun. I will buy him as many lap dances as he wants. Especially if he takes care of me like that night. It was so good."

"Oh God, that's TMI. Next subject," I said, almost choking from laughing.

"Okay, enough about the gentleman's club. Guess who I talked to?"

"Who?"

"Tia."

"That's nice," I said as my mood changed. I don't know why she was wasting her time telling me about Tia. I was not being bothered with her at all.

"You know she moved to Columbia, South Carolina."

"So."

"After losing her job, she didn't want to be up here anymore. She invited me and Michael to come down there for a visit."

"She did? And you told her no, right?" I asked with an attitude.

"No, I didn't tell her anything."

"How could you even think about going to visit her after all that she did to me and my mom?"

"So, I'm not allowed to talk to her?" Reshaun asked, perplexed.

"No," I said with a straight face.

"You are so funny. This is not second grade. We are all grown. Tia asked me the same thing. She wanted to know why I am still talking to you."

"She said that?"

"No, but now you see how silly that sounds." I didn't appreciate Reshaun playing me like that, but I didn't say anything. She had a good point, but

I really didn't want her talking to Tia. I didn't want any reminders of her in my life. Reshaun was now my friend and my friend only.

When Dre came back, I had already planned our night out. I had bought him a watch and I was going to take him to The Venus Room. After that we were going to come home and have an explosive, sex-filled night. I was a modern woman. If Reshaun could go to a strip club, I could be adventurous and go to one, too!

"Dre, I'm taking you out tonight, so don't make any plans. Oh yeah, wear something comfortable."

"Where are we going?" he questioned, sitting up in the bed.

"I can't tell you. But don't wear anything that you don't want to get wrinkled."

"You not going to tell me where we are going?" he asked as I stood in front of him. He nestled his face into my breasts, trying to seduce me into staying home.

"Come on, Dre, stop playing around."

"I'm tired. I don't feel like going out. All those hours in the airport. I just want to relax."

"This is going to relax you, trust me. Come on." I pulled him up from the bed. "I'll give you a clue . . . it is every man's fantasy."

"I don't have a fantasy."

"Yes, you do. All men have a fantasy. So put your clothes on and let's go."

By the time Dre was dressed, he was still trying to figure out where he was going, saying he was really sleepy and he felt sick, and could we go home? I didn't want to deal with his semi-bitchy mood, but I didn't want to cancel my plans. I wanted to do something fun.

"Fine, Dre. We're going to this little place that I heard about. It's called The Venus Room."

"That's a strip club. I don't want to go there. Take me home."

"It is not a strip club. It's a gentleman's club. And I know you are going to love it." I was acting like I knew what I was talking about, but I was really going off Reshaun's word. I had tried to call the club and ask for the protocol. Like what I should wear and how I should tip, but the person who answered the phone wasn't very helpful.

We parked the car. He got out reluctantly, dragging his feet like he was still so tired. I grabbed his hand and we walked in. As we entered I saw a few other couples and people with suits on, which calmed my nerves. I ordered us two French martinis and we got a table. The décor was electric blue neon, with average-looking women who thought they were beautiful swinging up and down from poles. *I wish I had that much power in my legs,* I thought, as one of the exotic dancers came slinking down the pole.

We had a seat with our drinks. Dre was still uncomfortable. I gave his shoulders a quick squeeze and told him to relax.

A woman came over and introduced herself as Sapphire. Her skin was rich chocolate and her wavy, store-bought hair landed right in the center of her high, perfect butt. Her body was densely covered in a red firefighter outfit and red patent leather, six-inch, clear-heeled boots.

"Would you like a dance?" she asked Dre. He shook his head no, but I politely told her yes. She began to dance seductively in front of him and then she bent and dropped down to her knees and did all types of movements with her hips, legs, and ass.

Initially, Dre was looking at her like she wasn't any good. But as her performance went on, I could tell by the way he was holding his mouth open, he was enjoying his private show. So, we paid her to entertain us for two more songs. As she danced, Dre guzzled four straight shots of Patrón. I was still nursing my martini. His eyes followed Sapphire's every movement. She flipped her hair over her shoulders as she was moving side to side. Then she perched her body inches away from Dre's lap, and swayed her body in a seductive rhythm. I didn't feel the least bit threatened by Sapphire. She was doing exactly what she was supposed to and that was to get my man ready for me. Dre was so into it, he was ready to go home and give me what I needed. I waited for the waitress to come back and paid our tab, and then slipped four twenties in Sapphire's red firefighter boots. I whispered to Dre what I was going to do to him when we got home. I couldn't wait to get there. We were going to tear each other up. Yup, I was the cool, new-age girlfriend and my man was loving me for being so open-minded. He was driving with his left hand on the wheel and the other one was all over me. We pulled up to the house, and before we got all the way inside, my shirt was coming off and my pants were sliding down.

"Did you like your surprise, baby?" I said as I kissed him and simultaneously took off my shoes.

"It was okay," he said in a disinterested tone as I followed him up the steps.

"Just okay? You sure? I thought you would have really enjoyed it."

It was dark in the bedroom, but I could feel that Dre was upset. In the dark he yelled, "Have you ever, or do you want to, have sex with women?"

"No, baby. Not at all."

"Then why the hell would you think it would be a good idea to take me to a god damn strip club? If you got something to tell me, tell me now."

"What are you talking about?"

"You know."

"Whatever, no, I don't. Go to sleep, Dre. You are drunk and acting silly."

"I'm not drunk. I saw you touch that dancer," he slurred. I didn't know what he was talking about. I never touched that girl. I tipped her for his dance. "I don't want to ever see your hands on another woman. I don't want you to go back to that strip club anymore."

"When was my hand on another woman? Babe, all I did was give her a tip. It was my first time there, too!"

"Yeah, right. You seemed real comfortable to me."

"Okay, whatever. You are overreacting. Look at what I get for being the good girlfriend." I totally didn't understand what was going on. I felt stupid for taking him. I should have just stayed at home when he asked me to.

The entire night, I didn't get any sleep and felt

like I was being verbally abused. Dre went from accusing me of liking a stripper to saying I was probably completely gay. During his vicious attack on my sexuality he had to run into the bathroom and he began making all types of demon noises. Every few seconds the toilet flushed. I walked in the bathroom and he was collapsed on the floor. I guess the Patrón had got the best of him.

"You want some water?"

"No." He was sick on the floor and still being an asshole.

"Are you sure you okay, Dre? I can go and get you something to drink or something."

"No, I'm fine," he said. So, I left him there and went back in the bedroom. I turned the television up so I wouldn't have to hear his beastly cries all night.

An hour later he called out my name. I answered him and he said, "Can you go to the store and get me a ginger ale and soup or something? I still feel like shit." The only thing that was open this time in the morning was 7-Eleven. I didn't want to go out that time of night, but Dre had to be really sick to ask, so I did what I had to do. At 7-Eleven the lonely clerk was reading a magazine and said hello as I filled the little red shopping basket with overpriced saltines, chicken noodle soup, and a two-liter ginger ale.

By the time I returned, Dre was still on the floor, complaining about how his stomach hurt. He finally felt well enough to leave the bathroom. I brought a bucket in the bedroom that was filled halfway with water, just in case. He sat on the bed and began slurping down the soup. He asked me for water too. I'd told him he should have water.

Anyway, I went to the kitchen and came back up the steps with a glass full of ice water. He took a few sips, but immediately brought it all up. As I witnessed his stomach heave in and out, I almost wanted to throw up myself. Dre looked so sickly. He turned to me as little pieces of everything were in the corner of his mouth.

"I feel a lot better," he said as I gave him a towel. "I think that was the last of it." He tried again to drink the ginger ale and have a little more soup. The minute the ginger ale and chicken noodle soup touched his stomach, it was back in the bucket again. He looked helpless. I didn't feel sorry for him, because he was going off on me for no reason. Dondre Hill was getting paid back for being evil. He was looking sick and sweating profusely. I thought that there had to be something other than the shots of Patrón making his body do all of this. I considered taking him to the emergency room.

It was almost twelve hours later before Dre was back to hisself. He took a shower and went out, without saying a word. Any other woman would have left him after a night like that. He deserved to be left, and that's when I knew I must really love him because I didn't. When he left I thought about going home, but instead I took a nap. When I awoke he was sitting at the edge of the bed.

"Babe, I'm sorry," he said softly.

"It's fine."

"No, it's not. I think I'm getting a little scared. Sometimes people do crazy things when they think someone is getting too close to them, so they can protect themselves."

"What is that supposed to mean?"

"I love you a lot and I just want us to be perfect, with no lies and no dishonesty."

It was a half-ass apology and I wasn't sure I accepted it. Instead of saying anything I closed my eyes and continued to rest.

If you have a new boyfriend and your old boyfriend calls to invite you out to just meet up, you can go, right? I thought it wouldn't hurt to "talk" to Malcolm. But just because I thought it was okay doesn't mean I wasn't scared. It must have been my nerves or my conscience or just the fact I knew I was doing something sneaky. I was tripping. I could meet up with Malcolm if I wanted to. It wasn't like Dre had a tracking device on me. I was just having a conversation with an old friend.

That's what I told myself the entire ride to the Lucky Strike Bowling Alley. Malcolm was bowling with a few coworkers and invited me. I don't know why I even showed up. I don't know why I was here, especially after me and Dre just had our long talk about honesty. But I think I just wanted to confirm that I was really over Malcolm. Malcolm gave me a kiss on the cheek as soon as he saw me and said, "Nicole, hey, gorgeous."

"Thank you, Malcolm." I was real cool, not grinning or being overexcited, like I used to do whenever I was around Malcolm.

"So, how are things going?"

"Great," I said.

"I've been working on my future," Malcolm said, shifting from foot to foot. He was the one who was nervous.

"How so?" I asked, slightly curious. But I really didn't care about his future anymore.

"You know, finding the right attorney and what not. What have you been doing?"

"Not too much. Working hard. I got a boyfriend now," I said as I looked him directly in his eyes. I wanted to see how he would react.

"A boyfriend! What? You trying to make me jealous?"

"No, not at all. His name is Dre and he's really a great guy." I continued to study his expression. He was twitching and biting his tongue. I think he really thought I'd be with him or waiting for him, forever.

"It's only been a few months. You can't be too serious with him, are you?"

"We are very serious."

"Wow, Nikki, but do you still love me?"

"No," I said, shaking my head.

"You don't love me at all?" Malcolm asked.

"Nope," I said confidently. Malcolm no longer being able to have me made him want me more. The rest of the night he asked to take me to a hotel. I told him no repeatedly. It was different to see him beg, within a few feet of friends and co-workers.

But then eventually I gave in. I didn't have anything to blame it on. I wasn't drinking and I wasn't upset. I wanted to test myself and see if I was truly over him like I thought I was.

I must be over him, completely over him. Because our once incredible sex was now lackluster. Malcolm used to have the ability to make me have seizures. His touch used to give my body earthquakes, but this time I didn't even feel a tremor. I shouldn't have even went there with him in the first place. Plus, I felt so bad for sleeping with him. The only thing creeping with him taught me was how much I loved Dre and how over Malcolm I was. It was really over. I told him I had to go and that I would call him. But I really intended never to see him again.

Chapter 19

I could smell a barbeque aroma as I exited Dre's truck and I could hear loud laughter and music playing in the distance. Dre was about to introduce me to his family at their Fourth of July cookout. I hadn't met anyone's family in years and was excited. The only people I knew who were close to Malcolm were his friends that were always his alibi, so they didn't count.

We walked through a gate and down a narrow little walkway. The closer we got, the louder the voices and music became. At the end of the walkway was a huge yard full of people in every direction. There were a bunch of tables with green umbrellas that were adorned with patriotic red, white, and blue decorations and flags. A few people were engrossed in playing cards. They had two grills going with all different types of meats. There were tables with checkerboard tablecloths with aluminum foil–covered dishes of food on top. I noticed a cake with the American flag—whipped cream and blueberries served as the stars and strawberries patterned as the stripes.

"Hey, Dre!" everyone screamed, like they hadn't seen him in years. He went around giving hugs and kisses. And I didn't know what to do, so I followed him. He sat down and I sat next to him. We got up and weaved through the crowds of people. I recognized his brother, Brandon, and Syeed. I waved and said hello. They were both with their families, sitting back, eating and drinking.

"Mom, this is my lady, Nicole."

Dre's mom wiped her hands on her apron and said, "Oh, Dre, she is so cute." Then she gave me a big smile. "Honey, you just the cutest! I'm Ms. Pam." She was a very tall, stocky woman with full lips and an inviting smile. I felt like a new puppy, the way she kept gushing over me. Then she announced to everyone at the barbeque, "Look, y'all, this is Dre's new girlfriend."

His mom put me on blast and everyone turned and stared at me. But judging by their smiles, everyone approved. Then Dre walked me over and introduced me to his youngest sister, Pumpkin. She looked like a little thug. His middle sister, April, seemed like the conservative one, and his sister, Mercedes, was petite and friendly. I don't think she was even five feet. If I saw her walking down the street I would think she was a little kid, but she was a year younger than Dre. They were all cute and no one was overweight, which was not at all how I imagined them. Since he said he and his sisters grew up eating tons of junk food, I pictured his sisters all being heavyweights. After all the introductions were done, I had a seat and Dre said he would be back. I saw him walk out of the yard. I wondered where he was going and why he had left me alone in an entire yard full of strangers. I just pulled my phone out and pretended like I was looking at some text messages. Damn, I felt so uncomfortable. His mother came over to me and said, "You can help yourself to the food, sweetheart."

I said thank you as she handed me a heavy white Styrofoam plate. I wanted a little of everything, but decided to sample a few chicken wings and celery and carrot sticks with dip. I sat there by myself, quietly nibbling on my food, waiting for Dre to return.

Then I heard a voice say, "Dre bringing another woman around already, that's just wrong." I turned around to see who had made the last comment. It was Dre's thugged-out-looking sister.

Then another voice said, "I think she heard you."

Then Little Miss Thug said, "I don't care if she heard me. He must really be done with Jocelyn this time. 'Cause he ain't never brought no girl around the family."

"Who cares. I hate Jocelyn. I'm just glad he got rid of that girl. My brother needs to be with someone else," another voice said.

Although I could hear their conversation very well, when they looked over at me I acted oblivious. Luckily, Dre came back carrying his daughter over his shoulder and was holding his son by his hand. His family took the kids and began passing them around, showing them off to the people at the cookout.

Dre ate and danced with his mom, between being silly and spoiling his children with lavish affection. They ran around the cookout nonstop all day. Mikal really liked me, but Sabria was not as receptive toward me. She was basically on some *who is you?* type stuff. She was only three years old, but she was acting like a jealous woman and wouldn't take her eyes off of me. Every time Dre came and sat next to me, she came and sat on his lap and glared at me. He said she was acting funny because he hadn't seen her in a while. But I wasn't convinced.

Aside from the whispering they'd done earlier, I came to realize that Dre's family was nice and they were so loving. We stayed until it was dark and the lightning bugs began blinking through the yard. Dre's children were getting restless; it was past their bedtime. He told everyone we were leaving. When we got up, everyone walked us to the car and told me it was nice to meet me.

Once we were in the house Mikal and Sabria were running up and down the hallway. They were jumping and screaming even though Dre told them it was time for bed. He calmed then down, bathed them, and made them change into their nightclothes and put them to bed. Then Dre took his shower and came in his bedroom with me. His lower half was wrapped with a towel. His torso was looking so edible, I was ready to attack him. Then Sabria moseyed in his bedroom, rubbing one eye while the other eye was following me. "Who is she, Daddy?"

"I told you, Bria. This is Miss Nikki. Say hi, Miss Nikki."

"Hi, Miss Nikki," she said quickly and then

turned back to Dre. "Daddy, I need you to pat my back so I can go to sleep."

"Daddy will be right there."

Sabria left the room slowly and walked down the hall holding on to the wall. Dre threw on a T-shirt, boxers, and gym shorts and walked out of the room to go put his daughter to sleep. By the time he came back I had fallen asleep watching the news. He woke me and grabbed my waist tightly and asked, "Are you ready for all this? I love my children and they are always going to be around me. Nicole, you really think you're ready?"

"Yes, I'm ready. Mikal already likes me and I have to work on Sabria," I said as we both laughed and held each other to sleep.

CHAPTER 20

"Hello . . . hey, what's her name again?" I heard a voice ask.

"You're calling my phone. Who is this?" I asked with my face scrunched up in irritation.

"Dre's sister, Mercedes."

"Oh, hey, Mercedes." I looked down at the phone like, *Okay, what can I do for you? Why are you calling my phone?*

"The reason I was calling was because my mom wanted to ask you if you wanted to go with us to Commons Premium Outlet in Tannersville. It's an outlet mall. We all going shopping on Saturday. After shopping, we are probably going to dinner and just have some fun."

"Uhm, that sounds good. How y'all getting there?"

"My sister, April, has a big truck. You can meet up at my mom's house." Dre wasn't even going to be there, so was I supposed to go? I didn't want Dre to think that I was trying to make myself a part of his family.

"Okay, that sounds nice, but I'm sorry, I won't be able to make it."

"You can't? Well, maybe next time," she said, disappointed. I hung up and a few minutes later, Dre called. "Yo, why you not going out with my sisters and my mom?" he yelled into the phone.

"Dre, first of all, I don't know them like that and secondly, I don't really have any money to shop."

"Nikki, just go shopping and whatever you spend, I will give you back when I get back. Okay?"

"Okay,"I said reluctantly.

"And the next time my family invite you somewhere, don't be acting all funny, just go. My mom and sisters are good people. You have to get to know them."

I met everybody at Dre's mother's house. They were all sitting in April's Ford Expedition. It was Dre's mom and his sisters April, Pumpkin, and Mercedes. Mercedes brought some guy who was dressed better than all the women in the car. I got in and sat on the third row with Mercedes and her friend. She introduced us. "Alex, this is my brother's girlfriend, Nicole. Nicole, this is my cousin, Alex."

"Hi." I gave the cousin a friendly smile.

"Hey, diva," he grinned through shiny pink, glossy lips. His hair was in a short, cropped, midnight-black bob and his makeup was stunning.

"What kind of work you do?" April asked from the front seat.

"I'm a manager at a hotel at the airport."

"Free rooms when my boy comes to town," Alex squealed.

"Shut up, she doesn't even know your boy," Mercedes laughed.

"I know you, girl, don't I? I like her better than Jocelyn already. Welcome to the family, girl. And you know I do hair. So I can hook you up. Get me some rooms and I'll be all in your hair, girl." We all started laughing.

"What are y'all talking about back there?" Dre's mom, Ms. Pam, asked.

"Jocelyn's free-loading behind," Alex said.

"No, Mom, Alex was welcoming her into the family, saying he doesn't like stupid Jocelyn. And Alex ain't even really in the family."

"Yes, I am. Auntie Pam, I'm in the family, right?"

"Yes, you are in the family, but stop talking about that girl."

"Auntie Pam, stop fronting. You don't like her either."

"I'm not going to say anything bad about her. She is the mother of my grandchildren, but she is drama. I've never been so happy to see two people break up. I'm not saying anything else about her. Plus, Nikki don't want to hear that mess."

"I don't care what you say, I still don't like her mom," Mercedes said.

I just listened as they went back and forth about Jocelyn being no good. Maybe she really was. I wanted to add to the conversation and tell them how she got my tires slashed and my radio stolen. But I decided against it.

Once we arrived at the mall, I gravitated toward Mercedes and Alex. Mercedes seemed the nicest from the cookout. There were all these outlets everywhere. I wasn't a shopaholic, but I couldn't help but get excited.

"Divas, help me pick out an outfit," Alex said as he pulled dresses off the rack. He sashayed up and down the aisle of the Charlotte Russe store. I didn't see anything I wanted, so I went next door to the Ralph Lauren store. Pumpkin walked in behind me with her arms loaded down with bags. One of her bags was from Bloomingdale's and there wasn't a Bloomingdale's in this mall. I watched her as she wrapped polo shirts around her arm then slid them inside the bag. She walked up to me as I got to the register and paid for my shirts, trying to make light conversation.

"Did you see my sister?" she asked.

"No, she might still be at Charlotte Russe's."

"Oh," she said. Then, right in front of the cashier's face, she stuffed socks into her bag and walked over to another rack of clothes. She was fast and I was impressed by her boosting skills. But I was not getting locked up with her.

I left her right in that store and tried to locate Mercedes. I ran in the store, not knowing what to say. But Alex could read the expression on my face, because as soon as he saw me he said, "Are you okay?"

"Yeah, but Pumpkin is in that store."

And before I could complete the sentence, Alex shook his head and said, "Stealing. That's a damn shame. Somebody should have warned you. Poor child."

"She's doing what?" Mercedes said, not amused. She picked up her phone and began dialing.

"Who you calling?" Alex asked.

"My mom," she said as she aligned the phone with her ear. "Mommy, Pumpkin up in here stealing again. Yeah, she was doing it while she was in the store with Dre's girlfriend. Okay, me neither. All right, bye. We'll meet you at the car around seven."

"What she say?" Alex asked as he held a pair of Michael Kors jeans up to his waist.

"Not much. She just said to let her get locked up, because she is not going to get her out and she said she warned Pumpkin before we got to the mall."

By the end of the day, we were all tired and spent out. It was worth it, though, because I got all these deals and cute clothes that Alex handpicked. I was excited that they accepted me into their family like I was one of them. I was smiling all the way home. I was in a good mood, but I don't think Lolo appreciated seeing me so happy. She was sitting on the sofa and she noticed my bags and rummaged through them.

"How you going shopping and didn't ask me to go?"

"When do you ever want to go anywhere with me?" I asked.

"Always, Nicole. But that's okay. It's all right, you want to make me feel like I don't even have a daughter. You never here and now you are going shopping. Who did you go shopping with?"

"A friend of mine's mom and sisters."

"Really? The same friend that you practically live with? I've been wondering if you're ever going to get around to introducing us, 'cause something's wrong with him anyway."

"Ain't nothing wrong with him."

"Hmph, so you say. Either you are embarrassed of him, or me and Ernest. Now, which one is it?"

"It is neither. Mom, I will bring him to meet you and Ernest."

Chapter 21

I was so scared to bring Dre home to meet Lolo. I knew he would get along with Ernest but my mom—that was another story. I heard men look at their girlfriends' mothers to see what they are up against in twenty-five years. In the looks department he will say okay, I'm good, but personality-wise, Dre is going to run. I was so nervous and scared that Lolo would chase Dre away.

We pulled up in front of my mother's door and all I could think about was my mom embarrassing me in some kind of way. As we approached the house I tried to warn Dre about Lolo. But there was no easy way to say that my mom is crazy, so beware.

"Now, Dre, I have to warn you, my mother is very different than your mother."

"Different how?"

"You'll see just how different. I'm going to apologize right now for anything she might say tonight," I said as I knocked on the door. I wanted to prolong them meeting as long as possible. I didn't even want to use my key.

Ernest greeted us as soon as we entered. Dre walked over to him and shook his hand. "Nice to meet you, man," Ernest said as he shook Dre's hand enthusiastically. It was like Ernest couldn't believe I had brought a real man to the house to meet him and my mom. Dre had a seat and I walked toward the kitchen to get my mother. I figured, let me hurry up and get the inevitable over with. But it was too late. Lolo walked in the living room on her own, all fast. I didn't have enough time to get my thoughts together.

"Hi, Mom, this is Dre, and Dre, this is my mom," I said, almost stuttering as she approached the living room.

Dre stood up and said, "Nice to meet you," and offered her a handshake. Lolo didn't extend her hand back. She just stood in place and looked Dre over. She twisted her lips and stared him down, hard enough to see his soul. I knew it was about to go down. All I could say to myself over and over was *Be nice, Lolo. Please be nice.* Dre could sense how tense I was and asked was I okay.

"Yeah, she okay. She always gets nervous when she brings someone to meet me. But I got to say I haven't seen her with a boyfriend in years, so you must be special. I'm Lois, but you can call me Miss Lolo."

"Nice to meet you, Miss Lolo." Dre smiled and handed her a bottle of wine.

Over the next hour, my mother and Ernest threw a barrage of questions at Dre. From where he met me to how many children did he have. But any questions they presented him with, he answered perfectly. I didn't know why I was shocked. I knew Dre was intelligent, but I thought Lolo was going to find a reason not to like him. But she didn't. She didn't even get smart with him. Surprisingly, she asked him to come over for dinner.

Later that night when I spoke with her, she admitted that she didn't like the fact he already had two young children, but other than that, she loved him and thought he was a good match for me. I was relieved because I know Dre is my soul mate. Dre had defeated the big bad monster named Lolo.

I love Dre so much. And he feels the same way about me. Me and Dre can't go three hours without talking or texting each other. I know it is still early, but I know he loves me and I love him. I love his family too. I've been to Ms. Pam's house twice this week to have dinner. There were always so many people there, it was hard to keep up with everybody's names. Dre's family had friends, but they didn't really need any because they are all each other's best friends. They are super close. They get together for movie night, bowling night, and all kinds of get-togethers. I wish I grew up with a big, tight family like theirs. His entire family is so nice, but I've grown the closest to Mercedes. I think she is my new best friend. I don't know why, but me and her have hit it off. I'm actually surprised. I usually don't make friends fast or easily. Mercedes is so funny, though. She is the girl version of Dre—silly and loves desserts. And the two of us just laugh and joke all the time. We like the same things, own the same perfumes, and she also reminds me a lot of Tia. It is like we've known each other for our entire lives. I find myself giving her advice on her relationships. She has a nice stable of guys who she's talking to, but she said she's really interested in this married man who works at her job. I confessed to her about Malcolm and warned her to stay away from the married men. I shared a lot of personal stuff. I mean a lot. I was running my mouth so much that the next day I had to write down what I told her and evaluate whether or not I had revealed too much. She is just becoming my friend, but she is always going to be Dre's sister first. I like her, but I feel a little funny being so close to her. I would hate for her to share anything I told her with Dre.

I drove Dre to the airport because he had to go out of town to look at a few more properties. Then I came in and went to work. My trainee program would begin in a few weeks. The transition team was gone. I had recommended Maritza for my position and was steadily trying to keep the standards high. Who knew the next time we would have a surprise inspection? Just as I got settled to get ready for my day, I got a call from Ms. Pam. She wanted to know if I had seen Dre.

"I just dropped him off at the airport. He went out of town on business, Ms. Pam."

"Nicole, if you talk to him, have him call me. Tell him it is important."

"Is there anything I can do?"

"No, Pumpkin is in jail and she needs bail money. I wish she would learn to leave other people's stuff alone. What's wrong with this girl?" Damn, he had all these family problems, it was crazy. I knew I couldn't help her, so I told her I would try to reach him.

I called Dre and updated him about everything and told him to call his mother. Minutes later he called me back. "Nicole, go to my house and in my closet, behind my shoe boxes, there is a safe. The combination is fourteen, six, thirty-nine. Take ten thousand dollars and go meet my mom and give it to her."

"Hold on, so I can write this down. You said fourteen, six, thirty-nine?"

"Yeah. I have to go—I'm on the plane and they are asking me to turn my phone off. Leave me a message when you are done."

I told Maritza to hold the fort down while I drove to go pick up Dre's money to give to his mom. Once I reached her house she asked me to drive her to the police station in Chester County to get Pumpkin out. Once we got there, we tried to give them cash and they said they would only accept a certified check. We had to ride around and find a bank and then pay five dollars to get the check.

It was nearly one when it was over. I was exhausted. Ms. Pam told me I could leave while she waited for officers to release Pumpkin. I knew I couldn't leave her so I waited, and that took another two hours. Pumpkin walked out of the courthouse like it was a regular day and me and her mom hadn't wasted our entire day trying to secure her freedom.

"Thanks, Mom. I'm going to pay you back."

"Don't thank me. Thank your brother. He got

you out, and Nicole brought me up here and ran around with me all day."

Pumpkin turned to me and said, "Oh, thanks. Tell Dre, I got him. I should have never went in the Gap. They are so lame. I saw the security guard looking at me, so I put the jacket back. And they still locked me up. The guard was going to let me go, but the girls behind the counter insisted on calling the police."

"Don't be blaming the cashiers. How about don't steal at all, Pumpkin. I'm sick and tired of having to constantly bail you out of jail," Ms. Pam yelled.

Pumpkin just sighed, acting like her mom was getting on her nerves. It was obvious she had no remorse whatsoever. After all of the running around, I still had to go back to the office and work. I didn't know how much more I could take of Ms. Pam, Mercedes, Pumpkin, and everybody else. By the time Dre called me I was knocked out. I was emotionally drained from all the running around for some unappreciative person.

"Yeah, thanks for earlier. My mom said how helpful you were. I really appreciate it. I know my mom can be a little bit overwhelming at times. If they call you too much, just don't pick up." He didn't have to tell me that twice. "When they can't get to me now, they going to try to get the closest thing to me, which is you."

"I'm the closest thing to you?"

"Yeah, you are."

"Whatever." I played it off like I wasn't flattered, which I was. "So, did you like any of the houses this time?"

"Yup, I bought a house."

"You did!" *That was fast,* I thought.

"I'm going to move down here. I really like it."

"That's good. Well I'm going to rest a little. I'll call you back." I had to get off the phone with Dre. He bought a house and I felt a little hurt. I guess we weren't as strong as I thought we were since he went and bought a house and was planning a major move without bothering to discuss it with me.

CHAPTER 22

Dre had Brandon and his team in my house on a daily basis and they were almost finished. They even kept Smokebreak and Pee Wee around to help on my house and some other jobs. Dre said they both were good workers. I was a little surprised. But I guess you have to make money to buy beer some kind of way. I've been staying with Dre until they finish it. Then I guess I'm going to move into my house.

I hadn't called Reshaun in a long time—she'd been leaving me messages, but I had been overwhelmed with work and Dre. Now I had some free time, so I dialed her up. "Don't be mad at me."

"I'm not. You must be in love. I know you'd better have a good excuse for not calling me back."

"No, just been tied up with my house being remodeled, and Dre and his family."

"You met his family?"

"Yeah, I'm all in good with his mom. She's real nice and two of his sisters are cool. But the baby sister is crazy. I had to bail her out of jail. But I don't know what's going to happen with us. Dre just bought a house in Georgia and he said he is moving down there. He didn't even ask me how I felt about it. How's everything going with you?" I asked.

"Good. I was calling to tell you Tia had her baby."

"Oh, she did? That's good. What she have?"

"A girl."

"Oh, that's so sweet. That's really nice. What she name the baby and who the baby look like?"

"She told me what she named the baby, but I forgot. But she had a little girl. She sent me the picture on e-mail. I'm going to forward it to you."

"Don't forward me the picture. Stop telling me about her. I don't care. Tia is not my friend no more. You know I don't mess with that girl like that."

"I know you say that, but I know, deep down, y'all still want to be friends."

"No, I don't. I'm good. But I'm happy for her. I'm sure she'll be a good mother. Like I said, I'm really happy for her. But that's as far as it goes."

"Nicole, you should really call her."

"No, I shouldn't!"

"Yes, you should, because Lamar left her. And she down there all alone. Her mom and none of her family is helping her out the way you would expect them to. They ain't doing right or supporting her, because they never liked Lamar anyway. The last time I talked to her, she sounded real down and I'm sure if she heard from you, that would make her day."

"Reshaun! Tia is never going to hear from me. Stop trying to be the peacemaker. I'm not calling her. That's on her. This is what happens when you do dirt. You get dirt. You think all of this is an accident? Nope, it's called payback."

"You wrong, Nikki."

"Whatever. I'm out; I'll talk to you later." I hung up on Reshaun. Truth be told, I really did feel sorry for Tia. I was so happy she had a baby girl. But I was also mad. I was supposed to be there when she had that baby. We were going to name our kids after each other, but she messed all that up over a couple of dollars that she ain't never seen. I wished she wouldn't have ever stayed with Lamar. This was the great part of her life that I will never get to experience with her. I should have been there when her baby was born. I didn't get a chance to give her a baby shower or help her decorate a nursery. She messed all of that up. It was supposed to be me and her against the world. I never thought it would ever be her against me. I sat there thinking about Tia and her dumbness until the phone rang. I picked up, ready to yell at Reshaun again.

"What's wrong with you?"

"Nothing's wrong, what's up?"

"You in the house?" Dre asked.

"Yes, I'm in the house."

"Are you sure?"

"Why are you always asking me am I sure? I hate when you start that checking-up-on-me shit. It's irritating."

"I just have to make sure. What's with you? Why does it seem like you have an attitude?"

"I don't have an attitude—it's just my old best friend just had her baby. Reshaun said her boyfriend left her."

"That's messed up. Maybe you should call her if it is like that."

"I'm thinking about it. When you going to be home? I need you."

"I'm on my way home now. Your house is done. We going to check it out tomorrow."

"Okay, bye, Dre." Even hearing that great news, I couldn't be happy. I was still kind of in a bad mood. I wished I never called Reshaun.

Dre covered my eyes and walked me into my new house. He opened the front door. I couldn't wait to see all the changes. Dre took his hands off my eyes and said, "So what do you think?" I opened my eyes and was amazed. My living room already was furnished.

The entire house was so bright and open. I had all new walls that were painted a crisp off-white. They had knocked down the wall that separated the kitchen and dining room. With the wall gone it was one huge room. I could see the beautiful kitchen from the front door. I excitedly walked into the kitchen. It had black Silestone countertops, ceramic tile backsplash, and the dark brown cabinets were huge. I opened the cabinet doors and saw empty shelf space. I turned to Dre and gave him a hug.

"Babe, this is so nice."

"There's more to see. Go upstairs."

"Okay," I said as I jogged up the stairs and gazed at my new bathroom. I had a shower in one corner and a large, deep, claw-foot tub in the other. From there I stepped into the middle room, which was plain, but my back room was already set up like a study. Dre had a silver-metal computer desk and bookshelves. I came out of the office and spun around toward my bedroom. It had white track lights on the ceiling and a big cappuccino-black canopy bed in the center of the room. Across from the bed was a thirty-two-inch television on the wall. I stood in shock, a little bit in disbelief. It was so pretty. I needed a moment. I was about to cry. I never thought I would see my house look like this.

"What's wrong?"

"Nothing, it is just so nice. You did all this for me?"

"Yeah, I did it for us. I'm going to be staying here too. So I have to make it comfortable," Dre said, bringing me into his chest and holding me.

"That's the only reason why you made it nice," I said, pulling back from him and lightly punching his arm. I took a long sigh of relief, because I was finally home.

Chapter 23

All this time I wanted my house fixed and now that it was, I never stayed there. I officially lived with Dre. All my belongings were at his house. His house really looked like our house. I rearranged the living room and we bought a new television. Our bathroom was filled with his-and-her body products, and I had almost taken over his closet. He complained about my shoes and hair products. I transferred all of my mail, and I go past my real house every few days just to check on things. A few months ago I would have given a kidney to have that house completed. Now it didn't mean that much. Now that I've moved, Lolo finds reasons to call me. She'll ask me if I've seen her hair dryer or a sweater she hasn't worn in years. She found any reason to call me. I saw her number and answered.

"Hey, Mom."

"No, it's me, Ernest. How's it going, Nikki?"

"Good."

"Well, that's good, real good. I wanted to ask you can you come over for dinner? Sometime this week."

"I'm going to try. I'm really busy at my job. So I'm going to see."

"Your mom really misses you. She won't tell you but she does. Now I know you have your house and new life, but please come over today or tomorrow. Just come and sit and talk to her."

"I can't, I have something to do today."

"Well, how about tomorrow?"

"Okay, I'll be there tomorrow."

Ain't life funny, Lolo missing me. I would have to go and hang out with her. But not today. Today, I had a hair appointment with Alex. Mercedes and I were going to get our hair done and go to dinner.

We arrived at Alex's hair salon. He put us in front of all his clients and no one said a word. His clients like to hang out at his shop to get a good laugh. Alex was so damn funny, plus he could do some hair. I was in his chair and he was curling my hair and telling me another story about Dre.

"So, y'all, these boys was bothering me, right? And they said they wanted to fight me. I was so scared. I didn't want to fight. So I called Dre and he was right there. He was not letting anybody mess with his cousin. But it was like six of them and two of us. But I didn't care, so I start windmilling on them, right?" he said as he started demonstrating for us, waving his hands and arms in all directions. "So Dre saw me fighting like a cat and called me out in front of everybody. He was like, 'Alex, stop fighting like a girl and put your fist up.' I didn't know what that meant, but I balled up my fist and we beat the whole school yard. Ain't nobody ever fuck with me again. That's my cousin. He is all right with me. Ever since then I be like, 'Cousin, whatever you need I got you.' I told him I would cut his hair."

"He don't want you in his hair, Alex," Mercedes chimed in.

"Why not? I would hook his hair up. Give him waves for days," Alex said, returning to my head.

"That's exactly why you won't get in his hair," Mercedes laughed.

"Whateva. Tell Dre I'm here for him. And look how pretty you look, Nicole. You are a baby doll. I knew you were a diva," Alex squealed as he turned me to the mirror to see my hair. I thanked him and paid him. I loved the way he had my hair bouncy and flowing.

Me and Mercedes left the hair salon and went to the Outback for dinner. Mercedes was telling me one of her many dating horror stories. I felt so bad for her. She was going through exactly what I was going through all these years. From the married men to the clowns who didn't deserve another date. And I just couldn't understand it. She was petite, cute, had a good job and nice home. I didn't understand why someone wouldn't see that and take her off the single circuit.

"I don't know what I'm doing wrong," Mercedes said.

"It's not you, it's them. I don't think there are any good men out here." In the middle of me comforting Mercedes, her brother called.

"Hey, Dre."

"Where are you?"

"At dinner with your Mercedes."

"Where at?"

"Outback."

"Oh, you have to get me the Chocolate Thunder from Down Under."

"Okay, Dre, I got you. You don't want anything else?"

"No, just that, and I see you when you home."

"What my brother want?"

"Some dessert." We both laughed and continued to try to come up with a plan to get her a good man.

I walked in Dre's house and called his name. He said he was upstairs. I grabbed a spoon out of the kitchen and brought him up his dessert. He was sitting in the bed all relaxed. I sat on the bed and handed Dre his plastic container filled with sweetness.

"Can I come home to you every day? This all I need, some good food and a beautiful woman."

"That's not food. I wish you'd eat some real food. You are going to develop diabetes. You need some vegetables and protein."

"I had a mushroom cheesesteak earlier today." He laughed.

I undressed, took a shower, and went to lie next to him. Dre was already finished eating and just about asleep. He sat up and looked at me very seriously and said, "Let me ask you something."

"What?"

"You ready to move with me to Georgia?"

"I can't move to Georgia."

"Why not?"

"Dre, it's thousands of reasons. Mainly because I just can't pick up and move to Georgia and sell my house."

"But if I'm down there and you are up here, I guess we breaking up?" Dre asked, confused.

"No, we don't have to break up, we can do the long distance thing."

"The long distance thing—are you serious, Nicole?"

"Very."

"Why?"

"Because, Dre, that is your house and not mine, and what happens if I sell my house and give up everything here and then we break up?"

"We are not going to break up again. It's your house, too."

"No, it's not our house. I'm not your wife. You can kick me out at any given time."

"You think I would kick you out? I love you too much now. You going to be my wife one day. We stuck with one another."

"Dre, I'm not your wife yet, so I can't leave everything. If anything happens I'm going to look crazy."

"What is that supposed to mean?"

"It means exactly what you think it means. I'm not making no big moves like that. Not as your girlfriend."

"Forget it, we'll talk about this another time. Because I know you are moving with me. I'll convince you."

Okay, if you say so, I thought as I lay in the bed and dozed off.

CHAPTER 24

"There is a guest complaint," Maritza said, tapping on my office door with a cheesy grin.

"It never stops, does it? Why don't they go stay at another hotel," I murmured under my breath. "What's wrong this time?"

"I don't know. The woman said something about being double-billed on her credit card."

"Pull up the file and tell her I will contact her before the end of the day."

Maritza nodded and then walked out of my office. A few moments later, she came back and said, "She needs to speak with a manager, right now."

I eyed the piles and piles of paper on top of my desk. I had so much work to do. I really didn't have time for this, but I reluctantly got up from my chair and came up to the front. I walked up to the front desk and didn't see any irate guest. All I saw was Ms. Pam and Mercedes. "What are y'all doing here?"

"We were in the area and wanted to see if you had time to go get lunch with us."

"I can't. I have all this work."

"Oh, okay." And then I saw Dre walking behind them. I felt really confused. "What are you doing here?"

Dre walked up to me and said, "Nicole, you want to spend the rest of your life with me?"

"What is he talking about?" I turned and asked Ms. Pam and Mercedes. They didn't answer me. I was frozen. We had been playfully talking about marriage, but nothing serious. I knew it might happen one day, but not right now. I knew Dre wasn't proposing to me.

"Nicole, I know you are the one. I want to spend the rest of my life with you. I want to ask you something, but first I need you to get this box out of my back pocket."

At first I was speechless, and then I thought I would play with him some before I gave him an answer. "You want me to get a box out of your back pocket, so you not going to get on your knees and say, 'Will you marry me?'"

"No, I'm not getting on my knees. You want this ring or not?" he joked as he reached in his back pocket and pulled out a small red box with gold trimming. Then he slowly bent down on one knee. I felt tears streaming down my face. I was trying not to cry. "Are you going to marry me or what? I know you said you won't move to Georgia with a boyfriend, but will you move with your husband?"

"Dre, you for real?" I asked as I shook my hand fast in front of me, trying to wake up from my dream.

"Yes, I'm for real. Nicole, will you marry me?"

I stared in his eyes before I responded. He

pulled a shimmering white-gold, infinity diamond ring out of the red box and held it up to me.

"You better say yes," Mercedes shouted out.

I said yes, he stood up, and I hugged him. He slid the ring on my finger and said, "I love you, Nikki, and I want to spend the rest of my life with you. I promise you that I will be the best husband to you."

First, Mercedes started crying, and then Ms. Pam joined in. Ms. Pam was crying harder than me. She turned to me and said, "I prayed for you to come into his life. And now that you are here, I am so happy for both of you."

Everybody started getting emotional. Dre pulled me close and hugged me tighter, like I was a prize that he didn't want to let go. I called Lolo and told her. She was so excited. Then I dialed Reshaun.

We all went to have a quick toast at the full-service Marriott that wasn't too far from my job. We were all sitting in a booth. I was leaned over on Dre, staring down at my ring. It was so beautiful, I just couldn't stop looking at it. He kissed me. "So right after our wedding, we are moving to Georgia."

"I kinda figured that out already."

"So, we moving?"

"I guess so."

"Good. I thought it was going to take a lot of convincing."

Ms. Pam and Mercedes were in their own little world, calling people and telling them how Dre had proposed to me.

"But wow, babe, we moving fast. It's only been six months. You sure this is what you want?" Dre asked.

"Yes, I'm sure."

"Are you sure? You accepted my ring."

"Of course I'm sure," I said again. I could hear my phone ringing. I sat up and searched for my bag. It had fallen over by Mercedes' foot. "Reach in there and get my phone."

Mercedes answered the phone and then she passed it to me. "It is somebody talking about getting a divorce."

"Huh?" I took the phone from her.

"I got my divorce! Babe, I got my divorce," a male voice kept repeating.

"Divorce? Who is this?" I asked. I noticed Dre looking over at me suspiciously.

"I need to see you, Nikki. Please. Please, Nikki. I can come to your mother's house. I miss hearing your voice."

"Who is this?"

"It's Malcolm. Ever since we left each other, I've been thinking about you and I just want to let you know it is official. I just left my attorney's office. I'm getting divorced in a few weeks and I want to be with you."

I couldn't even say anything. It was the words I had waited to hear for years and now they didn't mean anything. "No, I'm sorry, you have the wrong number," I said as I turned the ringer off. I then excused myself from the table and walked to the bathroom. I could feel my phone vibrating inside my bag. Malcolm was being persistent, and all I can say is, he sure had some bad-ass timing.

"Why you hang up on me, Nicole? Why you tryna act like I had the wrong number?"

This was an awkward moment. I paced around the bathroom and quietly said, "Congratulations, Malcolm, but I'm getting married."

His voice raised and he said, "What the fuck? After three years of us being together and I finally go get myself together and you going to tell me you getting married?"

"Malcolm. Stop it. I can't do this right now. I will talk to you later."

"You will talk to me later? I can't believe you, Nicole. How can you do this to me?"

"What did I do to you, Malcolm? I'm living my own life. Got my own man. I waited for you for years. This conversation is over."

"Man, meet up with me, and stop playing."

"No, and I'm not playing with you. Don't call my phone anymore." Did he really think all these months later I would be here, sitting and waiting for him? He must have been on some type of drugs. I turned my phone off completely. As I came out of the bathroom, Dre was standing right there, asking if everything was okay.

"Yeah, everything is fine. It was so noisy at the table, I couldn't hear. I had to tell someone else the good news." Dre gave me a look like he didn't believe me. I felt bad for lying to him, but I was really through with Malcolm and it didn't make sense to bring him up now.

Chapter 25

A loud knock signaled me that someone was at the door. "Dre, are you at my door playing?" I asked, cradling my phone. Dre was always surprising me, so I assumed it was him.

"No. I'm on a job."

"Then who is at my door?" I asked him as I looked out my door and saw Tia standing there, holding a pink blanket around a little baby.

"Dre, let me call you back," I said as I opened the door. I didn't say anything to Tia. I just hugged her and we both began crying uncontrollably. We stood there for a minute just weeping. Then I wiped under my eyes with my hand and said, "Come in. How did you find out I moved in my house? I'm barely ever here. Girl, you are lucky you caught me."

"Ernest told me."

"You went to my mom's house?" I asked, surprised.

"Yeah, I figured your mother wouldn't be as

mad at me since I dropped the suit. I don't know what I was thinking about. I'm really sorry."

"It's okay. I know. My mom told me. But you better be glad you bumped into Ernest instead of my mom."

"Is she still mad?"

"Lolo don't get over anything, but she is changing. But forget all that. Let's talk about her." I held my arms out. "Let me hold the baby. What's her name?"

"Timarnet."

"What? Say her name again. How you pronounce it?"

"Tee-mar-net."

"What the hell, Tia?" I said as we both started laughing.

"I know, I'm thinking about changing it. It was supposed to be a combination of Tia and Lamar."

Once inside, I pulled the blanket away from the baby's face. "Aw, look at her! She is so adorable. I can't believe you had a baby. How does it feel?"

"It feels good."

"She is so pretty," I said as I stared down at the little life in front of me. "Hi, baby girl." The baby just stared up at me, giving me a sweet smile.

"What is that on your hand?" Tia asked. I almost dropped the baby when I stood up and told her I was getting married.

"Oh, my God," we screamed together. I stretched my arm out so she could get a better look at my hand.

"I can't believe Malcolm finally got his divorce," Tia said, shaking her head in awe.

"I'm not marrying Malcolm. My boyfriend's name is . . . I mean my fiancé's name is Dre."

"I am so happy for you. Oh, my God, this is wonderful. Congratulations. And seriously, Nikki, I'm so sorry about everything."

"Me, too!"

"I know, we were so stupid. While all that drama was going on, I was pregnant with her."

"Girl, that's horrible. That last night I saw you, I was so mad, I was trying to kill you."

"We was acting like we was back in high school. I know I was tripping, listening to Lamar."

"You was. But that's over. Right now I am so mad at you. Look at what I missed out on. Tia, I really felt like you turned your back on me. Like you neglected me, like we weren't ever friends. I mean, when you took his side over mine, that hurt me so much. You never let a man come between us before." Images of me and Tia out in the parking lot, fighting, scrolled across my mind. Tears started spilling from my eyes.

"I know. I know. Stop crying, I'm so sorry. I just didn't see it as being a big deal. I wanted to say I was sorry back then, but I was being stubborn. I am so . . . so sorry, Nicole. It went too far."

"You right. Well, guess what else I've been doing? I got a semi-promotion at my job, my fiancé fixed this house for me, and everything has just been coming along for me. It is just the grace of God. So, how is it in South Carolina?"

"Slow. I thought I would like it, but I didn't. I didn't get a lot done. I was pregnant and it was lonely. I know Reshaun told you me and Lamar broke up. You know he wasn't even there when I had the baby. He came back to Philly and was like he didn't want to be with me anymore after six long years."

"Damn."

"And, you know what? It's crazy—he left me while I was pregnant with his first child and he got me fired from my job. And the minute he came back to Philly, he got locked up. He is saying he is sorry and wants me to bring the baby up to the jail to see him. But I don't feel like I want that for me or my child."

"No, Reshaun didn't tell me all of that."

"So, how did you meet your fiancé?"

"At the gas station."

"What?"

"Yes. He has kids, two. They're three and five."

"Wow! You about to be a stepmom."

"I guess so, but his kids are sweet. Now my mom keeps talking about me having a baby. Strange as it sounds, I don't even want any kids. Dre says he'd like to have one or two more, but I don't know. And, oh, my God! I met my sister and I talked to my brother on the phone. I even got a seventy-seven-year-old grandmother." I was talking so fast, trying to bring Tia up to speed with my new life, that I found myself running out of breath.

"You really did a lot in the last seven months."

"You did too. Look, you had this beautiful baby. I can't believe you are a mommy."

"Me neither. I'm happy to have her, but now I don't know what my next move is going to be. I still have the house, but I got to find a job and get her in day care and all of that. It is going to be hard, but I'm going to do it. I do wish sometimes I would have left Lamar's ass alone. I would still have a job and be sexy, young, and free."

"What you always tell me? Everything happens for a reason." I smiled, trying to make Tia feel a little better about the terrible situation she'd allowed Lamar's no-good ass to get her into.

"I guess. I'm really happy for you. You are doing well," she said as she looked around my home. "I really got to catch up. Timarnet need a step-daddy."

I gave Tia a hug and walked her to her car. We hugged one more time after she put Timarnet in her car seat.

"I am sorry again," Tia said as she got in the car.

"Me too."

"Let's act like it never happened."

"No problem."

"Love you, girl."

"Stop making me emotional. Bye, call me later," I said as I walked back to the house, so happy my friend was back.

CHAPTER 26

Mercedes was pressed on giving us an engagement party. I told her no, like three times, but I have come to the conclusion that Dre's family loves having parties. Our cake read: *Congrats Nik and Dre.* It was a big, royal dark-chocolate cake with mint green writing.

I moved around the party. Mercedes and Ms. Pam introduced me to all these people, uncle this, aunt whatever, and so-and-so from the old neighborhood. My head was becoming dizzy. I took a picture with Ernest and my mom, the only two people who were there to represent me. My family seemed so small compared to Dre's big tribe of family and friends. I wanted another drink but was too scared to be tipsy and make a bad impression. Where were my other family members and friends? I didn't even see Dre, the man I was about to marry. I dialed Reshaun. "Where are y'all?"

"We are on our way. I'm trying to find a parking space." I went to the door and waited for her and Michael. To my surprise, Reshaun brought Tia instead of her husband. I was glad to see them both. I gave them a three-way hug. I walked them to the back of the house and we went out on Mercedes' huge pinewood deck.

"This is a real nice party and house," Tia said as we all walked around to the back of the house and sat on the lounge chairs.

"I know. His sister set this up."

"So, how you feel?" Reshaun asked.

"I feel good. I'm still in disbelief. My life just changed. But on some real shit, I feel like I deserve all of this and then some," I said as I looked around to see if anyone was in hearing distance of my conversation. "Like, after all those years I wasted with Malcolm, I finally get a good man. Please, and you know Malcolm tried to call me to tell me he got a divorce."

"And I know you hung up on him," Reshaun said.

"I sure did. How about if I was still with him? I would still be sitting up in my mom's house and missing out on all of this. Being dumb and stupid and getting constantly disrespected by someone who only cares about himself."

"Are you hiding?" Mercedes asked as she slid open the glass sliding door and came out on the deck.

"No, girl, these are my friends," I said as I introduced them.

She turned to them and said, "Hi, friends." Then she grabbed me and said, "Get your butt back in here. You have so many people you have to meet."

I fluttered my fingers, motioning *See you later* to Tia and Reshaun. I followed Mercedes, who then introduced me to another half-dozen people with names that I didn't remember. Then Dre came behind me. He kissed my neck and squeezed my hand.

"Where you been at?" I asked.

"Making moves."

"Well, don't go too far, I need you to meet my friend. The one who just got back from South Carolina." I noticed Mercedes was involved in a lengthy conversation so I pulled Dre's hand and brought him to the back deck. Tia and Reshaun stood up. They both was smiling so hard. It's like they couldn't believe Dre was all mine either.

"You better take care of my friend. If not, you are going to have problems," Reshaun giggled as she pointed to herself and Tia.

"He takes care of me now. Did you see this ring?" I teased. "Tia, this is my Dre."

"Nice to meet you, Dre."

Tia said a soft hello, never taking her eyes off my ring. I could tell she was a little uncomfortable. She was fidgeting and obviously a little jealous. She probably thought she was going to be the first one getting married and having all this. But it will happen for her too. She just has to recover from all this Lamar nonsense. I gave her a little smirk and she smiled a little and then Dre said, "Nice to meet you ladies again. Excuse us, we have a lot of people to see before the night is over," and rushed me back over to Mercedes.

"Why did you walk away? Aunt Linda is looking for you two. Plus, I want to get some more pictures," Mercedes said.

"Mercedes, give us a minute. I just got here. I need a drink." Dre went over to the table and poured two shots of Patrón and took them both back with no chaser in less than two minutes. He coughed a little and then wiped his face with a napkin and stood up straight and coughed a little more.

"You okay, baby?"

"Yeah, I just don't need Mercedes pulling us around our party. But I'm fine, Mrs. Hill. Now let's enjoy our party," Dre said as he kissed my hand and led me in the opposite direction of Mercedes and Ms. Pam.

CHAPTER 27

At work I was slowly going back to my old ways of not doing work. It wasn't intentional, but my life had become consumed with planning my wedding. Over the weekend I picked out my dress. It was a classic, ivory, strapless chiffon dress with gold trim. Dre, Syeed, and Brandon were fitted for their suits. Reshaun, Mercedes, and Tia were going to be my bridesmaids. Pumpkin got locked up again and couldn't get bail. So she was not going to be able to make it to the wedding. I wasn't that close with April, but I invited her and her husband.

We mailed out invitations last weekend and everyone started calling me and asking if I was pregnant. People thought we were rushing the wedding. But Dre and I were not in a rush, we just didn't want to wait until next year. We both thought it was a good idea to get it over with before the holidays. We were registered at Macy's and our honeymoon was going to be in Maui. Every time I needed some more money for the wedding, Dre gave it to me without thinking twice, but he was not the least bit interested in picking out color schemes, selecting items for the menu, or anything else.

Lolo was helping me do everything and trying to overrule all my decisions. I wanted simple, chic, and classic. She insisted on fabulous, flamboyant, and over the top, even though we only had fifty guests. Like I didn't want a bridal shower, but she said she was giving me one anyway. I wanted a deejay, but she said I should get a band. She wanted to serve our guests champagne from expensive, personalized glasses that people were going to break and never drink from. I had to put my foot down and told her absolutely not! I chose photo cookies. They were going to have pictures of me and Dre. They were cheap and cute, giving people the option of eating them or saving them if they wanted to. The color scheme was gold and white and I was still deciding on centerpieces. The one thing I was noticing was that everything was really expensive. It started out as, *Oh, that's only twenty-five dollars, I can afford that,* and the next thing you know—that's twenty-five dollars times ten, because you need a couple for each table. I had to remind Lolo daily it was not her wedding. She was getting on my nerves something terrible, yelling at me about my menu selection. Some things will never change.

"You can't have chicken on your menu. Black people always serving chicken at their weddings. Be creative. Why not have lobster, shrimp, and scallops on your menu?" Lolo asked.

"Some people have seafood allergies. Everybody eats chicken."

"Chicken. How typical. But if that's the way you want it, fine. Fine, Nicole, have Popeyes cater your wedding! I give up. Here, look at the seating chart," she said, shoving the chart in my hand. I looked down at the seating chart—it was all wrong. My mom had all the Hills in the back of the banquet hall.

"Why is Dre's family all clumped together?"

"It wasn't intentional. I just sat them all together. I figured they would be comfortable sitting with they own kind."

"Their own kind? Undo this. Everybody has to get to know each other." I handed her back the chart. "Change it, Mom. Mix everybody up."

"If you say so, but I know it is uncomfortable sitting next to people you do not know."

"Mom, it's my wedding."

"I know whose wedding it is. I'm just saying. Why you so worried about his family?"

"I'm not. I just want everyone to mingle and enjoy themselves."

"Yes, you are. I guess you going to get married and forget about me."

"No, I'm not. Weren't you the one who told me to get married? There is no pleasing you, lady. Mom, I don't have time for this. I will do my own seating chart," I said, and grabbed the chart out of her hand and put it in the bag and got ready to leave.

"Just make sure I get it back tomorrow."

"I will. I have to go, thank you." I knew her feelings were hurt and I honestly didn't want her to feel like she was being kicked to the curb, but I really didn't have time to deal with her insecurities.

* * *

Dre insisted we share a quiet evening at home together. But it seemed crazy to be sitting up in bed with him, munching on popcorn and watching *American Gangster* for the thousandth time when I could be taking care of important wedding business.

"Write your vows," I blurted while Denzel was gunning down some dude who stole money from him.

"Hold up!" Dre leaned forward as if seeing the scene for the very first time.

"Damn, Dre. A wedding is the most important day in a woman's life. I am so stressed from handling everything by myself. Why won't you take our wedding more seriously?" My voice was shaky and I made it extra high-pitched, like I was about to break down and cry.

Dre put his arm around me. "I'll try to take it more seriously. Okay?" He kissed me on the cheek. "I'm sorry I'm not acting all excited, but, baby, I want to marry you and whatever you decide I agree with it."

"So, you want me to write your vows?"

He grinned. "Yeah?"

"Dre!" I punched him playfully. "Come on, baby. That's the only thing you have to do. Please."

"Okay, I'll get on it tomorrow." His eyes flitted back to the TV screen.

"What about your children?" I asked, bringing him back to the topic of the wedding. "We have to get them fitted and buy them shoes."

"She said they couldn't come."

"Who said they couldn't come?"

"Jocelyn."

"How can she make a decision like that? You are their father!"

"It doesn't matter. She is trying to start some shit. I'd rather she say no now, rather than let us get everything together and then they don't show up on the day of the wedding."

Dre was right. I couldn't argue with what he'd said. But even though I had never met this Jocelyn, I really disliked her and I didn't like the way she treated my future husband. I got up and went to the kitchen to work on the seating chart. Dre put the movie on pause and followed me. He sensed that I wasn't feeling the way his ex had control over him and his relationship with his kids. I took that shit personal. He grabbed my hand and stopped me just before I sat down at the table to work on the seating chart. Dre lifted my chin up and looked me in the eyes. "Baby, the only thing that really matters is on October fourth you are standing in front of the preacher and us becoming husband and wife. After that, we out! Boarding a plane to Hawaii." He smiled and kissed me.

"You right," I said as I kissed him back, feeling reassured. The important thing was that we were getting married. Jocelyn or nobody else could stop that. He leaned me back on the kitchen chair and began trying to unzip my pants and kiss me. I sat up and pushed him off me and zipped my pants back up.

"No, I have to finish doing this seating chart."

"It's starting already. Syeed said it was going to happen," he said, shaking his head.

"What's starting? What did ya boy, Syeed, tell you was going to happen?"

"He said that as soon as I put a ring on your finger, you was going to stop giving me some."

"Well, tell him he right," I laughed and started working on the seating arrangements, which was as difficult as putting together a five thousand–piece jigsaw puzzle.

Chapter 28

"Where are you? I really need to talk to you, Nicole."

"Hey, girlie, where the baby girl at?" I asked Tia.

"With my mom."

"I'm at my job, catching up on some work. I have been slacking off bad with all the wedding planning and everything. Don't forget, we are going to pick up the dresses on Saturday."

"I won't, but listen, I need to meet up with you today."

"Okay, you can meet me at my house. What's up? What's so important?"

"I'll tell you when I see you."

I told her I would meet her at my house at six.

Tia was already sitting in front of the house when I arrived home. Her facial expression told me she was going through something. I knew it had something to do with that no-good ass, Lamar. I hoped she didn't take the baby to the jail to visit him. "What's wrong, girl? You look really upset," I said as I unlocked the door and went in the house. I placed the mail down on the mantelpiece. Tia took a seat and began rocking back and forth.

"Listen, sit down. I have something to tell you. Actually, I have a whole lot to tell you. Now, I wouldn't be a real friend if I didn't come clean about a few things." She looked at me and said, "I know Dre. I know Dre, very well."

"What the hell are you talking about, Tia?"

"I used to have threesomes with his girlfriend, Jocelyn, and him."

In my mind, I felt like I had just been kicked in the back of my head, but I managed to keep my cool. In a real calm voice, I corrected her and said, "You mean his ex-girlfriend, Jocelyn."

"Yeah, and Jocelyn is my ex, too. We just kind of broke up, too."

"Your ex? What? Okay, you right. I need to sit down." The room was starting to spin a little. Tia was coming at with me some crazy shit that I wasn't the least bit prepared for. She needed to explain what the hell she was talking about.

"Nik, when I was in Columbia, I was living with Dre's ex, Jocelyn. Me and her been dealing with each other, but we both still had boyfriends. So when Lamar left me, I called her and she came down and stayed with me. And from the moment she started staying with me, Dre started going crazy. He kept calling me, threatening me and her. Nicole, he is still in love with her. I can't believe he is trying to marry you. He was just in Columbia, begging Jocelyn to come back home and be with him." *What the fuck?* That was the only thing that went through my mind. Did she just sit here and tell me she was bisexual and that Dre's been chasing his ex the whole time we have been together? I couldn't believe what I was hearing. I needed a drink.

"What? When? How has he been down there when he has been here with me and he is always working? How could he? How far is Columbia from Atlanta?"

"Like four hours. Listen, I saw him with my own eyes. When did y'all start dating?"

"I met him in, like, February."

"So, it's September. I don't know exactly what month he stopped coming, but it was real hot when he came down for his last few visits."

"Did he come to see his kids?"

"No, I'm telling you he was there for Jocelyn. She was back and forth with the kids. She sent them up all the time. He was there for her," Tia insisted.

"Why are you just saying something? Oh, my God. I feel so stupid," I said as I got up and paced the living room, back and forth. I couldn't believe Dre, the man who claimed he loved me, was still begging another woman to be with him.

"Nicole, I wanted to say something sooner, but I was trying to mind my business. When you said his name, I was like, what a coincidence. Then I was thinking, no way. There are a million and one Dres. It's a common name. I had no idea he was the same person, until you were walking him over to me and I'm like . . . oh, shit! Dre *is* Dre. I swear. I never put it together. And before I could react, you walked away and I didn't want to cause a scene, and it wasn't appropriate at the party. I wasn't going to say anything at all. I really wasn't. Then I thought about it, like I would be on some real shady shit if I don't say something."

"So, Dre, you, and Jocelyn. I don't understand, how did all this Jocelyn stuff start?"

"It is a long story. I met her through one of my coworkers. And at first we just talked a lot. I could tell her shit about Lamar, and she was listening to me and telling me her problems. We hung out a couple of nights. And one of the nights, she invited me to her house. When we got there, she started teasing me and began kissing me and I don't know, one thing led to another."

"One thing led to another doesn't make sense. Did you know she was gay? This is so unbelievable. You never been into women. I would have never dreamed you got down like that."

"I didn't. She was my first. I didn't even know how to feel in the beginning, but little by little, I was with it. So, then she was like, 'Can my boyfriend join in?' And I met him a couple of times, so I tried it. And it was all fun in the beginning. But he wasn't really with it one hundred percent. 'Cause every time we would all get together, he would cuss her out and call her a gay bitch the next morning. Then he would apologize. So, we stopped the threesomes 'cause he couldn't handle it. But then he started calling me, like he wanted to get together with me one-on-one. I told him no, and he started feeling some type of way, and was like he didn't want me around her by myself."

I shook my head. "None of this sounds like Dre."

"It's Dre, and remember when I was pregnant

the last time? It was his baby. He said it wasn't his, but it was because the condom bust and Lamar was in jail that month."

Now I was ready to pass the fuck out. "Oh, my God! Don't tell me your Timarnet is Dre's daughter?"

"No, definitely not."

I could feel relief washing over me. "So, you think he still really wants to be with her?"

"Yeah, no doubt about it. Nikki, he is never going to stop loving her. You should not marry him. If you marry him, he is going to still cheat with her. She got some kind of magic over him. She would tell me that Dre does whatever she tells him to do. They one of those couples that been together forever who ain't never going to really break up. They would go in the room and I would hear things move and I would usually just leave out for a few hours. And when I got back they would always be lovey dovey, talking and whatnot, and then he would go."

"I know they were together for years, but he said he was tired of her and the back and forth, and his whole family hates her."

"They hate her because no matter what they say or do, he always goes back to her."

In the middle of us talking, Dre called my phone several times. I didn't answer it.

"Is that him that keeps calling?"

"Yeah."

"I knew it. That's another thing. He is real possessive and he always want to know where you are and what you doing. And he try to put you with his family, so he can always have tabs on you. Jocelyn got tired of that bullshit and his crazy family. She said they were all fake and full of shit."

My phone started ringing again. This time, I picked up. I couldn't hide my disgust, and said, "Yeah, what's up?"

"What's up? Where you at, Nikki, and why you talking like that? What's wrong with you?"

I could barely talk. All I could get out was, "You already know. Damn, Dre. Wow! All I can say is wow."

"What are you talking about?"

"So, you been begging Jocelyn to get back with you. Huh? While you planning a wedding with me, you begging that no-good, don't-wanna-work, ain't-got-nothing bitch to take you back?" Tia probably didn't expect me to confront Dre while she was there, but I couldn't hold back. I was fired up.

"What are you talking about? Who told you that?"

"Don't worry about who told me. Just answer me. Is it true?"

"No, it's not true. Where are you?" As soon as he began lying to me I couldn't take it. I just powered my phone off. Minutes later, he walked in my house and walked past Tia like she wasn't even there.

"Come upstairs. Let's talk."

"Ain't too much to talk about, Dre," I said.

And then he looked me dead in the center of my eye and said, "Nik, listen, baby, whatever has happened in the past is in the past."

Before he could complete his sentence, Tia was like, "He is a liar and he been lying all along."

"I'm a liar?" he said as he got in her face.

"Yeah, you are a liar and you know it."

"Bitch, you need to mind your business."

"I got your bitch." Tia pointed at me. "Nikki is my business. You telling her you left Jocelyn and you know damn well you didn't leave her, she left you! Tell Nikki how you been calling Jocelyn for the last six months, begging for her to come back to you. Does she know how you was flying to Columbia every time you had a chance?"

"Why are you going to sit up here and make shit up? Are you crazy?" Dre asked her, shaking his head.

"No, I'm not crazy."

I turned my attention to Dre. "Is any of this true?" I sniffled and tried to keep my nose from running. He didn't say anything. As I screamed for Dre to get out of my house, I saw Tia leaving.

"Let's talk." His tone was soft and pleading. I could see the pain in his eyes.

But I wasn't having it. I folded my arms across my chest. "There is nothing to talk about. I don't know her and I most definitely don't know you."

"Nicole, I promise you there is nothing going on between me and Jocelyn. I did go to South Carolina a couple of times. I don't know what Tia is telling you, but I was not constantly trying to get back with that girl. The first time I went down there, me and you wasn't even speaking. That was after your windows were busted. Now, I'm not gonna lie. I did ask her was it really over then. All the other times that I went down there were to visit my children. But we didn't even sleep together."

"Somebody is lying. Tia doesn't have any reason to."

"She has a lot of reasons to lie. You know what, fuck it, Nicole. Believe what you want to," Dre hollered as he left out my house, leaving me behind with so many unanswered questions.

CHAPTER 29

The other night I was in my house and I pulled out my ring and just stared at it. It was so pretty, but yet it was so damn ugly. It represented deception. The love it was supposed to symbolize, I no longer believed in. It was supposed to represent the union of me and Dre, but we were no longer a unit. I'd been hiding out from Dre and Tia. I really didn't want anyone all up in my business, asking questions and starting rumors, so I'd been wearing my ring to work. This was some crazy shit, though. I couldn't believe it. I didn't know if I ever would understand why this happened. What are the chances that I'd meet a stranger at a gas station and fall in love with him, only to find out that my best friend, who was living out of town, had already fucked him? The thought of them being together made my stomach ache. They had seen each other naked and been extra intimate with one another. And how could Tia be gay and not tell me? Why would she keep that a secret? I wouldn't have judged her. Then I was mad at her for coming to my house when she got back from Columbia, having this big meeting with me. She gave me this elaborate story about Lamar leaving her, and how she was down there all alone, when she was really booed up with Jocelyn. And I didn't know if there was any truth about Dre still being in love with Jocelyn. I didn't know what to believe. I felt like a fool. Like I had been living a lie for all these months. I was so embarrassed. I didn't want to tell my mom, but I had to. Surprisingly, she was so understanding and, of course, she was really on my side. I think she was disappointed too, because I think for the first time in my life she was proud of me. But she kept her opinion to herself, which was a first for Lolo.

I know nothing ever works out the way you plan it. However, you could not tell me I would be in my house all alone. I hated being in my house alone. I really didn't know what to do with myself. I wandered from room to room, feeling abandoned and betrayed. But I was so sick of my every-night pity parties for one. I looked at my beautiful ivory gown hanging in the closet and thought, *Why me?* I turned my head away. I really couldn't look at my wedding gown. It hurt too much and I didn't want to start crying again. If I was going to be miserable and sulk I needed someone to do it with me. So I invited Reshaun over, hoping she could cheer me up and give me some words of wisdom.

"So what are you going to do?" Reshaun asked as she sat on my sofa.

"I have no idea. It would take a Nicole, right?" I laughed, trying to make humor of my situation.

"This is just so crazy, Reshaun. As soon as I think I got it all together, something like this has to happen. Never in a million years could I have thought up this shit."

"Right," Reshaun said, agreeing.

"I don't know. It's like I can't believe either one of them. I'm just trying to figure out why Tia would wait until weeks before my wedding to tell me some shit like this. If she had something to say, she should have said it when I introduced them at the engagement dinner. Right? That would have made more sense than playing it off like she didn't know him. Tia is the most fucked up person I know."

"You're right."

"I mean, I cheated too. I'm not perfect. I got with Malcolm once. I mean, it happens. And I can accept he had somebody before me. But what scares me is that he might really still love her and want to be with her."

"I don't think so. I think he was with her because he was used to being with her. And probably for his children."

"He said something like he was going down there for his kids, but that's too hard to believe."

Suddenly, someone knocked on the door and we both jumped.

"If it's him or her, I'm not here," I said as we both peeked out the window. It was my mother. I was so relieved. She motioned us to hurry up and open the door. Reshaun flipped open the lock and my mother came in.

"So, is this wedding happening or what? Are you canceling? If we act fast enough, we can maybe get some of the deposit money back," my mom said as she bust inside my house.

"I still don't know. I don't know, Mom."

"It is not that hard. I wouldn't be bothered with either one of them. After you fuck me, I'm done with you. But I don't know about you. You got a lot of forgiveness in your heart, Nikki."

"No, I don't. It's just that I already mailed out the invitations."

"That don't mean you have to still marry him. He ain't the only man out here."

"How can I cancel the wedding? How do we get in touch with all those people and tell them not to show up?" I asked.

"Easy. I can send out an e-mail and make some phone calls. You don't have to go through with this if you don't want to."

"I can help your mom with the calls and everything. You really don't have to do this," Reshaun added.

"I just always knew it was something going on with that girl. She always had that bull dagger look in her eye," my mom said out the clear blue. I looked over at Reshaun and we both began laughing and shaking our heads.

"Mom, hold up on the calls and e-mails 'cause I really don't know what I'm going to do yet."

"Whatever you decide, I will support you. Either way I am here for you. Make your own decision. Because no one has to live with this but you."

"She is so right, Nikki. Let me just say this—I know it is hard, but I tell you one thing, that man loves you more than anything. And you can't let Tia walk up in here and ruin everything for you," Reshaun said.

"So I should trust him? He lied to me. He said he broke up with her. Oh, my God, I'm so confused. I wish this didn't happen. Tia could have really kept this shit to herself."

"She should have," my mother said, grabbing her purse and standing up.

"I think Tia has changed, and she is not the same person anymore. Call me if you need me. I have to go," Reshaun said as she kissed me on the cheek. "Be strong, girl. I know you're gonna do the right thing."

When they left, I sat in my living room all alone. I didn't answer the telephone or watch television. I just kind of meditated and went into a deep thought process. I was weighing all the possible scenarios in my mind. The shoulds and the shouldn'ts. Should I believe Tia, someone who had already done me wrong, or should I believe Dre, the man who came into my life and loved me the way no other man has ever done before? I had to make a decision and I had to make it fast.

CHAPTER 30

I didn't have to give out an explanation. I made up my mind, the wedding was off. I was not marrying that man and that was my final answer.

I dialed my mother and yelled, "Cancel everything. Everything! I'm not marrying him and I don't care. Write a letter and sign my name. Say something like, 'Sorry, there will not be a wedding. Thank you.' Keep it short and sweet."

"Are you sure about this?"

"Yes, Mom, I am sure."

"I don't know, Nicole. Just think about it some more."

"There is nothing else to think about, Mom."

"So, you want me to cancel the bridal shower, too?"

"Yes."

"Cancel the wedding, call everything off?"

"Yes."

"And you're sure?"

"Positive. I've made up my mind and it is final."

Lolo took one long breath and said, "Okay." I

could hear her still talking before she hung up the phone, saying something about, "I don't believe this shit."

If she couldn't believe it, how did she think I felt about me and Dre's future together being over in the blink of an eye? It was a hard decision to make, but it came down to honesty and trust. Dre was not truthful about our entire relationship. I do believe he loved me, but I wasn't sure if he was over Jocelyn. And I was not marrying with all that doubt hanging over my head. I didn't want the what-ifs to drive me crazy for the rest of my life. He had those two children and they were always going to be there. He was going to have to interact with their mother, and I didn't want to be scared each time he dropped them off. No. I couldn't live my life that way. He had been trying real hard to talk to me, but I didn't have time for him. I had to handle him and all of this from afar. I felt so mortified and let down. I had a beautiful wedding dress, I'd mailed out invitations, and now I was not having a wedding. *Did I really think I was going to walk down the aisle and get married, for real? Nope!* Deep down, I knew something was going to happen before the wedding actually happened. That's the kind of luck I have.

Ms. Pam kept calling me, trying to plead Dre's case, but there was nothing to talk about. And when she was not on my phone, Mercedes was. And my relationship with her was on the line too! Because although she had been trying to remain neutral, she had been grappling with her loyalty toward her brother, and lately she'd been speaking on Dre's behalf. But it's finally over. I wrote Dre a letter, listing all the reasons why I couldn't marry him. I went to his house at three in the afternoon when I knew he wouldn't be there. I ran up the steps with my two empty black suitcases and began filling them up with all the things I'd left behind. I took everything hanging up on my side of the closet. My shoes, my suits, dresses, belts. I threw them in my suitcase. I went in the bathroom and took all my perfume, body wash, everything that belonged to me, down to my toothpaste. I saw the watch I'd bought him sitting on the dresser. I put that in my pocket, too. He didn't deserve it. I could give it to Ernest. I looked under the bed, and then checked the drawers. I saw some of my bras, so I picked them up and slipped them in my bag. I took a long look around the room to make sure I didn't miss anything. Then I placed my letter on his pillow. I went down the steps, my suitcases thumping at each step and making it hard for me to stand up straight.

As I walked out of his house with all my belongings in tow, I turned around and said good-bye to what might have been. And even though I cancelled the wedding, I really didn't want to speak to Tia, either. She had done so much, I was not sure I knew her. My girl, my friend since the fourth grade, the ride-or-die chick I would do anything for—I didn't know where she was. The Tia I knew would never do her sister like this.

I was happy I made it out of the house without running into Dre—that confrontation would have been drama. I placed the suitcases in my backseat. I opened my cell phone and saw I had two missed calls from Lolo. I checked the messages—she said she had started calling everybody. And her voice just seemed to quiver as she spoke, so I pressed One and played the message again. I needed to hear that she said, what I thought she said. She had called everybody and told them. I was instantly sad. *Why me? Why me?* I thought. I am going to be so humiliated. People are going to call me, asking me what happened. I started tearing up again. All this crying was getting old. I took my engagement ring off my hand and rolled down my window and tossed it out onto the expressway. Fuck Dre, and anybody that plays for his team.

I came home to my empty house and didn't have the strength to do anything. I was tired from crying. I turned my phone off. I would deal with that shit tomorrow or maybe the next day. I just closed my eyes and wished none of this had ever happened.

I must have fallen asleep, but when I opened my eyes, Dre was sitting at the edge of the sofa. I screamed loudly until I was able to focus in and see that it was him.

"What are you doing here? Get out my house. How did you get in here?"

"It don't matter. I'm done dealing with this shit," Dre said with his head and hands in his lap.

I sat up. "You done. I been done. You need to leave. Nobody invited you over here."

"I'll leave, but let me just say what I have to say." He cleared his throat and continued, "I promise you there is nobody else I want to be with. I haven't been one hundred percent honest with you about me going to visit my children. However, there is nothing else I lied about. I don't want to be with anyone else besides you. I love you more than anything and I can't believe you would think I would try to hurt or play you. I would never. I am here, willing to do anything. But `I can't take no more, Nicole. I really can't. Now listen—yes, me, Jocelyn, and Tia had threesomes a couple of times. Yes, I was originally thinking it was something that I was interested in, but each time after it happened, I didn't feel right. I wasn't with it. I didn't want to see anyone I care for with another person. So I told Jocelyn, don't bring her around anymore. I didn't enjoy it. We were already on bad terms and I think that made it worse, and by then it was too late. They were already into each other and Jocelyn wouldn't leave Tia alone. I mean, we wasn't together anymore. But then she took my kids back and forth to South Carolina to be with this chick and that made me mad. I didn't want my children raised by no lesbians."

"So you had a threesome and didn't like it. And you didn't try to keep a relationship with Tia going on the side and you got mad because she wasn't with it? And you still not fucking Jocelyn, but you never mentioned it to me that you were visiting her? Yeah right. Do you think I'm stupid?"

"Nicole, I haven't touched, slept with, or tried to get back with Jocelyn in over a year. When I was going to Atlanta, I was really checking on real estate and it was so close to Columbia, so I checked on my children. I wanted to make sure they were okay. I didn't tell you, because I didn't think it was a big deal. I don't know what Jocelyn was telling Tia about my visits, but think about her motives. She probably did say I wanted her back, or maybe she really felt that way, but I don't want her at all. I want to be with you, Nicole. You are the only person I want to be with. I can call her right now and she can tell you." He opened up his cell phone and turned his speakerphone on. The numbers dialed loudly, then there were long pauses between rings and a sleepy woman answered the telephone.

"Jocelyn," Dre said.

"Yeah, what's up? The kids are 'sleep. Call back tomorrow."

"I'm not calling about them."

"Then what do you want?" she said nastily.

"I need you to tell my fiancée that me and you are not together and haven't been together for over a year."

"Oh, my God! I know you not waking me up for this bullshit."

"Jocelyn, she is right here. Tell her," he demanded.

"No, we not together. I don't want you or any man," she finally admitted. Dre looked over at me and I gave him a *so-what?* expression. I didn't care what she said or what he said. As far as I was concerned she wasn't a credible source for information. Everybody said she was crazy and a liar anyway. Dre noticed I wasn't the least bit swayed by their conversation. So he kept going on and on, asking her more questions in hopes that she would say something that would convince me that they weren't a couple.

"When the last time I've been down there?"

"I don't know. A couple of months, I guess."

"Do I try to get back with you?"

"No! No, I don't want you and you don't want me and I'm hanging up now."

Dre hung up his phone. "Now do you believe me?" he asked as he attempted to hold me.

I snatched away from him and said, "What did that prove, that you are not seeing her anymore? Huh? What about in the beginning of our relationship? Listen, you have a lot of issues that I don't think you have worked out. Everything Tia said makes sense."

"What Tia says makes sense?" Dre shouted as he got off the sofa and kicked my wall. Then he screamed, "Shut up right now, Nicole. You sound so stupid. This is the same hoe who sued your mom, tried to fight you in a parking lot, didn't speak to you for six months until her baby father left her. And now she is the most honest person you know? You got to be kidding me. You are being so loyal to her and she ain't even loyal to you. She don't really care about you. Did Tia tell you that she used to call me, asking to be with me? She was telling me how I needed to leave Jocelyn all the time and how I should be with her. She was talkin' that shit even this summer. Did she tell you that?"

"I don't believe that. She said that you were trying to get with her."

"Tia doesn't want to see anyone happy. She got a lot of fucking issues. She ruined one relationship for me and I refuse to let her ruin another one." I still didn't believe him. He cupped my face and said, "Nicole, listen up. Look at me. I am so done right now. I can't take anymore. I am not joking or playing. This is my life. Hear me out. I would never do anything to hurt you."

"I don't believe you, Dre, and I think you need to leave."

He grabbed my arm and said, "I'm not going anywhere. If I leave out this door, I'm going for good. I'm sick of all this back and forth shit with you."

"You are going to get out of my house or I'm going to call the police on you."

"Call the police. Do whatever you want, but whatever you do, you better mean it. I'm really done with acting like we are fifteen. I love you and I want to marry you."

"I don't love you. I hate you. Now leave!"

"I'm going to stay right here. You need to think about this. I'm serious. Is this what you really want to do?" I tried to go upstairs, but he pinned me down and I began crying in his arms. "I love you, Nicole. I'm not going to hurt you. I love you. I'm not leaving you. I'm never going to leave you. I'm not walking out of our life. Look me in my eyes."

I kept my head down, refusing to look him in his eyes. He started tilting my head upward, so I closed my eyes and turned my face away. I wanted him to let me up. But he wouldn't loosen his grip. I was getting mad. So mad, I screamed, "Let me go. Let me up. You don't love me."

"Yes, I do. I can't leave you. I'm not going anywhere. We are going to stay right here until we work this out."

I got tired of struggling so I lay still as Dre's body heaved up and down on mine. I felt his tears dripping on my face. "I love you, Nicole, I'm not leaving you."

We sat in the living room on that sofa in a deadlock for hours. I finally gave in and let Dre convince me that he loved me and that if I didn't marry him it would be the biggest mistake of my life. I could not give up on him. I couldn't give up on us. I wanted to be with him. I loved him and was going to make a way for us. We were still getting married in two weeks as planned. Nothing was going to stop that.

Chapter 31

When I told Lolo to cancel the wedding, she had tried, but it was too late to get any of my money back, so she left everything in place just in case I changed my mind—like I did. Our only real issue was calling everyone, reinviting them to the wedding. After I called the wedding back on, I told Dre what I did with my engagement ring. We went back to the expressway and searched for it. I couldn't remember exactly what stretch of the highway I threw it out on, but I remembered it was right before my exit. I felt bad and stupid for throwing it and I knew we weren't going to find it. But it was at least worth the effort. Dre and I double-parked on the side of the highway, put on the truck's hazard lights, and began our search. We searched inch by inch as cars raced past us on the expressway. After a half hour I wanted to give up, but Dre didn't. I said forget it and I went and sat in the truck.

But Dre kept looking for it and he found it amongst the gravel and dirt. He came back in the car and said, "Look what I found." My ring was a little bent, but my diamond was still in place. I was surprised he found it, but I knew that was a sign that it was meant to be. If I forgave him I had to forgive Tia too. The way I saw it, she is like my sister and we have been through so much. Sisters and families fight all the time, and I figured if I could forgive Dre then I could forgive her, too. I knew she slept with my soon-to-be husband, but I also knew that it would not ever happen again. We made up two days after me and Dre called our wedding back on. At first, he said she couldn't be in the wedding, then he said he didn't care as long as it made me happy.

The night before the wedding, we were all staying at the Embassy Suites hotel on the Benjamin Franklin Parkway. I had just picked up my shoes and finished getting my nails done and was on my way. Everybody was at the hotel waiting for me. I called Reshaun to check on everything.

"Nikki, hurry up. Your mom is telling people they shouldn't even be here. She's starting with Tia and Ms. Pam. She is even bothering Mercedes," Reshaun told me.

"Oh, no. What is she saying?"

"I can't keep up with all the insults. There were so many. Let me see . . . Oh! She said that Dre's mom should have got Botox before the wedding. And what kind of woman wears black to a wedding? Uhm, it was actually kind of funny because Dre's mom came back at her and said she can wear whatever the hell she wants to wear to her son's wedding. And then your mom said it wasn't her son's wedding. It was her daughter's wedding and that Dre's mom wasn't running this shit. Then your mom turned on me. She said that I should have lost weight and Mercedes better put some concealer over her tattoo," Reshaun said, laughing hard.

"Oh, God. No. More drama. I can't take no more."

"Well, hurry up and get here. Before it go down."

"Keep Lolo and Ms. Pam apart. I'm on my way."

Meanwhile, as soon as I hung up from Reshaun, I called my mom.

"Mom, how you going to insult my future mother-in-law?"

"I call it like I see it. She need a shot of Botox under her eyes, and her daughter, that little one got a big ole ugly-ass snake going down her back. Just ghetto!"

"Mom, leave Mercedes alone."

"If somebody doesn't say anything, your wedding pictures will be a mess."

"You not paying for my pictures, Mom, so don't worry about it."

"I hired my own photographer and he will be there. And I don't want to see that mess in pictures that I'm going to be looking at for the rest of my life."

"Mom, I'm going to see you in a few." I hung up.

By the time I got to the suite, my mom had stopped insulting everyone. But her victims were still looking wounded. I apologized and pulled my mother out the room. Reshaun followed and closed the door for me.

"Mom, please calm down. You can't talk to people any kind of way."

"All I said was the damn truth."

"Mom, it doesn't matter. Either calm down, relax, or leave, and I'll see you in the morning."

She blinked and shifted from one foot to the other, making it clear that she was offended. "So you choosing those people over me?"

"No, but Mom, you really need to stop it."

"If you don't want my help then I'm leaving." I looked at her like . . . *Leave!*" She glared at me and then went into the room, grabbed her purse, and stormed down the hallway. I thought about chasing her, but I had to let her know who was in charge. She needed to realize whose wedding this is.

"Dra-Ma," Tia laughed as I came back in the room where everyone was gathered. I came in and gave each person a hug.

"I just want everybody to be themselves. This is my wedding. All the pictures and everything are going to turn out fine. It is going to be a relaxed wedding."

Lolo did get over herself. She came back to the suite after a couple of hours and behaved as if nothing had ever happened. We had cocktails and a late dinner at the T.G.I.F. next door to our hotel. Dre was somewhere having his bachelor party. Syeed promised me he wouldn't let it get too crazy. Reshaun asked me if I wanted to go over there and check on him.

"Nah, I'm secure." What happened before was in the past and I trusted that we were good. If I had any doubt that we weren't ready or strong enough, I would have cancelled or postponed the wedding. It was back like old times. Me, Tia, and Reshaun were having a good time reminiscing, but something was troubling Tia. I asked her what was wrong and she said it was her first time away from the baby and she missed her. She stepped in the hallway, called and checked on her daughter, and then she was back to acting like herself.

On the day of my wedding, I awoke at six in the morning. I had seven hours until I was Mrs. Dondre Hill, and surprisingly I wasn't scared or nervous. With everything that had happened I just wanted to get it over with. And I was not trying to be a Bridezilla. I didn't want to be frantic, rushing around acting crazy, and cussing people out. I wanted to be the opposite of all of that. From our room, we could see the city skyline and the Art Museum of Philadelphia on the horizon. It was just beautiful, and shaping up to be the best day of my life.

"Good morning, bride. Are you ready?" Reshaun sang as she knocked twice on my door, cracking it open.

"Yes, I'm ready. I'm sitting here asking myself, is this real?"

"It's real. What time is Alex coming?"

"Around ten."

"What are you going to do for the rest of the day?"

"I got a massage scheduled for all of us, then we can get the finishing touches on our hair."

"Here you are. I wanted to give you this," she said as she handed me a gift bag.

"What's in here?" I opened the bag and there were Mr. and Mrs. light yellow, embroidered towels and matching robes.

"Thank you. These are pretty. I am going to put these in our bathroom."

Tia walked into the room. "Don't leave me out—I have something for you too!" She handed it to me and I pulled out a mint-colored box and pulled out a silver wedding frame.

"Oh, Tia. This is beautiful. Thank you so much. Both of y'all. Thank you for being here." We sat and talked and ordered room service.

At six in the morning it seemed like we had the entire day. But after breakfast and our massages, time started flying by. It was ten before I knew it. Then Alex arrived with his makeup and hair tool belt on his hip, screaming, "Divas, who is going first? Let's get started." He set up a makeshift station in the living-room area of the suite. He did Mercedes' hair and makeup first and then moved on to Lolo. Right after Alex got there, the photographer arrived and he began taking pictures of everything. At that very moment, I began feeling a little something in the bottom of my stomach. All this time I wasn't nervous, but now I was. Something came over me. I knew Dre was the right man, it wasn't that. I think I just couldn't believe all of this was for me. All these people, all this preparation. It made me scared, because nobody ever made a fuss over me. Now everything was all about me. I escaped the madness by going into the bathroom and taking a shower. Then I just sat on the toilet seat and looked at pictures of me and Dre that were in my cell phone. Dre called and we started talking on the phone like it was a normal day. I shared with him everything that had happened and he told me to relax.

"I can't wait for this all to be over and we are on

the plane. All I want to do is be alone and in love with my baby."

"Aw, Dre. That's so sweet."

"So, I'll see you when you are walking down the aisle and all this is over. I love you."

"Baby, I love you too!" Hearing his voice made me calm down. I could do this. I was ready. I was building my confidence meter up. It was almost energized until somebody knocked on the door.

"Nicole, come on and get in your dress before you are late for your own wedding," Lolo yelled.

"I got an hour, Mom. And I'm getting my hair and makeup done before I put on my dress."

"No, you don't have an hour; it's already twelve. You're going to put the dress on first and drape a sheet or something around you, and then you are going to get your makeup done while I get dressed," she said in a firm, no-nonsense tone.

It didn't seem like I had been in the bathroom that long, but I really had less than an hour to get ready.

"Okay, here I come. Hand me my overnight bag."

Lolo handed me my bag. I put on my underwear, stockings, deodorant, and perfume. Then she passed me my dress. I stepped into it. She came in the bathroom and zipped it up and the sides began drooping.

"My dress doesn't fit."

"Let me see," Lolo said as she tried to make my dress stay up. As soon as she pulled it up it slid right back down.

"I can't believe this. I just got fitted a week ago."

Ms. Pam came in and took one look at the situation and said, "We going to have to pin you up. How did you lose so much weight? Call down to the front desk," she ordered Lolo. I couldn't believe my mom was taking orders from somebody. But I guess she was scared my drooping dress would mess up the pictures her photographer was going to take. Minutes later, the bellman was at the door.

Ms. Pam got on her knees as Lolo took the pins and they cinched the inch of extra material together under my arm and down the seam of the dress. After they were done you couldn't tell they'd had to make those last-minute adjustments.

"I don't know how you going to get out of that dress, but it doesn't matter. You look so pretty," Ms. Pam said as everyone came in and admired me.

"You do look beautiful. Now, go get your makeup done," Lolo said as she pushed me to Alex.

Once I was seated and Alex was doing my hair and makeup, everyone went back to their suites and scrambled to get dressed.

Thirty minutes later, Alex put the finishing strokes on my makeup. My head was full of perfect, loose spiral curls. The final piece was when he pinned my gold-and-white tiara veil on my head.

He looked at me and said, "I knew you were a diva. Hey, diva, you look gorgeous."

I thanked him and took one fast look at myself and headed for the door. It was time to go. My mom rounded everyone up and we huddled into the elevator. The limo bus was waiting for us. We boarded and all took a seat. The limo bus was spacious and nice. It had gray leather interior and ceiling lights. I felt like a princess and finally began to calm down and enjoy the moment. The hard part was over. All I had to do now was show up.

Ms. Pam was wearing a tight, black wrap dress. My mom had on a ginger-brown suit. Tia, Mercedes, and Reshaun looked stunning in their gold, strapless bridesmaid dresses. I looked over and Lolo was talking with Ms. Pam. They had finally gotten over their differences. Reshaun was taking pictures and I was just taking in the moment. Everything was perfect until Tia moved over to my side and whispered, "Don't go through with this."

I looked at her, shook my head, and said, "Huh?"

Then she repeated herself and said, "Don't go through with this."

"Don't start this again, Tia," I said as I looked out the window, hoping nobody else noticed what was going on. I ignored her. I hoped that would make her shut the hell up. But instead of stopping, she kept whispering in my ear that I was making a mistake. I didn't know what to do. I didn't want to become upset, so I got up and went and sat next to my mom. I knew Tia didn't have the heart to say out loud the things she was whispering.

But I was so wrong. She actually got out of her seat and stood up on the bus and yelled, "Nicole, don't ignore me. You know I'm telling the truth."

"Tia, sit down, you are tripping," I said.

"No, we have been friends for too long for me to let this go down."

"Let what go down? Please, Tia. Look, I love you like my sister, but enough is enough. We already had this conversation. Whatever you say right now is not going to change my mind about Dre. Everybody on this bus knows what happened. If you're my friend, get over it. I love him." At this point I didn't care who heard or knew about what was going on. Everybody in that limo cared about me and loved me.

"So if everybody on the bus already know what happened, how come everybody is letting you marry him?" Tia was shouting like a crazy woman. I was trying my best to stay calm and not go off on her ass. I could picture us fighting and her ruining my dress, and trying to pull out my hair.

"Stop trying to make a scene. Why you feel like you want to embarrass me in front of my mother and my mother-in-law? What can you really say, Tia? Why are you worried about why I am marrying him? I love him, he loves me. That's all you need to know. My marriage doesn't have anything to do with you. Why are you taking it all personal and shit? You the only one on this bus who got a problem with it."

"I just want to know why you want to marry a man after finding out all that you now know. He is no good, Nicole. He was still trying to get back with Jocelyn while he was with you."

"Says who? You? I don't believe you, Tia. I know Dre is ready to commit to me today. If I'm willing to accept that then you should be able to accept it too."

"Well, I don't think it is right," Tia said defiantly, standing her ground. "Did your fiancé tell you that he ate my pussy? Oh, yeah . . . I already told you that he got me pregnant and none of that matters to you. So, you tell me, Nikki . . . how can you think about marrying someone your best friend has been with?"

I stared at Tia with my fists balled up, but I refused to resort to violence on my wedding day, so I calmed myself down and spoke softly. "I'm starting to question if you are my friend at all."

"She is not your friend. Nicole, I warned you about this jealous hater-ass bitch," Lolo said, lunging for Tia. It took a quick reaction from everybody to hold her back.

Tia stepped back a little, but continued running her mouth. "He is only marrying you to get back at her."

"That's not true," Mercedes said, jumping in. Everybody was slowly starting to react to Tia. I knew all I had to do was say the word and everyone on the bus would have pounced on this dumb bitch.

"Tia, I forgave you for everything you did to me. I have tried to make this friendship work, but your happiness is not going to come before mine. For once in your life, are you going to think about someone else beside yourself? This is not about you, it is all about me."

"I am thinking about someone else. I'm thinking about you. I want you to be happy, Nicole, but he is all wrong. Is this really the man you want to wake up to every morning for the rest of your life?"

"Yes, he is. Listen, you know what? I'm getting married today. This is the last time I'm going to tell you. I'm done with you and all your shit. We are not the same anymore. You changed. I'm the bride and it's my day. You are not going to ruin it." I turned and yelled to the driver, "Stop this bus now!" He didn't slow down quick enough so I screamed, "Right now!"

The bus stopped suddenly and the doors flew open and the driver looked back at me through his rearview mirror. I didn't care about anything now. I was ready to kill Tia.

"Tia, get off this fucking bus right now. I'm marrying Dre." You could hear a pin drop. Everybody was being quiet. Surprisingly, my mom didn't utter a single sound. I think everyone was in a state of shock. No one expected me to throw Tia off the bus like that.

"Where am I supposed to go?" she asked, trying to sound pitiful.

"I don't know, but you getting the hell off of this bus."

With her head hung low, she stepped off the bus. I looked away. I really couldn't bear to watch her being ejected off the bus. As soon as she stepped off, the driver closed the doors and pulled off. I held back my tears and peeked out the limo window, looking at Tia wearing her gold bridesmaid gown and standing on the side of the road. As soon as we drove away, she called my phone. I didn't answer. She had already shown that she intended to ruin my day. I couldn't deal with her anymore, ever.

We made it to the banquet hall five minutes before the ceremony began. We all lined up and took our places for the biggest event of my life to begin. I stood at the entrance of the hall. I could see Dre in the distance. Cameras started flashing and everyone stood up. I began my approach to the altar. I stepped delicately on the blush-colored aisle runner that was lined with white rose petals. I was trying to live in the moment, concentrating on not falling as I floated down the aisle. On my way down, I saw all my friends and family. I wanted to speak to everyone, but I kept my head up, looking forward.

At the altar Dre, Syeed, and Brandon were standing to the left, each dressed in a black suit, with a gold-and-white vest and tie. I turned to my right and Reshaun and Mercedes were smiling back at me. I couldn't even focus on Tia not being there. I refused to cry. I just grabbed Dre's hand as the minister began the ceremony. He said a brief introduction and then said, "Now the couple will say the vows that they have written for each other."

Dre faced me, grabbed my hand, and said, "Nicole, I think I loved you ever since the first time I laid eyes on you and you got smart with me at the gas station. But I saw past the attitude and saw a great woman that I wanted to get to know. And once I got to know you, I couldn't be without you. Nikki, you are the one and only person I want to spend my life with. You challenge me and love me. I have never been so happy. For the rest of my life, I want to wake up and make you happy and be a great husband to you until we are old and gray. I promise to take care of you and never let anyone come between us and I will always put you first." As Dre spoke and looked into my eyes, I believed every word he said. I was proud of the good job he'd done in writing his vows. I still couldn't believe I was marrying Dre, even though we were in the middle of our wedding ceremony. He was in front of me, professing his love in front of all our friends and family. He really loved me and I was about to start tearing up. Instead, I said the vows I wrote to him.

"Dondre. Dre. I love you. You have brought happiness, peace, and love into my life. I take you to be my husband and I will be your wife. I will love and cherish you each day that I live. I will stand by you in good times and bad and I will even love you when you eat dessert for dinner." There were chuckles in the audience. People who knew Dre well and were familiar with his love of dessert, laughed the loudest.

After we said our vows, the minister continued with the ceremony. Then we kissed and lit one white unity candle, signifying our oneness. We were pronounced husband and wife. Dre lifted my veil and kissed me. We turned, hand in hand, and walked up the aisle. I tried not to cry, but I couldn't hold back that single tear that escaped my eye. It was so emotional. Everyone was cheering and clapping. My mom and Ernest, the entire Hill family, Reshaun and Michael, Maritza and Vincent. And my sister, Candice, was there with Nana. It was bittersweet. I had everything I could have ever dreamed of in life. My husband, my friends, and all my family. It was exactly how I pictured it, except Tia wasn't there. But you can't have everything. Nobody gets five out of five, even Tia said that herself. I can't see Tia ever being my friend again. I've lost her friendship forever, but I gained Dre. Though it hurts, I am happier to be Dre's wife than Tia's friend. I'm no longer dating somebody else's man. I have a man of my own and it feels like heaven.

If you enjoyed SOMEBODY ELSE'S MAN,
don't miss Daaimah S. Poole's newest
delivery of drama,

ANOTHER MAN WILL

Turn the page for a special excerpt from the novel, a Dafina trade paperback on sale now!

Chapter 1

Crystal Turner

"Dana, don't forget that I have to take the DNA test tomorrow."

"Right, right, okay. I'm glad you reminded me. I have a meeting, but as soon as I'm done, I'm coming straight to you. Ooooh, I hate Kenneth so much for making you go through this."

"I know, but once he gets the results, I think he will step up and do what he is supposed to do."

"He better, because this doesn't make any sense. My beautiful niece doesn't deserve this, and neither do you. I'll see you tomorrow."

"Okay, see you then," I said. Then I took a few deep breaths and prepared to go back into work. I was on minute eleven of my fifteen-minute break, and I didn't need another write-up. I hurried back inside.

I boarded the elevator and rode back up to my floor, the ACR Cable Vision headquarters. I thought about what my sister Dana had said and had to agree that nobody should have to go to court to prove the paternity of their child. Let me take that back. In some situations paternity tests were very necessary, but not in my case. I knew Kenneth Dontae Haines was the father of my three-month-old daughter, Kori. I was positive because we were in a committed relationship for several years, and during that time I wasn't with anyone else. I asked my younger sister, Dana, to go with me because she was levelheaded, and I want to have support just in case he brought his sometimes bigmouthed butch sister, Syreeta, with him.

Negotiating a maze of cubicles, I made it to my desk with only a minute to spare, just enough time to log back on to my phone. I put my headset back on, and instantly my phone began ringing. The air-conditioning made it very cold in the building, so I put my gray wrap sweater over my skinny frame and began taking calls. "Thank you for calling ACR Cable Vision & Internet. This is Crystal. How may I assist you today?"

"I have this blue screen on my TV," the caller complained. I could tell from his voice that he was old. I didn't know why people always called about the blue screen. They knew what the blue screen meant. It meant that they hadn't paid their cable bill.

"Okay, I'm reviewing your account," I said, as if there was a chance that there was mistake, but I knew better. "Unfortunately, your account is showing that you have a past due balance of one hundred and eighty-nine dollars." I hated giving the old man that bad news.

"What! Is that for one month?" the old man asked me.

"No, sir. Two months."

"Hmm. I gave my grandson the money, and he didn't pay the bill! Now I'm about to miss all my shows. If I mail you a check today, will you turn the cable back on?"

Aw, this was so sad. I hated this part of my job.

"No, sir, full payment is due at this time. However, I can take a check by phone."

He made an irritated sound. "I can't see this goddamn number on the check. Look, never mind. It's a shame how y'all rob the elderly. Can't even watch my television. All I can do now is just sit here and look at a blue screen." He grunted in aggravation. "You goddamn robbers, making people pay to watch TV, anyway."

I heard the man continue to mumble, and then he hung up on me. *Just one of our millions of loyal, happy customers,* I thought as I took the next call. I'd been a customer service representative for five years. The only really good thing that came with the job was the free cable and Internet. As I answered the caller on hold, I waved to my returning coworker, Gloria. She always tried to pop her head over my cubicle and make conversation between calls. But I wasn't interested. I kept it at "Good morning," "Hello," and "See you tomorrow."

I was more of a loner. I barely spoke to my supervisor, Delphine. I kept to myself, and I didn't have a lot of friends. My kids kept me busy enough. I didn't have time for catty, petty, drama-filled women. That was why I didn't deal with any of the women on my job. I'd seen it happen so many times. Two coworkers were besties; then the next thing you knew, they were enemies, telling everybody on the job each other's business. No thanks! The same women that ran to your desk with juicy news about someone would do the same thing to you. I came to work and then went home to my babies—Kori, who was three months old; Nasir, who was five; and Jewel, who was nine.

After work the pending test was still on my mind. I just couldn't wait until all the dumbness was over. I just wanted to be happy. Ever since I was a young kid, all I had ever wanted was to have a family and be happily married like my parents. My mom and dad had been together for thirty-five years. You'd think I'd follow in their footsteps, but it was hard for me to stay with anyone for more than a few years. I had three kids and three different baby fathers. The minute I told someone this, they automatically formed a negative opinion of me. Sometimes it bothered me, but most times it didn't. I hadn't planned for it to turn out like this. I had really believed that I was going to be with each one of my children's fathers forever, but it didn't happen that way. So, I just got up and went to work every single day and provided for my children as best I could.

Jason, who was my oldest daughter Jewel's father, and I were together from eighth grade until I was twenty-one. Jason got locked up when I seven months pregnant. When he first went away, I did the jail thing: the visits, sending letters, putting money on his books. But he eventually told me to stop. He said he didn't want to hold me back, and to go and live my life. That was eight years ago. He still had another seven years to go before he got out.

Then there was Maurice, my son Nasir's dad. I really cared about Maurice. He was very smart and motivated. I met him in the coffee shop down the street from my job. We were truly opposites. He was working on his third degree, while I had finished only high school. Initially, we were inseparable. He taught me so much about the world, and I really thought we had a chance. I was in love with him, but something about our relationship couldn't work. I think it was because Maurice saw me as his little project, like I was his "ghetto girl," whom he was going to refine. I wouldn't have minded being his project, but he wasn't trying to make me a better person. He was trying to mold me into something that I wasn't. After a while I got tired of him talking down to me. He wasn't physically abusive, but I knew he would never consider me his equal. His treatment of me probably bordered on emotional abuse. He rarely gave me money for Nasir, and he married some older woman, so I just acted like he didn't exist.

And lastly, there was Kenneth, the deadbeat baby daddy of my youngest child, Kori. In my defense, I could honestly say that Kenneth begged and pleaded with me to have his child. I loved my daughter, but I wasn't ready to be a mom again. I was actually on birth control, but obviously, it didn't work. I had planned on aborting her, but Kenneth cried. The man actually shed tears, whole tears. Trying to make me feel guilty, he said, "You had two babies for dudes that didn't love you. I'm the one here with you, loving you and your kids, but you wanna kill my baby?"

So I caved and went through with the pregnancy. And at first it seemed like we were going to make it. Kenneth was great during my entire pregnancy. He went to every doctor's appointment, was in the delivery room, holding my hand, telling me to breathe and to push when I went into labor. Kenneth even cut the umbilical cord and began kissing and snapping pictures of our baby daughter as soon as he saw her. He was a doting father for the entire half hour before his sister, Syreeta, arrived. Once she got there, everything changed. From my hospital bed, I saw her in the corner, whispering to him. I didn't know what they were talking about, but I soon found out.

Syreeta had a major issue with Kori's complexion. She said my baby looked like she was mixed with something, and that she was too light to be Kenneth's child. Now, I would admit, usually when two brown-skinned people had a child, you got a brown baby. However, I was smart enough to know about something called genes. Genes could cause traits and characteristics, like a child's complexion, to skip a generation.

Unfortunately, Kenneth and Syreeta weren't aware of these things, because all of a sudden Kenneth started having doubts. He was asking me questions like "Is Kori mine?" "Did you cheat on me?" "Why is she so light?" I thought it was funny, because when would I have time to cheat on him? I had a full-time job, two kids, and since Kenneth practically lived with me, he got a lot of my time and attention, as well. A part of me understood that in his sister's mind, she was looking out for her little brother, but Kenneth should've stood up like a man and told his sister that Kori was his daughter. He should have, but he didn't.

He asked me to take a DNA test, and I told him to kiss my ass. I asked him if he could just look at her and see that she was his. She had the same mouth, ears, nose, and had a head full of hair, just like him. But the only thing he could think to say was, "I don't trust a face test." Then he mumbled something about this bull on his job who got burnt that way. His denial of his daughter was unacceptable. He even refused to sign her birth certificate, so I broke up with him. My response to all of that was, "Fuck you." I wasn't about to poke or swab my baby for him or anyone else. If he didn't want to be bothered, then fine. It was his loss, not mine.

I eventually changed my mind and agreed to have her tested, and I suggested that we order an at-home DNA test. We could get the results online or in the mail, but Kenneth wouldn't go for that. He said that his sister had warned him that with an at-home test, I could tamper with the results, and so they wanted an official test done by professionals. So tomorrow was D-day, and I hoped we could finally put all this ghetto mess behind us. He'd have proof that Kori was his child, and his sister could shut the hell up.

Chapter 2

Dana Turner

The marketing firm I worked for was having its annual customer appreciation dinner at the Arts at Piazza in downtown Philadelphia. It was a big event where we got to wine and dine with our clients, all on the company's tab. Meeting clients socially was always good. They were relaxed and not in business mode. You could do the right amount of schmoozing without looking like you were kissing up to them.

The night was going extremely well; actually, the night was almost perfect. I was wearing an off-the-shoulder, lilac-colored dress that hung great on my size-six curves and accented my cherrywood brown skin. I had on my favorite pair of peep-toe shoes, which made my five-three look like five-eight. My beautiful, big layered silver necklace was making a grand statement and rested right above my cleavage. My long, wavy weave was pulled up into a sloppy, loose bun, which was set off with just the right amount of makeup.

The food was delicious; the cocktails had the perfect blend of sweetness, and only a trace of liquor was detectable. I was in the great company of my coworker Reshma Patel and her fiancé, Zyeed, and my other coworker, Leah Oliver, who had brought her boyfriend, Stephen. The only thing that was off was the empty chair that was next to me. It was reserved for my no-call, no-show date, Todd.

Leah was from rural upstate Pennsylvania. She was bubbly and fun and always made me laugh with her off-color humor. She had a few freckles, rust-colored hair, and brown eyes. Leah and I had interned together, and Reshma had come in a few months afterward. Reshma was a quiet, sweet-hearted first-generation American of Indian descent. We all got along so well, yet we were all so different, but we made the perfect little marketing dream team.

We all worked for Millennium Concepts Agency. We provided marketing and branding services for small and large companies—from the huge billboards you saw on highways to the tiny advertisements above your head on the train.

"So where is that boyfriend of yours, missy?" Leah inquired.

"He should be on his way. I was about to call him and see where he is," I said.

Reshma grabbed my hand and tried to contain her laughter as she pushed her straight black hair in front of her wheat skin to block her smirk. "It's okay, sweetie. You can stop lying. We know you don't really have a date."

I frowned. "Reshma, this is not funny. That's really sad that you would think I would make up having a date. I told you, Todd said he was coming. He'll be here."

Reshma looked at Leah and made a face. They both began to laugh at my expense as their guys stood around, looking bored and making light conversation with one another.

My eyes were focused on the entrance. "I'll be right back. Let me see if he is on his way," I said as I excused myself from the table. I was trying to act nonchalant, but I was so angry at Todd, I could feel my blood pressure rising.

I exited the crowded party, hoping to see Todd parking or walking toward the restaurant, but no such luck. I didn't see him. So I called his phone and listened to it ring about four times and then heard, "You have reached Todd Montgomery. Unfortunately, I'm not available. . . ." I listened as I looked up and down the street once more, before leaving a message. "Todd, where are you? I hope you are on your way. I'm still at the Arts at Piazza on Fourth Street. Call me and let me know what's going on." I really hoped Todd would make it. He said he would. But he said a lot of things. Todd was not my real boyfriend. We were in a six-month relationship about a year ago; then things got complicated. Our relationship was going so good. I mean, really, really, really well. But then work got in the way.

He said our relationship was taking up too much of his time and that he needed to focus on his architectural career. He said I required so much and he couldn't give me everything I deserved. So we semi-broke up but never stopped seeing each other. Our relationship was downgraded to that fuzzy place commonly referred to as "friends with benefits." Which meant that we hooked up occasionally. I kept thinking if I hung in there for a while, he'd realize that we should be back in an official relationship. Plus, I loved a career-driven man, and Todd was definitely that. Believe me, there were far worse things that a guy could be doing besides working nonstop. Especially in this economy, when so many people couldn't find jobs and others were losing their homes. And I knew he didn't have anyone else, unless she lived under his desk at his job. But then it was evenings like this one, when he stood me up, and it didn't seem worth it or fair.

I walked back to the party, and my phone rang. Todd's name appeared on the screen.

"Hey. Are you on your way?" I asked.

"No, not exactly," he said.

"What does 'not exactly' mean?" I already knew what that meant, but still I asked.

"Sorry. I can't make it. Listen, don't be upset with me. I can't leave this office. I have so much work. I really want to be there with you, but my work is my priority."

Instead of giving him the artificial "Okay. I understand"—that was what I usually said—I just gave a defeated, "You never can make it, can you, Todd?"

"Why are you being sarcastic, Dana? What do you want me to do?"

"I don't know. You promised me. I told you about this party how many weeks ago? And you said, 'I promise I'll be there.' "

"Yes, I said I would be there. However, I can't always predict what's going to happen. Things change on a daily basis at this company. . . . Once again, I'm sorry, Dana. I have to go. I didn't eat, and I'm very frustrated. I'll be at the office for a while. Feel free to stop by."

"Okay," I said as I twisted my mouth and tried to control my anger and not let tears escape my eyes. He wasn't able to be with me, but at least I could be with him later. I felt a little better, even though I was at another event alone. I walked to the restroom to make sure my eye makeup hadn't smudged. Leah and Reshma were exiting the ladies' room.

"We were looking for you. Are you okay? So is he coming?" Reshma asked.

"No, he is working."

"Well, one thing is for sure, when you get married, you will be provided for," Leah joked as they walked me into the restroom. I began to fix my clothes and reapply my eyeliner and blush. I tried to remain calm, but I was so upset.

Leah looked at me in the mirror above the sink and said, "Dana, I can't understand why you put yourself through this. You are a beautiful girl. You can find someone else.

"You deserve a real boyfriend." Reshma giggled, breaking the serious tone.

"You guys are full of jokes tonight."

"No, really, you need to be dating, having fun. You need a guy that doesn't stand you up all the time," said Leah. "You're beautiful, you have a great personality, and you're successful. I'm sure lots of guys would love to date you."

"If it was only that simple," I snapped back at them. "Listen, ladies, there aren't that many black men like Todd."

"And what is that supposed to mean?" Reshma asked.

"It means it is different for us," I replied.

"What do you mean, us?" said Leah.

"Us means black women. We don't have as many options as you guys. There aren't thousands of black architects running around Philadelphia."

"I don't believe that. That's just a myth. It's all the same. There are as many jerks who are white men, Asian, and Indian men as there are those who are black," Leah responded.

"Nope, not the case. There are plenty of white men for you to marry and lots of Indian men for Reshma. I have to work with what I have. Todd is a great catch, and I'm not letting him get away."

"Great catch or not, he doesn't treat you well. Seriously, I don't like seeing my friend upset," Reshma said.

"I have to say one thing. You won't find anyone as long as you won't let go of an old relationship," Leah retorted.

Reshma nodded her head in agreement and said, "Remember that crazy Indian guy I dated before I met Zyeed? After him I didn't think there was any hope that I was going to ever meet anyone—and now I'm getting married in two weeks. As a matter of fact, there will be a lot of single guys at my wedding."

"And I could introduce you to one of Stephen's friends if you like," Leah added.

"I don't want to be hooked up with anyone. I'm happy with what and who I have. And besides, I want a black man."

"You're telling us you'd rather have a so-so good black man over a nice guy of another race?" Reshama asked, perplexed.

"Yeah. I mean no. I just want a good man, but I would prefer if he is black. Besides, I have one, and we are not having this discussion anymore."

"If you say so." Leah looked at me like I wasn't making sense. I wasn't . . . but I was. I knew what I wanted.

I left the party and stopped at Todd's favorite restaurant, Laverne's, to pick him up dinner. He always got the classic turkey-spinach burger, sweet potato fries, and a strawberry milk shake. *He's going to be so pleased that I brought him dinner,* I thought.

Todd worked on the twenty-second floor of a tall office building at Twentieth and Market Streets. The building was lively during the day, but at 10:00 p.m. it was eerie and empty. I said hello to the security man, signed myself in, and rode the elevator up to his floor. I walked down the hall and could see Todd steadily working. I tapped on the glass door, and Todd came and opened it. He gave me a quick kiss on the cheek and said I looked beautiful. I was glad that he noticed.

"You said you hadn't eaten, so I stopped and got your favorite."

"Wow, and I'm starving. Thank you, sweetheart." He took the food out of the white paper bag and took big bites out of the sandwich and stuffed the fries in his mouth. As he ate, I admired the blueprints lying out on his desk and the color model on his computer. I was always so amazed at the intricate drawings that eventually became buildings.

"What project is this?"

"The new athletic center for Temple University. The deadline is next Friday, and we are so behind. I'm going to be working nonstop on this. There is so much that has to be done."

"Oh, this is what kept you from being with me tonight," I said as I poked out my lips.

"Yeah, this is it."

"I really wish you could have been with me tonight. I get so tired of going places alone. My friends at work think I'm lying when I say I have a date. They think I'm making you up."

"I don't know why. We've all met before. They know that's not true."

"Yeah, they were just being extra silly tonight, I guess. So, how much longer are you staying here tonight?"

"Actually, I'm trying to get out of here now. I have to be back in here by seven, and what I have left, I can do from home. Do you want to meet me there? I'll be home in, like, half an hour."

"Okay."

At Todd's loft, he continued to work and I didn't distract him. I took off my dress and cute shoes and showered. Once I was out of the shower, I put on one of his T-shirts, and I watched television in his bed, making myself comfortable. Todd was right in the other room, but I wanted him closer. I could smell his scent on his sheets. However, I knew not to bother him or force myself on him while he was in work mode. When he was ready to come to bed, he would join me and I could show him how much I missed him.

Around 2:45 a.m. I got the nudge I was waiting for. I was barely awake when he began lifting my T-shirt over my head. The room was dark. I couldn't see Todd, but I could feel his hands all over my breasts. Once his hands touched me, everything was right in the world. I forgave him for standing me up, making me angry and embarrassing me in front of my friends again. I was so caught up in the moment that nothing else mattered.

"You ready for me, baby?" he murmured in my ear.

"Yes," I responded sleepily as I wrapped my arms around his neck tightly, sliding my body down on him, until he was all the way in. My pulse sped up the moment our bodies connected. My clitoris was pressed hard up against the base of him. I could feel hot sensations coursing through me. I was just enjoying the way he gripped my waistline and controlled my body, moving my hips as fast he needed to.

"Todd!" I moaned as he panted on top of me. Our bodies were sweaty. The sex was so good, and I was just enjoying it so much that I couldn't help whispering, "Baby, I love you and don't want to be without you anymore." I waited for him to respond and say he loved me, too, and he needed me, as well, but he didn't speak. More strokes brought out more emotions. I couldn't control how I felt or what I was saying. "I love you so much, Todd. I miss you when we're not together. Baby, we really need to figure out what we are going to be."

Todd still remained quiet and placed his finger over my lips and kept pushing his firm body in and out of mine. I didn't like that he was ignoring me. I couldn't let it go any further without him giving me an idea of what we were doing. He had to explain why we just couldn't go back to being a couple.

I pushed him off of me mid-stroke, sat up, folded my arms, and asked, "Todd, when are we going to be together again?"

"Let's not talk about this right now please, baby." He pushed me back down and squirmed back in me and began our beautiful experience again.

I was becoming a little frustrated. I felt like crying, but tears only made Todd upset. So I kept them in check and momentarily forgot all my troubles by focusing on the pleasure on the horizon. Within minutes I exploded. My body shook so hard, I thought I was having a damn seizure. All the shaking I was doing must have excited him, because a few seconds later he collapsed on top of me. We were both satisfied so it was the perfect time to ask him the status of us again.

"Todd, what are we doing?"

"I don't know."

"You do know. What is this? Where are we going?"

"Uh, Dana, can we talk about this later?"

I said okay, but the minute he was in the shower, my brain started spinning again. I began to get angry and I decided I didn't want to spend the night. If he couldn't define us then I didn't want to be bothered with him anymore. I huffed loudly as I threw my dress over my head and slipped on my heels. Todd walked back in the bedroom in his open navy robe, brushing his teeth.

"Where are you going?" he asked with a mouth full of toothpaste.

"Home."

"Why?"

"Because I can't keep getting hurt by you. I asked you a simple question, and you can't answer it."

He stepped back in the bathroom and spat out the toothpaste and said, "That doesn't mean you have to leave."

I didn't hesitate. I finished getting dressed and walked out the door.

"Dana, hold up," Todd called. "Wait. Let me throw on some shorts and walk you to your car."

The cool summer air was refreshing and woke me as I climbed in my white Honda Accord coupe. Todd made it to my car door just as I started the engine. I rolled down the window and waited for him to speak.

"Yes?" I said, staring straight ahead.

"What's wrong with you? Why do you always get like this? I told you I don't want a relationship, not with you or anyone else, right now. You know what we are."

"No, I don't know. That's why I'm leaving."

"Dana, you're being extra . . . Just call me when you get in."

I wasn't thinking about Todd right now; he frustrated the hell out of me. I pulled out of the parking space and dialed Tiffany, my friend since college. We had been roommates at Maryland Eastern Shore. In college we shared books, food, clothes, and gained a lifelong friendship. If her mother sent something for her, it was for us, and vice versa. I missed college, the good old days, when I didn't have a lot of responsibility and every day was a party. Nowadays Tiffany was sometimes up in the middle of the night, doing lessons plans, preparing to deal with the twenty-one kindergarteners in her class, and we would talk. I took a chance and called her.

"What's wrong? Why are you calling this late?"

"Todd is the problem. I'm just leaving his house. He stood me up again, and then I asked him where our relationship was going and he acted like he couldn't speak."

"Dana, he always does this to you. I don't like Todd for you anymore. He had all this time to get himself together and still hasn't. When are you going to realize it is never going to be the same?"

"I know. I was just hoping that maybe one day it would. That's what's kept me around. I hoped that one day he would change. He is everything I want in a man and husband. And I'm not in a rush to leave him, because what else is really out there, anyway?"

"You have a point, I guess. But is a little of something better than nothing?"

"I don't know."

"You should think about it. Good night."

I drove back to my apartment and went inside. Now that I was in my apartment, lying in my cream silky sheets alone, I regretted leaving Todd's. I should have just continued my fantasy with Todd until morning. But no, I shouldn't have—because he was not giving me what I wanted. What I wanted was for a man to treat me like royalty. Like the love of his life. Like I'm the only thing that matters.

Like how my daddy treated my mom. I wanted a good man who took care of his family, like my father.

My dad, James Turner, worked long hours at the Tastykake factory to provide for my mother, me, and my two sisters. Tastykake was a well known Philadelphia baking company. My dad would bring us home treats all the time, including Butterscotch Krimpets and lemon pies. Every time he got his paycheck, he would take all his girls out. And on our birthdays he would give us a hundred dollars and let us pick out whatever we wanted at Toys R Us. My dad was the closest thing to Superman. He could do no wrong, and even now he still treated my mom like a queen and me and my sisters like princesses. I guess they didn't make them like him anymore.

It was morning, and I didn't have time to think about last night with Todd. I had to concentrate on my presentation at work. I was in my office's huge conference room. It had three large windows and a twenty-foot-long, shiny maple boardroom table that could seat ten on each side. I pulled down the projector and made sure everything was set up for my 10:00 a.m. meeting.

Reshma and I had thirty minutes left to prepare for our PowerPoint presentation. We were scrambling to get our notes together for our initial meeting with Cell Now. Cell Now was doing really well in the southwestern part of the country, and the company wanted to expand its services in the region stretching from Philadelphia to Atlanta. We planned to do a viral campaign through social media and have lunchtime contests and giveaways at local colleges. The service was good, but the phones were kind of cheap. Still, they were highly marketable to the eighteen-to-twenty-five demographic.

Our presentation went okay, though I flubbed a few lines of my prepared speech and then the computer kept freezing. I had to present most of the figures from memory, instead of being able to refer to all the attractive graphs and charts I had prepared. Overall, it still went well, I thought, as everyone from Cell Now exited the boardroom. They seemed excited about our ideas. I would know in a few days if they were going to go with our agency or not. I looked down at my cell phone. I had to hurry up and get to Eleventh Street to meet up with my sister Crystal.

"We are ordering food. Do you want Greek today?" Leah asked as she tapped on the door to my office.

"No, sorry. I have to go take care of something with my sister."

"Is everything okay?" Leah asked.

"Yes, everything is fine."

I arrived at the family court building to find it crowded, with long lines in every direction, and they made everyone go through a metal detector. I was truly annoyed by the way the horrible, power-hungry security people kept speaking to me. They were very demanding and questioned me. "Take off your earrings." "Do you have any change in your pocket?" I gave a hefty security guard an evil stare, and he responded by saying, "Miss, I'm just doing my job."

After the invasive security screening was over, I finally was able to go upstairs. I walked into the room and saw Crystal, her baby daddy, Kenneth, and his sister. I gave Kenneth and his sister both a stone-faced glance. I had to make sure they knew that my sister had support.

Kenneth should be executed for having the audacity to deny that he was Kori's biological father. However, Crystal should have known better than to mess with a nothing ass like Kenneth. Crystal was a classic example of a middle child. She wanted to save the world, be nice to all, and help everyone, but honestly she needed to save herself. Every relationship she had ended in disaster. And, of course, it was never her; the men she chose were always the ones to be blamed. But I blamed her for picking such horrible men. She believed everyone had the best intentions for her, and obviously, they didn't. I'd been telling her this her whole life. Sometimes it was hard to believe she was not adopted, because it didn't seem possible that two people who were less than two years apart and had been raised in the same household could turn out so differently.

Chapter 3

Yvette Turner-McKnight

Some women hated to walk past groups of men, because no matter what you were wearing, they found a way to objectify you. I wasn't one of those women. I would not say I welcomed it, but I couldn't help the way I was built. Early on, I just embraced it. I had always been tall for my age and built like a little woman, my mother would say. My father would always try to make me wear baggy clothes and didn't like the way boys looked at me, wanted to walk me home, and rang the phone for me. He hated it so much, he tried to keep me under his supervision as much as possible. I was not allowed to spend the night at the house of a friend who had brothers, and I could never get off the porch. All my dad's efforts were in vain, because I was still boy crazy. I moved out and married at eighteen and left my younger sister, Crystal, to deal with my punishment. My dad put a tighter vise grip on her life. She couldn't do anything or go anywhere. That didn't work, either, because she got pregnant early and the dad went to jail. By the time they got to my baby sister, Dana, my dad had refined his approach and molded her into the perfect overachiever.

I walked past a group of men who worked at the same place I did. They were dressed in dark blue Dickies pants, work boots, and T-shirts and were leaning against the dingy white work truck. They were staring at my short, tight, tan pencil skirt and my navy and white short-sleeved blouse. The most noticeable glance came from Hector. His eyes were roaming up and down my legs, and he didn't look away, which made me feel slightly uncomfortable. I had asked him before not to stare at me like that.

As I made my way past them, one of them called out, "Yo, Miss McKnight. Can you tell Frank we are burning up in these work trucks? They need to be serviced. It's ninety degrees outside. They have to get this AC fixed. I shouldn't be sweating like this when they got all that money."

"Okay, I will. I'll let him know."

"Please, 'cause someone should tell him that air-conditioning is not a luxury. It is a necessity."

"Okay. I'll call him as soon as I go in the building."

"Miss McKnight, I have to give you my time sheet," Hector said.

I didn't bother to turn around. I just kept walking and said, "Make sure you get it to me by the end of today."

I sashayed off of the showroom floor, filled with

hanging rugs on display and living room, bedroom, and dining room sets, and headed upstairs to my office. I worked as the front office/human resources manager—and any other title they decided to give me—for Zinoloi Rugs, Carpets, and Exotic Furniture, with seven locations in New Jersey, Delaware, and Pennsylvania. Mr. Zinoloi, the owner, was really nice and gave me a job almost nine years ago, and then he retired and his son, Frank, took over and started cutting corners everywhere he could, like not getting the air-conditioning fixed in the work trucks. I entered my spacious office and dialed him. He never answered, so I left him a message.

"Hey, Frank. Listen, the guys are complaining that they don't have air in the trucks. Please give me a call so I can get approval to have them repaired." Before I could complete my sentence, Hector walked up to me, grabbed my butt, and lightly bit my lip. He was a twenty-four-year-old, sexy-ass Puerto Rican from Kensington—a rough North Philly neighborhood. He had a low, wavy haircut and a trail of colorful bad-boy tattoos going down both of his muscular arms. From afar, someone would mistake Hector for a thug, but he was not one. He was one of the sweetest men I knew. He would be my man if I hadn't married and wasn't now divorced, and if he were a few years older and didn't have a girlfriend and a kid. Because of all our obstacles, he had to be content with just being my YB, or young boy.

"You better be careful and make sure no one followed you up here," I warned.

"They didn't. They made a McDonald's run. So we have, like, ten minutes."

"Uh-huh. Where is the time sheet?"

"Right here," he said as he patted his pocket, where part of a bulge was visible.

"Stop playing."

"I'm not playing. The way your ass was moving in that skirt . . . it took everything in me not to grab you. How's my lady doing, anyway?" he asked as his hands glided up my skirt massaging my ass.

"She's great. She misses you."

"Tell her I was thinking about her this morning in the shower."

"Okay, I'll be sure to let her know."

"When can I see her again?"

I walked from beside him and said, "Hector, I have a lot going on. I don't know. Sometime soon."

"How you going to give her to me, then take it away?"

"I'm not taking her away for good, but she can't right now. Hello. I just went through a divorce, Hector. I'll call you tomorrow. We will get together then. I promise you. Right now I have a lot of work to do."

He gave me a kiss on my cheek and told me he was holding me to my promise. I had a seat at my desk and began to prepare checks to pay a few dozen invoices. My work phone rang and interrupted my work flow. I hoped it was Frank approving those new air conditioners. But it wasn't; it was my best friend Geneva. "Are you going to come to Caribana and party with us Trini style?" Geneva asked with a fake island accent.

"I told you I can't go to Canada. I have so much going on right now."

"Vette, you need this trip. Every year I go, and every year when I come back, you complain that you should have gone. This is going to be the closest we'll ever get to Carnival. You're a newly divorced woman that needs some fun in her life. Plus, we want this to be your divorce party weekend."

"My divorce party weekend," I repeated back to her. "Who came up with that idea?"

"Stacey did. She is getting you a cake with a dead groom to sit on top of it."

"A dead groom. Really? You know what? That actually doesn't sound like a bad idea. Can you put the real dead ex on a cake, too, for me?" I laughed.

"Vette, you are crazy. Come on and go. We're going to have fun. Please come."

"It sounds like fun, but I have a few things called bills standing in the way. This is my rent check."

"What about your check from the house?"

"That check didn't come yet. It will be here any day. I have to call the Realtor."

"Vette, come on. You haven't been anywhere this summer. It will be fun with all three of us. You are going to miss it. Think about it. . . . When will be the next time all of us will be able to get out of town at the same time?"

"I don't know. Probably never."

"You're right—never—so you have to go."

"Let me see what I can do. Maybe I can pay everything when I get back. I'll think about it. Who's driving?"

"Stacey is driving."

"Good. Because you drive too slow. Give me a minute. I'll call you back."

I giggled a little at the thought of a divorce party and the fact that I was thirty-three years old and about to be twice divorced. If you started as early as I did, it was easy. I married my first boyfriend straight out of high school. He was leaving for the army, and I wanted to go with him, so we got married. Six years later I had two children and was divorced. I couldn't blame Doug for anything; it wasn't his fault that it didn't work. I was bored with him and tired of moving all around the world, and I cheated on him. Now, looking back, I should have worked it out. He was a very good man. My first ex-husband now lived in Panama City, Florida. The kids had just got back from spending their summer vacation with him. He was a good guy and father. He sent me money for them and coparented from afar.

I went into my second marriage like I was going to make it work and be a good wife. What a mistake! His ass cheated on me like crazy. My ex-husband Phil was a bus driver for SEPTA, and in case you didn't know, bus drivers had fans and groupies, too. Their fans were the ladies that sat daily in the front of the bus and talked their ear off the entire ride. Well, one young girl took a liking to my husband, and, well, he couldn't resist. She was only nineteen and was so in love, she knocked on my door, claiming she was pregnant by my man. This little girl knew everything about me—where I worked, my schedule, my kids' names, what kind of car I drove—and she said she had been to my house several times. So of course I wanted to leave my husband for cheating on me. But when I confronted him, he assured me it was over.

Most women that got cheated on were somewhere crying and asking why. I did the opposite: he cheated on me, and I said, "Oh, that ain't nothing, boo. I'll cheat on you, too, and I'll do it better." So when the opportunity presented itself for me to get revenge, I did . . . with Hector. Phil knew how to give it but couldn't take it. The minute he learned I had an affair, the world was over. I'd forgotten to turn my ringer off, and Hector had texted me all these messages from YB on my phone. They said that he was falling in love with me and couldn't wait to fuck me again. I came out of the shower, and Phil was in tears. He cried, "How could you? How could you think about being with another man? What? I don't satisfy you?"

I didn't know what to say. I tried to tell him I cheated because he did, but he was furious and was not trying to hear my argument. We had a long discussion that night, and he said he forgave me. I believed him at first, but then he would come in the house, slamming things and picking fights with me. Of course, I always said, "You cheated first!" But all he could say to that was "I'm a man." I guess that meant he got a pass and I didn't. He constantly questioned me about what YB stood for and who YB was, but I told him it didn't matter and we should work on our marriage. I promised him the cheating was a one-time occurrence and not a full-fledged affair. He would have died if he knew it was with someone on the job.

And I think our other issue was jealousy and him wanting to compete with me. He was envious of the relationships I had with my parents and my sisters. He would always tell me I was lucky I had good parents, because his mother and father had neglected him and had let him raise himself. His parents chose drugs over him and I think he almost resented the fact that my parents were there for me. Then there were other signs throughout our entire relationship. For instance, if I said I was thinking about going to the gym, then he suddenly got interested in lifting weights. If I said I was thinking about buying something, he would go buy the bigger, better version. We were having a lot of problems, and we finally went to counseling. I thought it would save us, because for a little while everything got good again, but it didn't last. Then reality set in: Phil would never get over the fact that another man had touched his wife.

So, after all the cheating and counseling, we decided to just get a divorce. We agreed on no high lawyer fees; we did a do-it-yourself divorce. It wasn't like we were rich, and we didn't have a whole bunch of possessions. The only thing we gained in our marriage was our house. Our house was a brick single-family home in Cheltenham. It was on a tree-lined street, with a big front lawn and a double garage. It was a few minutes outside of Philly, but it seemed like it was miles away. Our neighborhood wasn't affected by the recession, and we were fortunate enough to have equity in our house. I wanted to stay in the house, but we both needed the money to move on with our lives. We were going to split the profit and then go our separate ways. My share was twenty-five thousand dollars, and with that money I planned to find a house to rent, pay my daughter Mercedes's tuition for the year, get a nice used car, fix my credit up, treat me and the kids to a few things, and put the rest up.

In the meantime, while I waited to go to the real

estate settlement, I got a temporary small apartment with a month-to-month lease and put most of my big things in storage. All of this divorce stuff was so aggravating. I regretted meeting and marrying my ex Phil. I regretted our big, expensive wedding. Had I known I would be divorced after only three years of marriage, we would have just said "I do" at city hall.

During the drive home I realized Geneva was right; the summer was almost over and I hadn't been anywhere. My rent was due, but I could pay my landlord as soon as I got back with my next check. I needed to go on this trip. I called Phil to find out our exact settlement date. I hated his voice, the way each syllable came out of his mouth.

He didn't say hello or anything. He just answered, "Yeah, we are going to the settlement sometime next week."

"Okay. Well, I wasn't calling only about that. I was making sure you were okay, too."

"I'm fine. Yvette, don't act like you like me or even care about me. When I get the exact date and time, I'll call you," he grumbled, and then the phone went silent. He was a nasty, miserable-ass man. That was exactly why I was happy. I wasn't with him anymore.

I dialed my mom to see if Brandon and Mercedes could stay with her and my father for a few days. My father answered the phone, and I put on my baby voice, which had worked on him since I was three.

"Daddy, where's Mommy?"

"She is in the living room. Why? What do you need?"

"I don't need anything, Daddy. I was just wondering if maybe the kids could come over for a few days."

"Uh, I don't see why not. Sure, no problem. Where are you going?"

"Just getting out of town for a bit. You know, with the divorce and everything, Geneva thought it would be a good idea for us to get away and relax."

"Yeah, that sounds good, and I'll be home this weekend. Your mother won't mind. You can bring the kids. We'll probably get Nasir and Jewel, too."

"Okay, I'll bring them over now, because we are leaving first thing in the morning."

Now that I had a sitter, it was time to leave Frank a message letting him know I wouldn't be in tomorrow, and call Geneva back and let her know I was going.

I was now extra excited and began packing for my trip. I had so many things I needed to do. I had to do something with my hair, get a pedicure, go to the bank, pick a few things up from storage, and drop the kids off. I called down the hall to my son. Brandon was fourteen and was starting high school in a few months. He thought he was grown, but he was still part baby. He came in my room, smelling like an entire basketball team after practice.

"Go pack. You're going to Mom Mom and Pop Pop's for a few days."

"Why?"

"Because I'm going out of town with Ms. Geneva and Stacey for a few days."

"Man, I don't want to go over there. It's boring! Pop Pop's going to be telling all those back-in-the-day stupid stories."

"You don't have a choice. You can't stay here by yourself."

"Can I at least take my Xbox?"

"I don't care. Take your game, but take a shower and get ready."

My daughter, Mercedes, whom we all called Mimi, wouldn't be as hard to break the news to. I could leave her anywhere as long as she had a few books to read, her skates, and a rope. Mercedes came in my room, bouncing and lively. She was very thin and smaller than the other nine-year-olds in her class.

"Mom, where are you going?"

"On a little trip with Miss Geneva."

"Where are we going?"

"To Mom Mom's."

"No, Mom, please. I don't want to go there."

"Too bad. Get ready. I think Jewel will be there, too!"

"She will?" Her attitude changed a little, like maybe she could deal with her grandparents if her cousin was with her.

"And whatever you do this time, do not talk to her about Santa Claus not being real or her dad's college."

"Okay, Mom, but there isn't such a thing as Santa Claus, and her dad is in jail, not college. Why does Aunt Crystal tell her that stuff, and why does she believe it?"

"Because she does, Mercedes. Just go get ready."

I pulled up to my parents' West Oak Lane home. It was a semidetached brick home. The neighborhood had changed a little, but it was still a decent area, where everyone worked, trimmed their hedges, and swept in front of their home. My mom came to the black iron security door. I could tell she was surprised to see us. I was tall caramel brown and shapely like she was, but I didn't inherit her thick brown hair, which she kept flipped up at the ends.

"What are y'all doing here?"

"Daddy didn't tell you? The kids are staying over for a few days."

"Your father doesn't tell me anything. But, of course, they can stay." My mother reached her arms out to Mercedes and Brandon. Mercedes gave her a pathetic hug, and Brandon quickly patted her side.

We walked in the house that I grew up in. Everything was still the same: My parents still had the big black sectional, next to the the wall unit that took up the entire wall, pictures of all our proms hung on the wall. The pictures reflected a time when we had long ponytails, missing teeth, too many barrettes, and hadn't quite grown into our looks. My dad came out of the basement. He gave me a quick peck on the cheek.

"Daddy, why didn't you tell Mommy we were coming?" I asked.

"Oh, I forgot."

"Brandon, your grandfather was just saying he was going to call you to see when you wanted to finish working on the planes in the garage," my mother said.

Brandon looked over at me like, *Why, mom*? I turned away, laughing to myself.

"Here is some money if they want to order a pizza or something," I told my mom.

"A hundred dollars for pizza?"

"Yeah, Mom, and if they need anything else. Call me if you need me. Love y'all."

"Yeah, bye, Mom," Brandon shouted with an attitude as he lowered his eyes at me from the top of the steps.

Mercedes pouted, her lips poked out and her arms crossed.

"Don't worry about them. They'll be fine," my dad said.

"I'm not worried." I wasn't worried. They could spend a few days with their grandparents while their mother had much-needed fun.

CHAPTER 4

Crystal

It was a quarter to one, and the line was already wrapped around the corner of the family court building. I wasn't excited about taking a paternity test, but at least my sister would be there with me. The only problem with Dana was she thought she knew everything and she didn't. I never got why she was always in someone else's business and giving out advice. She was not married, either, and didn't even have a steady boyfriend that I knew of, but she was quick to tell someone what they were doing wrong in their life. However, she was the first one to go to college in our family and had a really good job and a nice apartment, but that didn't make her life perfect.

I walked into the dreary beige room filled with

rows of empty, blue, hard plastic seats and sat in the back. I wanted to have a full view of the room when Kenneth arrived. I looked out the corner of my eye and saw Kenneth and Syreeta walk in the room. He gave me an evil stare, like I was the enemy. Behind him was his manly looking sister, Syreeta. She was skinny and tall, dressed in sagging blue jeans and an oversize orange polo shirt. Her brown hair was two inches long and slicked back with gel.

Kenneth made me so angry. Here he was, a few feet away from his only child, and he wasn't even acknowledging her. I had to put my head down and try not to let them get to me. But even with my head down, I heard Syreeta say something like, "That baby ain't yours. Look at her." Instead of responding to her, I gave Kori her bottle and checked the time on my phone, because I was only minutes away from the truth.

A few moments later I heard the click of high heels approaching. I looked up and saw my sister. I smiled and spoke to Dana very loudly. Kenneth and Syreeta looked up, and I gave them a look like, "What now, bitches? I have back up, too." Dana grabbed Kori from me, gave her a kiss, and started playing with her, which garnered more hateful stares from "the uglies."

Finally, this older black man came into the waiting room and called out, "Mr. Haines and Ms. Turner, follow me please." I stood up and grabbed Kori and followed him down the hall. The man took us into a small room and instructed us to have a seat. A woman with a white lab coat came in and began to explain the testing procedure.

"I'm going to insert this in your mouth, and I

need you to hold it against the inside of your cheek for me. Okay?"

We both said yes and took turns opening our mouths and being swabbed. Afterwards the lab worker inserted the swabs into vials and then sealed them. She scribbled a few things down the side of each with a black marker and said that she was done and that we would receive our results in two to four weeks. I was surprised it took only ten minutes. I thanked the lady and gathered Kori and my bag and began walking out the door. Kenneth was right in front me. I had so much I needed to say to him. I sped up a little and tapped his shoulder.

He turned around, backed up, and said very rudely, "What's up?"

"So, when you get the results, are you going to come and get your daughter?"

"Yup, but if she ain't mine, then it is a done deal and you better not say anything to me"

"I don't say anything to you now. You are ridiculous; you know this is all stupid and unnecessary."

"No, I don't. That's why we are here."

I didn't know why I was still shocked that Kenneth was acting like an ass. "You are a fucking idiot," was all I could think to say.

"Whatever," he said as he flagged me, pulled up his sagging pants, and then bent the rim of his hat down and said to his sister, who was waiting for him, "Man, let's get out of here."

She rolled her eyes at me one last time, and I just shook my head.

"Kenneth, you got this," she had the nerve to tell him. "I don't know why chicks be trying to blame babies on dudes. You don't have anything to worry about."

I couldn't hold back anymore. Syreeta was always saying whatever the hell she wanted to someone, and no one was supposed to respond.

"Why don't you stay out of this, Syreeta? Kori is his. She is your niece, whether you like it or not."

She walked over to me, pointing her finger in my face, and said, "That's yet to be proven."

"Nothing needs to be proved. I know who I slept with, and so does your brother. You weren't there." I stood toe-to-toe with her and looked her directly in her face, as if to say, "Try me, bitch."

Kenneth grabbed Syreeta, and Dana began pulling on me. Syreeta was still talking trash, but I was happy that I had finally stood up to her.

"Girl, you lucky I don't feel like getting a case, because I would smack the bullshit out of you," Syreeta yelled.

"Syreeta, please! You still a woman, and I will fight you like one. Like I said, you need to mind your business."

"I ain't got to mind shit," she said like she was ready to throw a punch, but Kenneth grabbed her before she did. She kept trying to yank her arm away from him, screaming, "Get off me. I'm cool. I ain't even got time for this dumb bitch. She the one who don't know who her baby father is."

All she was doing was a bunch of hollering, making herself look foolish. People were staring, shaking their heads, and the security guard was on his way over. I thought I had won our match and felt like I had a victory, until she screamed, loud enough for the entire family court building to hear, "Crystal, your ho ass is nothing. You hear me? You have three babies and three baby fathers. Ain't none of them with you, and no one will ever want your ass.

Because you're just a whore-ass baby mom. Okay? Just a baby mom. You're not a girlfriend. You're not a wife. You're just a baby mom. Find out who your baby daddy is before you say anything to me. Okay. Let's get out of here before I snap on a bitch," she said and then walked off.

I wanted to give a quick rebuttal, but I couldn't think of anything to say back to Syreeta that would hurt as much as the words she had just hurled at me. I did have three baby fathers, but I wasn't a whore. And I knew for sure she had slept with more men than me, and she was a lesbian, but nothing came out. Her words stung, and she was kind of right. I wasn't a girlfriend or a wife. I was just a baby mom.

On Fridays I usually ordered pizza or made some kind of finger food for the kids. It depended, because my children were picky. On different days they decided what they would eat and wouldn't eat. Sometimes I'd end up making three meals: one for Nasir, one for me, and the other for Jewel. My mom said, "Don't fix a bunch of different dishes. Make them eat what you cook," but I didn't want them to be hungry.

While I prepared the ground beef for our tacos, Nasir played with his toys in the middle of the living room floor and Jewel entertained Kori as she sat in her bouncy seat. Jewel was my little helper, my big girl. She was only nine, but she was always telling me that when she grew up, she wanted to be a teacher and a mommy like me. She had a very nurturing personality and always helped me with her brother and sister.

My house was a three-bedroom house. Initially, I was renting, but then my landlord retired and sold it to me before she moved to Florida. It was a nice home on a quiet block, but by the time Kori got big, I was going to have to move because there wouldn't be enough room.

My living room had a big green love seat and sofa. In the middle was a large rug, which the children played and watched television on.

"Nasir, we are going to clean this living room and then your bedroom tonight. Okay?"

"My room is clean."

"No, *clean* means everything off of the floor and out from under the bed. We are going to clean this entire house."

My house wasn't dirty, but it is hard keeping everything together. But as long as we had a clean kitchen and bathrooms, who cared if there were a few toys on the floor? I didn't. I'd rather spend time with my kids and take them out for a day in the park than make them spend the day cleaning.

"Hey, Mom," I said, picking up the ringing phone after checking the screen.

"What are you doing tonight?"

"Cooking tacos for the kids and trying to clean the house."

"Dana told me about what happened in court. Don't worry about Kenneth or his sister. But I know one thing. He has to help you with that baby or he is going to deal with me. Anyway, I didn't call to talk to you about that. I just wanted you to know I have Brandon and Mimi over here, so if you want, you can brings yours over, too."

"The kids? Tonight? Mom, that's okay. I already started dinner, and I don't have any plans."

"It's Friday night. You had a long day, and you need a break. Bring them kids over here."

"No, Mom. I'm okay. Maybe next time."

"Next time, I don't know about that. I'm not going to call you every week and beg to watch your children."

"Okay, I'll bring them over after they eat."

I welcomed the break my Mom was about to give me, but I didn't have anywhere to go. Jewel would be happy to spend time with Mercedes, even though you could never tell they were the same age. My niece acted just like her name: spoiled and entitled. Yvette bought her everything; she even got her hair and nails done and my little girl still plays with dolls.

Mercedes was waiting on the steps for us to arrive. She called out to Jewel and ran over to the car as soon as she saw us. Her hair was in long rod curls and she was wearing all pink. Jewel was as excited to see her and jumped out of the car to hug her cousin.

"Mercedes, look at you. You look so pretty," I said as I gave her a sideways hug and grabbed Kori out of her car seat.

"Thank you, Auntie Crystal. Can I hold the baby?"

"Let me get her inside and I'll let you hold her."

I walked in my parents' big home. You could see both the kitchen and the dining room from the front door. It was one big, open space. Every time I walked through my parents door I felt like time stood still and I was a kid again. My nephew Brandon had already taken over my mother's television with his game. I spoke to him, but he was too busy killing people on his game to respond.

"Look at my baby. She is getting so big." My mom grabbed Kori, who then began to cry.

"She is probably still hungry. That's why she being fussy." I got her bottle out of her bag, warmed it up, and gave it my mother, and she began feeding her.

My mom looked down at Kori as she fed her and shook her head and said, "How can a man not want to be a part of this precious baby's life? Now that you took the test, explain to me what's going to happen next."

"We'll get the results, and everything should be okay after this. It will prove she is his."

"Okay, he better hope so, because he sure has a lot of nerve. I'll tell you, these men today have lost they damn mind. Making babies and then not taking care of them"

"Yeah, well I think he is going to get it together. At least I hope."

I talked to my mom a little more, then went upstairs to put the kids' bag in my and Dana's room. It was the back room. My half was the right side, and her half was the left. We used to jump on the bed and stay up all night in this room, sharing so many secrets, dreams about who we were going to be who we would marry, and where we were going to live. Back then I would never have thought my life would turn out like this.

"Mom, I'm going to get out of here."

She gave me a kiss on my cheek and asked if I had packed enough diapers.

"Yeah, and I already made the formula, so all

you have to do is put the bottle in warm water for, like, two minutes and it will be ready."

"I raised three babies. I'll manage."

"I know you will. Thanks for taking them, and I'll be here first thing in the morning," I said as I was leaving and tried to figure out what I was going to do with my free time.